GIN PALACE

Tracy Whitwell was born, brought up and educated in the North-East of England. She wrote plays and short stories from an early age, then in the nineties moved to London where she became a busy actress on stage and screen.

After having her son, she wound down the acting to concentrate on writing full time. Many projects followed until she finally found the courage to write her first novel, *The Accidental Medium* – a work of fiction based on a whole heap of crazy truth, which is now a trilogy, with more to come.

Today, Tracy lives in north London with her son, surrounded by a coven of friends as spooky as she is. Tracy is nothing like her lead character Tanz. (This is a lie.)

More by the author

Adventures of an Accidental Medium series
The Accidental Medium

GIN PALACE

TRACY WHITWELL

PAN BOOKS

First published 2020

This edition first published 2022 by Macmillan

This paperback edition first published 2023 by Pan Books
an imprint of Pan Macmillan
The Smithson, 6 Briset Street, London EC1M 5NR
EU representative: Macmillan Publishers Ireland Ltd, 1st Floor,
The Liffey Trust Centre, 117–126 Sheriff Street Upper,
Dublin 1, D01 YC43
Associated companies throughout the world
www.panmacmillan.com

ISBN 978-1-5290-8763-5

1 3 5 7 9 8 6 4 2

A CIP catalogue record for this book is available from the British Library.

Typeset in Stempel Garamond by Jouve (UK), Milton Keynes
Printed and bound by CPI Group (UK) Ltd, Croydon, CR0 4YY

Visit **www.panmacmillan.com** to read more about all our books
and to buy them. You will also find features, author interviews and
news of any author events, and you can sign up for e-newsletters
so that you're always first to hear about our new releases.

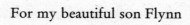

For my beautiful son Flynn

PROLOGUE: ENOUGH ALREADY

I am not getting out of bed. I've tried very hard for months on end to be a normal human being and it doesn't work, so I'm staying here until someone evicts me.

My mobile phone has been buzzing under the pillow, on and off, since 11 a.m. It's now three o'clock in the afternoon and I've had a really big bag of jelly babies and two large glasses of Merlot in those four hours (I try not to be drunk before six o'clock in the evening, otherwise I'd have drunk the bottle by now; I must have some standards). After several days of hiding, I suspect my bed smells, but I'm now immune to my own stink. Inka has alternately been under the covers with me, giving me feline love, or, as she is now, yowling at the end of the duvet, digging her claws into my feet, demanding her latest feed. She looks like a sexy panther when she's angry and it makes me feel sad, wondering whether she'll like it when we have to move into a cardboard box under Waterloo Bridge.

As I'm pouring my third glass of red, tactically moving

my feet six inches up, back and forward again to avoid those demanding claws, I begin to deliberate on who the missed calls could be from, just for fun.

I know it's not Pat because he left to travel the world more than six months ago and, after a couple of painful phone calls – where he described his new 'friends' on Koh Samui (far too many young, nubile females for my liking), the cocktails they'd been necking together and the parties they were about to go to – I called a halt; I told him to send the odd postcard instead, and to call me 'for a coffee' when he's back in London. He took it much better than he should have done and I've not heard from him since, apart from one dog-eared card from Chiang Mai with a picture of a sad-looking street-elephant on it. I wonder if he realized that painted, trapped, miserable animal would ring so many bells in my life right now.

Realistically, it could be my mam calling, as I've not been in touch for a week, but I don't want to speak to her at the mo. She'll ask how my job is going – the one I was forced to take, teaching 'drama' to endlessly disinterested teenagers in a local school populated by hooligans. The one I only started eight weeks ago. And I don't want to tell her the truth. The thing is, not one of those little shits could bear to lose face in front of their mates, so getting them to do a scene together was nigh-on impossible. The girls would go all hard-nosed and pouty, and the boys would drop their voices to 'mouse' level. They would all perform in a monotone; and the final straw came a few days ago when a boy called Golden was talking on his phone during class and I grabbed it off him and dropped it into my full mug of coffee. He went ballistic and the whole class erupted, as it was one of those iPhone-thingies and they're expensive. Meanwhile I stood up, having reached the end of my highly frayed tether, gathered my belongings and marched out, head held high, never to return.

It felt fucking fantastic until I emailed the principal to tell him I wasn't coming back. He replied within five minutes and said he could bring in a replacement teacher immediately, but I would be docked this month's pay; and that Golden had his phone in a bag of rice in the airing cupboard right now, but if it didn't work properly when it dried out, his parents were going to sue me. I couldn't give a damn about Golden's parents, or the horrible job that was destroying my soul, or the fact I can't afford a tin of beans, but my mam might have a few opinions, so I'm avoiding her for now.

Inka changes tack, crawls right up the bed and yowls directly into my face whilst shaking her tail. I spot a single overlooked cat treat on the bedside table and drop it into her mouth. It keeps her quiet for about one-point-seven seconds.

I doubt it will be Sheila who's been calling, because as soon as we found out that Mystery Pot was closing down, with no warning whatsoever, she got a job in another New Age shop as a tarot reader (her reputation as a top-notch clairvoyant went before her). This meant a trek to the other side of London most days for her, so we've hardly been in touch, compared with 'before'. Plus, I've cut myself off from all the spooky stuff – *closed down the receiving tower*, as it were – so there wouldn't be much to talk about. After what happened with creepy Dan and all of the supernatural shenanigans, I couldn't handle any more talking with dead people. It was just too much. I started having lots of nightmares; am still having them, so much so that I even stopped talking to my dead friend Frank. I feel bad about that now because I miss him, but I think it might be too late to make things better, because I've not heard his voice in my head for months; and when I tentatively tried speaking to him lately, I got nothing back. Not a whisper.

About a week ago I actually sat in my living room with tears rolling down my cheeks and a shawl over my shoulders, watching *An Inspector Calls* with Alastair Sim and wondering what it would be like to be dead. Really – what it would be like to end it all. I ran through the options and decided I didn't have the energy or the pain threshold for it. Self-pity was much easier. That's when it became apparent that I was going to have to sack off the horrible job, then go to bed indefinitely. Which I have. But the damn phone hasn't shut up and, unbelievably, is buzzing *again*.

So I take a swig of redders and reluctantly pull it from under the pillow. It immediately becomes clear that all of the missed calls are from my agent, Bill, and the current call is also from him.

Well, I'm not answering it. That way lies disappointment and doom. Bill's probably calling to say he's off on holiday, or there's some outstanding money I owe for new head-shots, or I have an audition for an underwear advert as the fat grandma, and the pay's a hundred quid.

I'm about to switch it to mute and go back to sleep when I hear a voice in my head, loud and clear, and behaving like the boss of me, like he's never been away: *'Get out of bed, you lazy cow. You've got work to do.'*

'Frank?'

'GET UP. You've got an appointment.'

'I'm tired!'

'You're just feeling sorry for yourself. Answer the call, then up, up, up! And feed your bloody cat.'

I can't lie – I've missed the mouthy sod.

I press the answer button on my phone.

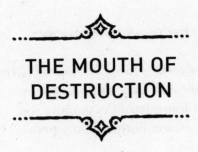

THE MOUTH OF
DESTRUCTION

Walking down Oxford Street feels weird. My legs are wobbly. I want to be back in bed. *Damn you, Bill. And you, Frank.* After several days of hiding, getting on the Tube today was quite a feat. I bought a coffee from the nice Italian man outside the station who always smiles at me, to try to get some energy from the caffeine. The sky is as miserable as I feel. Sheet-metal grey with a side helping of murky cotton wool. Before I left I mistakenly stepped in a bath that was so hot it almost peeled the skin off my legs. It was probably the exact temperature in which to boil crabs. This didn't improve my mood. Nor did my stupid, cheap hairdryer, which suddenly cut out for five minutes mid-dry. Why do they design hairdryers that cut out when they get hot? Surely that's *the point* of them . . .

'*Jesus, you're in a strop.*'

Frank. I'm so glad we're talking again, but I'm not telling him that.

'Suddenly got a lot to say, after disappearing, haven't you?'

'I didn't go anywhere. You did.'

'I didn't. I just got scared.'

'You got chicken.'

'Oi. Have you come back solely to abuse me?'

'Yes.'

'Well, don't, I'm stressed enough.'

'Stop being stressed. You're an actress – this is only a meeting.'

'Easy for you to say.'

'At least you're not dead.'

'Hey! What a cheap shot.'

'I've always been cheap.'

'Touché.'

Frank's right. It is only a meeting. But I'm so skint and so tired of being rejected. Why did I choose a job where I get rejected so much? I'm obviously a masochist. Someone once told me that you crave the foods you're allergic to. I've got a career that I'm allergic to. Unless I get the job in question of course, and then I'm not allergic at all. Well, not until later, when I'm moaning about the catering, or the Costume department, or the size of my dressing room. We thespians are horrible.

'You should just go in there and have a laugh.'

It's hard to have a laugh when you're staring poverty in the face and it's actually laughing back at you, with its tongue lolling out.

'I stink of desperation. They're going to hate me.'

'That's the spirit.'

'Shut up. Sorry, don't shut up. I'm simply anxious.'

'That double espresso you had on the way probably really helped with the anxiety.'

'Actually, do shut up.'

The place where I'm auditioning is dingy, stuffy and has another four actresses already waiting. They're sitting there, all perky, like primped hawks. All of them are regular 'character' faces on TV, and I know immediately I'm out of the running. What a waste of time.

I look at my lines. It's an episode of a northern thing I went for, ages ago. Then I was up for a leading role in the whole series. Now I'm up for four episodes playing a generic slut with four teenage kids who were taken away from her five years ago. *Teenage children!* I don't know why I'm surprised – my currency right now is about as 'current' as Buddy Holly on vinyl. What's galling is that everyone in the show is supposed to be a native of Newcastle and yet not one of them has a real Geordie accent. In fact several of them sound Norwegian; it's a bloody joke. Again I'm the only proper Geordie in this room today, but I don't stand a cat in hell's chance. I'm still smarting that my original part went to a Brummie who sounds like Björn from ABBA every time she attempts the accent. So much so that I have witnessed my mam and dad sitting there watching the show, mugs of tea in hand, tutting and asking, 'Where's she meant to be from?'

To add a cherry to this already irresistible cake, the script they've given me to learn is terrible. Milo, my best pal and a proper writer, would have a cow if he read it. He sweats blood trying to write quality stuff and often gets nowhere, and yet this is going to be on telly and is almost unintelligible. I really do despair sometimes. And I've got plenty of time to despair because, with four ladies in front of me, I have at least forty minutes to wait.

By the time the young casting agent comes out to call my name, in skinnies that must be cutting off the circulation to her torso and a 'vintage' T-shirt for a band whose lead singer choked to death on his own mediocrity, I have murder in my heart and a dead arse from sitting there so long. I'm quite sure my attempt at a smile must look like a cruel grimace, because I certainly feel like wringing her neck. Or crying. Probably crying, actually.

I stumble in behind her, trying not to stare at her tiny backside, and find myself in a claustrophobic, windowless room. Wedged in there are the producer and the director with a camera on a rickety table, pointing towards the chair I just fell into, like an ungainly baby rhinoceros. This is a child's chair, surely? I wonder if it's a deliberate attempt to make me feel low-status, this stubby, minuscule seat? The director is in his sixties, I'd guess, with curly white hair and a denim shirt. He nods, staring at me hard. He has very piercing light-grey eyes. The producer is younger, tanned and has a nose like a fish hook. He nods once, then goes back to reading something on his phone. I immediately dislike him. He has *smug* written all over his shiny jacket, and his hair is so carefully coiffed, it's basically a gleaming chestnut helmet. He looks like a conker. The director nods again, picks up my CV and photo, then looks at me like he's checking my passport.

'So, Tanz, I'm Brian Gordan. How are you?'

'Fine, thanks, Brian.'

'Oh, is that a real Geordie accent I hear there?'

'It certainly is – probably the first one you'd ever hear on this show. Ha-ha.' *Oh, fuck. Why did I say that?*

The producer's head twitches. The director stares even harder. The casting agent jumps like I kicked her in her non-existent balls and emits a tinkle of nervous laughter.

'Sorry, only joking. I was up for this before . . . Katherine Banner got the part. She's great, isn't she?' I'm back-pedalling at 400 mph. But it's too late, I know it's too late. The first thing I said, and I blew it.

'I don't believe you just said that.' I can actually hear Frank snickering.

'I'm nervous.'

'You're hilarious.'

Shit, shit, shit!

'So, you think we haven't got enough local talent on the show then?' The director has a dangerous light in his eyes.

I don't know how to reply. Probably with the truth, seeing as I've already messed up.

'Well, I know how TV works, so I don't think local talent will cut it if they're not big enough names. Sorry – I'm only bitter because I wanted to be in it and I'm not.'

'Hmm. Would you like to read scene twelve of episode four for me?'

Oh no.

I hate this scene. The dialogue is so embarrassing and fake, I have no idea how to make myself sound like a real person and not some autobot. As I open my script at the right page, the producer's phone rings. It's the theme tune

10

to *Mission Impossible*. Could he be any more of a cretin? He stands, throws me a look of disdain and leaves the room to take it. So rude. The director tips his head to one side.

'Anything wrong?'

'Oh, no. It's just . . .'

'Yes?'

The casting agent is wobbling her knee up and down, probably scared to death of what I'll say next. Then the devil seizes me. This is so excruciating, I can't help it – I have to speak my mind.

'It's the scripts.'

'What about them?'

The casting agent emits an involuntary high-pitched hum, which she quickly cuts off. She's gone pink in the face.

'Only one of them makes any sense. Episode six is good. The rest of them read like they were written by a monkey with a crayon.'

'You think?'

'Yes, I think. No Geordie in the history of the world ever said, "Away, man, canny lad, tha's too late." That's half Jamaican and half Yorkshire. Plus, some of the stories don't add up. If I'm confused reading them, what will the audience feel like watching them? Whatever happened to telling a story? How come the episode-six writer gets that and the other ones don't? Who commissions these people?'

The casting child has started to cough. I think she's choking on her own fear. Maybe her throat chakra just collapsed in on itself in horror.

Brian reaches for a bottle of water close by him on the glass-and-wood table and takes a sip.

'Well, Tanz, I would like you to read it anyway – make as much sense as you can of it. Sorry you don't think it's up to scratch.'

I am mortified and my cheeks are on fire. I so badly need cash. But I refuse to regret saying what's on my mind. I'll do that later when I get home.

It's only after I've read a few scenes, and Marcus the jackass producer has returned to watch the last of the whole sorry mess being recorded on tape for the executive producers, that Brian turns off the camera and cracks an unexpectedly dimply grin, the glint in his eye now rather saucy.

'Thank you, Tanz. I would like to say, on the record, that we are working on the flaws in the episodes you mentioned. In fact one specific monkey with a crayon will not be returning for the next series, will he, Marcus?'

Marcus looks from him to me, slightly nonplussed.

'Oh. You mean . . . yes, we've had a few little creative blips that need ironing out.'

Brian picks up a copy of episode six, this one properly bound with a front cover. Agents don't send hard copies any more, only scenes; I only had last night to look at my lines and the writers' names weren't included in the email. He points to the front: 'By Brian Gordan'.

Oh my God, he wrote the 'good' script.

'And I'm glad you saw the genius in my script. Very nice to meet you, Tanz. Be seeing you soon . . .'

Bloody hell. What just happened?

'*You flattered the one person you needed to flatter.*'
'Not on purpose.'
'*Who cares. High-five, Sister.*'

I don't understand anything any more. And, much as I'd love to, you can't high-five a ghost.

A NORTHERN ODYSSEY

'Where are you now?'

'About ten miles from Leeds, so about a hundred miles from you, me darlin'.'

'I'm so glad you're coming home . . .'

It's so wonderful to hear Milo's voice. He's my best friend in the world and he usually makes me feel a million times happier about everything, but recently he's had to endure a lot of ignored messages and calls while I moped about, feeling sorry for myself. Only now that I've left my shit job, and am on my way to my home town to do the job I actually trained for, does it occur to me that Milo sounds more than a little relieved that I'm coming to see him. He sounds positively needy. And also a little 'blurry'.

'Milo, are you drunk?'

'Yes.'

'But it's only three o'clock.'

Even by my standards, being drunk in the house by three o'clock in the afternoon is quite an achievement. I'm usually just 'merry'.

'I know. I only meant to have one, but then I had two, and all at once the bottle was half empty.'

'Of what?'

'Gin.'

'Argh. Wait, wait, my hands-free fell out . . .'

There's a bit of a panic as I bend myself double and drive with one hand, while I desperately feel about in the footwell with the other for that stupid little gadget that hooks over my ear and makes me look like I'm in *The Matrix*. I'm sick of this. I'm going to get a plug-in wire with earbuds instead. I don't care how untrendy that makes me. Eventually I locate the tricky little swine, after nearly snapping myself in half and getting within two feet of bashing into an enormous Royal Mail lorry. I push it back in place.

'Right. Why are you drinking gin on your own in the afternoon, Milo? You'll get depressed.'

I'm aware of the irony of this statement as it leaves my lips, but he doesn't need to know what I've been up to this past week.

'I *am* depressed. I sent that script off over a month ago – and not a dicky bird. They said to wait a week and they'd get back to me. They didn't. I'm skint and, worse, I can't write any more. I've got writer's shock.'

'Block.'

'Shock, Tanz. Shock. Their rudeness shocks me. I'm nothing without my writing. I'm a husk. An empty mussel shell. But I can't write another bloody word; my brain's shut down. Come and stay at mine. Please. We can hang out and watch films and drink loads of my booze.'

I watch the same Royal Mail lorry edge towards the

slow lane and almost send a car full of people flying into the hard shoulder. I wonder momentarily if all lorry drivers are lunatics, or merely a huge proportion of them.

'I can't. They've got me a room at the Copthorne and I've got lines to learn. Lines written in another language that only exists on *Pendle Investigates*.'

He gives a little shriek.

'I still can't believe you're going to be working with Caroline May. She's, like, an institution.'

'I know. That's one of the few perks of playing a thicko slag in a terrible series. I'll meet interesting people.'

'Jesus, sort yourself out. At least you'll be getting a wage and a hotel room. I'll bet you get a minibar as well. Remember there's no such thing as a small part, just a moody, ungrateful actress.'

'Fuck off, Milo!'

He's right. I'll walk away from four weeks on the show with six grand. Not a king's ransom, after tax and agent's fee, but not to be sniffed at. I know I'm being a brat. I'm going to live in a nice hotel, they're not making me stay with my parents (that would be the end of me); and they're paying me to learn lines, say them on camera and live in my home town. *What's my problem?* Plus, of course, I get to spend time with my lovely Milo, who sounds like he could do with some support right now.

'Okay, so you might have a point. I'm being a bit ungrateful. When I finish filming tomorrow, I've got the next day off, so let me take you for food and gins at six o'clock – on me – to make up for it.'

'And that's why I love you, Tania Bombania.'

'Don't call me Tania.'

'Oops. Sorry, witchy-poos.'

I'll let him off, this once. He's drunk. Plus, he doesn't know that I've been completely cut off from the witchy stuff for the past few months. I didn't want to tell Milo how scared I got, after I escaped from creepy Dan's clutches. Even the night I found out I'd got the part in *Pendle Investigates* I had another dream about Dan hanging himself in my bedroom, his deathly, blue-tinged face illuminated by the pale light from my CD player, his bulging eyes suddenly opening and blinking at me. I woke up wailing like a banshee, and only Frank's voice in my head could soothe me and tell me it was just a nightmare. But not even he could completely calm my terror at having my dreams haunted by a killer.

I'm hoping it'll stop, now that I'm away from London. I seriously want that nut-job out of my head.

PENDLE INVESTIGATES

It's freezing, and my common-or-garden-slut character seemingly lives in miniskirts, vest tops and silver sandals. It's even worse than I thought. The costume assistant is called Kelly and she's the most girl-next-door costume assistant I've ever met. She's around thirty and has shapeless long brown hair and a pleasant round face, and she wears alarmingly 'safe' clothes that make her look like a very nice primary-school teacher. She also seems to have no personality at all. I feel far safer with eccentric Wardrobe ladies and men, especially ones with kaftans and mad life stories. I try engaging her in conversation, but quickly ascertain that we would probably not find a point of mutual contact if we chatted from now until 2045. I'm guessing that, in Kelly's world, characters like mine dress as plastic chavs in horrid miniskirts circa 1988, and that's that. I doubt she'd have the imagination to go for something less stereotyped. I grit my teeth as I look down at my legs, which are top-to-bottom goosebumps.

Kelly smiles and nods approvingly.

'You look exactly how I hoped you would.'

I don't punch her. I just stare at my horrible sandals as she leaves smugly, satisfied that her work is done. I couldn't feel more unattractive if I tried.

They've got me in at 6.30 a.m. because I'm the newbie here, and the rule is that newbies take the Make-up slots at the earliest times, so the established stars get a 'lie-in' until 7 a.m., the lucky ducks. It's usually freezing at this time in the morning, but today it's especially biting. I'm on the Make-up bus, shivering, nursing a cup of disgusting instant coffee that the runner kindly provided. I don't remember his name, but he looks like a vole. My make-up artist is called Vicky and she gets up this early most days. She's very chipper, considering, and drapes a blanket provided by Vole over my shoulders as she messes with my hair, making me look as terrible as she can.

'Sorry about this, Tanz, but they told me to grease your hair and generally make it look unwashed.'

Oh, deep joy. 'That's all right, Vicky. I love looking like shit on prime-time TV.'

She laughs. 'It's a character part, you have to look like shit – it's the law.'

'Actually, apart from today, she has so few lines that she's more of an extra. Oscar material it ain't.'

'Take the money and run, Tanz. I know a lot of actresses who can't even get a line in one episode at the minute. It's dire.'

I like Vicky, she's no-nonsense. She's blonde, shapely, forty-odd and probably takes no monkey business from anybody. She smells of White Musk.

'I know, I know. I'm being a moan.'

'Pfff. You can moan all you like; you'll still not be as bad of some of them here.'

Oh, excellent – gossip. 'Come on, spill: who are the divas?'

Just then the room rocks. That means someone is climbing the caravan steps. All at once a chiselled head pops round the door, with eyes like emerald ping-pong balls. They really are big eyes. It's Jamie Brown, who's been on this show since day one. Handsome, northern, up-and-coming and in his twenties; all the young girls like him and he's tipped for the big time. His one problem is that even though he's very nice-looking – even more so in the flesh, as it turns out – he's as stiff as a wardrobe door onscreen. I'm speaking from the viewpoint of a sniffy actress, of course. I'm well aware that this will not preclude Jamie from having a long and prosperous career in Hollywood, which, as we all know, is bursting with famous, handsome, young wardrobe doors.

He nods at me. 'Hello there. Hi, Vicky, you need me yet?'

A curt nod, and that's it. *God I hate this get-up.*

'No, lovely, get yourself some breakfast first, then I'll shout you in when Claire arrives.'

'Cheers.' He's gone again.

'His eyes . . .'

Vicky chortles. 'Ridiculous, aren't they? He's like the snake from *The Jungle Book*. Once you look into them, you can't look away.'

'Is he nice?'

'He's fine. A bit obsessed with himself, but fine.'

'Have you ever met an actor who wasn't a bit obsessed with himself?'

Probably because it's early and cold, and a bit like Dunkirk, we start laughing. Girly giggling, actually. Then the coffee that I'm holding spills – thankfully on the blanket and not my costume – and Vicky takes it off me before I get into trouble, then drops it in the sink. That's the moment when the caravan wobbles again and a very upright head and neck appear, swiftly followed by a petite body in a pink towelling robe.

Caroline May.

The hair is honey-blonde, the unmistakable face is, to my surprise, as frozen as an Eskimo's ice-skate and the eyes glint like diamonds. Lilac diamonds with evil plans.

Vicky stops laughing. I stare.

'Hello, Victoria.'

The Jamaican/Yorkshire/Belgian non-specific accent that Caroline employs onscreen has been replaced with a cut-glass Queen's English that's almost comical. She used to have a lovely, soft face when she was in the long-running series *Terminus 5*. Now it's hard because it can't move. I'm so shocked. You could cut cheese with her cheekbones, and there's hardly a line on her. The woman's nearly sixty and her neck's ten years older than her face, so the effect is simply weird. I know I must not stare, but it's really difficult. Her hair is also about fifteen years younger than her neck. I don't understand why she's done this to herself. What I do understand, with a pang of sadness, is that she dismisses me on sight.

'Caroline, this is Tanz – she's playing Treena for the next few episodes. Tanz, this is Caroline.'

Caroline holds out an unwilling, manicured hand and shakes the ends of my fingers for precisely two seconds.

'Hello, Tammy. I hope they're going to give you something better to wear than that ghastly skirt. Has that Kerry girl gone blind? She really is awful, isn't she? Victoria, I am going to take breakfast in my trailer and wondered if you could come and set my hair in there – it's so cold in here.'

She doesn't look at me again. I've had my allotted moment, it seems.

'Well, the thing is: I've got a lot of extra people to sort today, so if you can hold on for Claire . . .'

'I don't want Claire, I want the senior make-up artist. See you in five minutes.'

And she's gone, trailing an industrial-strength cloud of expensive perfume that catches at the back of your throat like mustard gas. Vicky looks at me, lips tight. I'm flabbergasted.

'Am I mistaken or is she a fucking cow?'

Vicky releases a pent-up breath.

'She likes things just so.'

'Did she get my name wrong on purpose? And Kelly's?'

'Probably. Caroline can do what she likes. She's the money on this show, and she knows it. I'm not supposed to do her hair over there. I've got other people to get ready and I shouldn't have to cart my stuff around the place. Now Claire will have even more work to do in here and I

22

haven't briefed her.' She sighs and faffs unnecessarily with my greasy, preposterous hairstyle.

'What happened to her face?'

Vicky raises an eyebrow. More than Caroline could ever do.

'Jesus, Tanz – never mention her looks in front of her, or any "work" she may or may not have had done. She's very proud of her "naturally youthful" face. She will have you fired if you bring it up.'

'Wow. I never guessed she was a diva. She's so nice in interviews.'

'So was Idi Amin.'

This time Vicky giggles, but I don't. Everyone on this show is going to see me wandering about the place with oily hair and horrible clothes, which will already be a blow to my withered pride. Now it turns out I'll also be working with the Snow Queen's nastier sister.

What a let-down.

Think of the money, think of the money.

SELF-PITY AND GIN

We've had several gin-and-tonics. I'm on the slimline tonic and I had a salad (I don't want to be fat on TV, though it's a little late for that) as Milo tucked into his burger and fries. He has ketchup on his face now and looks the picture of foodie satisfaction. I, conversely, am still hungry and am eyeing up the two chips left in his bowl.

'Milo, I'm not overstating the case when I say she's a complete fucking shit.'

Milo is snorting. I suspect he was drinking before we met up.

'I think I like her even more now. She's the British Bette Davis.'

'You think Caroline May is as talented as Bette Davis? Bette Davis could move her bloody face. And she probably wasn't rude to the cameraman, nasty to the director and dismissive of the rest of the cast and crew – apart from Jamie blinkin' Brown, whose arse she basically licks off every time he comes on-set. It's obscene.'

'Oh my God, do you think they're shagging?'

'Don't be *stupid*. He's far too vain to cop off with an older woman who looks like an alien. But he's not daft; he laps up the attention and keeps Caroline sweet. He'd flirt with a radiator if it was famous.'

Milo giggles, shaking his head at me.

'You are such a bitter, bitchy actress right now.'

'I'm not an actress at all right now. I simply stand around a lot in the back of the shot and have the odd terrible line to say. The one thing Caroline was right about was the costume. Kelly from Wardrobe is obviously doing everything in her power to make me look appalling, so that everyone in the country who watches it thinks I'm a skanky old bird who can't act . . .'

He shuffles round in his chair so that he can put his arm around me.

'Hey, come on. You're not skanky. You're just old.'

I slap his arm. 'Look, I'm not stupid. I know I'd have been thrown into the workhouse if I'd not got this gig. I was on financial red alert. But I can't help thinking I've literally sold my dignity to Satan, simply to keep a roof over my head.'

'Tanz, that's so silly. You never had any dignity, to begin with.'

We both snigger. He has burger bun in his teeth.

'Look, fuck that corpse-faced bitch – I bet she can't talk to ghosts. You're much more interesting than her. From now on, you've got to promise me you'll parade around at work in your whore's skirt like it's Jean Paul Gaultier. They obviously think you've got nice legs if that's your costume, plus you can afford champagne again. What's there to be pissed off about?'

I smile at Milo's ketchupy face.

'You're the best person ever.'

He bows in mock modesty.

'I know, babes.'

I wasn't paying proper attention before, but close up Milo has new little lines around his eyes. Not smile lines – tension ones. I feel a pang. I haven't even asked how he's doing.

'Have you heard from the TV people yet?'

Milo sags over his drink. Just mentioning it saps his energy. He shakes his head.

'Oh, sweetheart. Have you managed to write anything new this week?'

'No. I can't do it, and I won't be able to until I hear back from those bastards. I've worked so hard for no money over the past year – I need a result or I'm going to go mad. I can't keep working for the sake of it; it's killing me.'

'It's not fair, darlin'. You're a genius. Another gin?'

He nods.

'Bombay Sapphires all round?'

He gives me a double thumbs-up and, as we sip and chat, the strain on his face begins to lessen.

By the time we finish up and decide to head down to the quayside to have a nightcap by the river, I've very nearly got my old Milo back.

BOYS IN GLASS HOUSES

As we exit past a squawking gaggle of smokers, the light is fading to dusk. This part of Newcastle is alive with bustle, as usual. Around me I watch the half-naked drunken girls (and older women who should know better) in impossibly high shoes, staggering towards the Bigg Market to flirt with boys in tight T-shirts, with tattooed necks and dodgy tan-jobs. I bet at least half of the young men I've seen tonight own their own sunbeds. I wonder what the skin-cancer rate is with boy-band aspirational males in this region.

'Should we go across the trip-trap bridge?'

I always want to go across the trip-trap bridge. I nod.

Milo leads us past the little alley we would usually go through to get to the quayside and guides us to the Black Gate.

The Black Gate is not a gate at all. It is a very old building that is, or at least was, attached to the actual castle that gave Newcastle its name. It's dark stone, tall, misshapen and a little higgledy-piggledy, as it's been modified and messed with over the years. Nowadays it has been spruced up and is open to the public by day but is still, at night when it's closed up, very spooky. Outside the front of it is a little bridge, which must have had the moat under it, not that there's any water down there now. There's just a steep grassy bank leading to a flattened piece of ground underneath. Sometimes, usually when we've been drinking, we go over it and walk under the tall stone arch to the front door, then dare each other to stand next to one of the floor-level stone arches that look as if they have dungeons behind them. In the gloom, they're shady and horror-film impressive.

As you pass through the tall arch there's a plaque that reads:

THE BLACK GATE
The principal gateway to castle built 1247–50
Upper two storeys built in seventeenth century
Restored, notably by R. J. Johnson 1883–84

Milo carries on a bit further to the walkway that leads across the grass and through the next set of stone arches to the castle itself, and attempts to replicate the music to *The Exorcist* (no mean feat) as I stand alone by the ground-level stone 'window'. As Milo pulls out a cigarette and starts freestyling a deep-voiced rendition of 'Ghosts' by Japan, I turn to look through the mesh that covers an opening into the building, trying to work out where the space behind it leads. I can't tell if it's a room or a corridor.

Just then I hear Frank's voice and simultaneously a

shadow moves in the gloom, almost beyond the reach of my vision.

'Uh-oh. Do you see him?'

Much as I'm relieved to have Frank back, I wasn't sure I was going to 'do' the other spooky stuff any more. But it looks like I don't have a choice right now. There's another shadowy movement. A frisson of cold creeps down my neck.

'Who is it, Frank?'

It's as silent as a tomb in there. But I'm quite sure I'm not alone.

I crane my neck and see the shadow move again. Close to the edge of light before the space disappears into total blackness. Natural as breathing, I quickly 'protect' myself as I feel the familiar pressure on my heart and diaphragm. There's a bloody ghost in there and it's coming towards me.

'Frank?'

'He lives here.'

'No shit, Sherlock.'

I try very hard not to run for it. After the trauma of creepy Dan, all things supernatural still intrigue me, but I'm fighting to stay calm. I turn to Milo, who's still humming and sucking on his fag. He smiles at me, then the grin dies on his face.

'What's wrong with you?'

I step towards him and attempt to look less freaked out. 'Nothing, just a bit chilly.'

I look back into the arch. The shadow is there. It's a 'he', as Frank said. And he's very short. Suddenly I can 'see' what he looks like. Not all the details, merely a dirty face with a cap and scruffy, messy hair. It's a young boy. He looks like an urchin. Not medieval clothes, more Oliver Twist than that. He has such a weird energy about him. I speak to him with my mind.

'Hello.'

He doesn't answer. Just stands there, staring.

'What's your name?'

The shadow is unresponsive. There's an unfriendly feel to this little fella. Suddenly Milo gets the heebie-jeebies.

'Tanz, is there something in there?'

I pause for a second too long.

'Yeah, it's a spirit boy.'

He jumps back like he's been scalded.

'Fucking hell – get away from it then.'

'It's okay, he won't do anything. He's just staring.'

'Jesus Christ, a staring ghost. I can't see anything.'

'Come here.'

'Fuck that. You come here.'

'Don't you want to learn?'

He takes a tentative step forward. His voice is quavery.

'I don't know.'

'He's still here, just standing. He's a child. He won't talk to me.'

Milo's eyes get more terrified as he slowly walks to the arch. He reminds me of a wild horse.

'Unfriendly or mute?'

'No idea. He doesn't seem too happy we're here.'

'Well, why the shitting hell am I walking towards him then?'

'He's a spook, Milo, he can't do anything.'

I'm conveniently forgetting Mona's spectacular floor-show at Dan's house.

'I still can't see owt.'

As Milo gets about two steps away from me, I 'see' the shadow move. In my mind's eye the boy quickly bends, stands again, then jerks his arm. This is followed by an unearthly screech from Milo, which causes me to yawp like a kicked dingo. I have never seen that lad move so fast. In a few seconds he's legged it over the walkway and only slows down when he trips over his laces and lands on his face in the grass.

There is no way I should find this funny, but as I hare over there to make sure he's okay, nerves get the better of me and I'm actually choking with laughter when I reach him. Milo is on his back by now, face like wax, having some kind of panic attack. In between my gasps of mirth and his gasps of fear he attempts to explain himself.

'Stop laughing. It – something – threw a stone . . . a stone hit me . . . really hard . . . on the shin.'

As I help him to a sitting position and try to control my hysterics, he pulls up the leg of his jeans. There's a mark there, already starting to bruise.

'Bloody hell, Milo. He cracked you a good 'un.'

I do my best to calm my anxiety-induced mirth as we sit on the grass. As I stroke his back his breathing slows down and he lights another fag, looking warily back towards the building and the trip-trap bridge. We're too far away to actually see the shadow, but I can feel the 'presence' around this place. He's still watching us, I know he is.

The little boy is called George.

'Thank you, Frank.'

'You've got some work to do.'

'Sorry?'

'He's not the problem. Laters.'

'Frank!'

He's gone. Cryptic swine.

'Tanz, that was horrible. Like a poltergeist. What the fuck?'

'Evidently he doesn't like visitors.'

'You know what: I need another drink. Can we go to my place?'

'Of course, come on.'

Poor Milo's got grass stains on his shirt. He's shaking as I link arms and lead him to the taxi rank. I still keep getting the urge to laugh. Partly because I'm so impressed. *That little spook threw a stone.*

I need to find out more about this George. He's hooked me back in.

SHEILA'S FEELERS

'It *threw a rock* at him, Sheila. I swear. Gave him a gorgeous purple bruise. It was phenomenal.'

I've had my day off. I went to see my mam and dad, then had a walk in the park. Milo's switched his phone off. I think last night was too much for him.

Sheila coughs, like she's bringing up a lung.

'Are you okay?'

Turns out she's been off work ill for a while now. I had no idea. I can't believe I was so up my own arse the past few months that I neglected my lovely friend. One thing I know, though: she should stop smoking. She sounds terrible. Just as I think it, I hear her sparking up. There's no telling that stubborn woman anything, so I keep shtum.

'Of course I am.'

The familiar cockney rasp that I love so well doesn't sound as assured as it did. I called because my spooky mojo is back and I wanted to share the good news. Now I strongly feel the need to go to London right this minute and visit Sheila.

'I'm fine. Plenty of bed rest, plenty of juiced veg and I'll be right as rain. How about you? How are you feeling?'

She knows better than anyone how our little adventure in St Albans knocked the wind out of my sails.

'Better. A new job and a change of scene have perked me up. I thought I'd run a mile if I connected with a ghost again, but now I'm thinking that ghosts aren't the problem. Dan was the problem.'

'That's my girl. I didn't think you'd cut off forever. You simply needed to lie low for a bit. I tell you what, though. I've been doing this spooky stuff for years and I can't believe how much you attract the live wires. Far more than me. Moving things around isn't the norm, you know. Ghosts usually only make the living feel bloody miserable, or stop them getting to sleep or whatever. It's all atmospheric. Not yours, though. Yours throw stones and make pictures fall off the walls. I wonder if it's because you're an actress – you get the ones with a more theatrical bent?'

I start to laugh and she joins in, but quickly dissolves into another raucous coughing fit.

'Sheila, that cough is scaring the bejesus out of me. Can I do anything to help?'

'No, love. Just don't nag me about the fags. Gets right on my nerves, that. A girl's got to have some vices . . .'

'I know, but—'

'Shhh. I'm trying to link into that George of yours.'

We both sit quietly for a minute. I hear Sheila's snaggly breaths as I look out of my hotel-room window over the River Tyne, watching it swirl and eddy, remembering the many stories I've heard of drunken revellers jumping in for a joke, never to emerge alive again. For a second I think I hear a ship's horn from the end of the quay. But there aren't any big ships on the river, so it can't be.

'Hellfire, he's hard to get a grip on, this one. I can see this imp with his little cap on. What a mucky thing he is. He looks like the Artful Dodger, doesn't he? But . . . there's something very dark about the energy around him, Tanz. You'd better be careful. All I get is that he's standing guard. That's it.'

'Yeah, he was staring at us and he wanted us to leave. He made that quite clear. Maybe he's guarding the building?'

'Maybe. But there's an extra layer here, something slippery. I can't tell what he's about, not at all. It's strange. What's he trying to hide? I think you should find out more about the building. Also you could find out if anyone has seen him or knows who he is. It may be documented.'

'Good idea. I've got a couple of standby days this week. They probably won't use me, but I have to stick around, just in case. I'll go up to the library and check then.'

'How's work?'

'Interesting.'

'What does that mean?'

'It means I might have a nervous breakdown.'

Her laugh turns into another cough, but she quickly gets it under control. Probably trying to limit how much I worry.

'Knowing you, you won't have a nervous breakdown – you'll give somebody else one . . .'

'Thanks.'

'I'm sorry I've not called you lately, darlin'. I don't like socializing when I'm ill. It makes me really cranky.'

I hear a male voice concur that she is cranky, and then a laugh. Sheila puts her hand over the receiver, then comes back to me, sounding amused.

'Sorry about that, Tanz.'

I get a stab of jealousy. Only a little one. She's been hanging out with this beautiful Jamaican lad since he came to her for a reading and she basically saved him from a prison sentence. He seems to worship her a bit, and I don't know if they're lovers or simply friends. She's such a cagey tart, she won't talk about it. But he certainly gets to see Sheila more than I do.

'Is that Troy?'

'Erm, yes, he came over to make me some soup. It's a healing thing that his mother taught him.'

'Yeah, right.'

'Watch it!'

'No socializing?'

'Yes, but . . .'

'Night soup. Really? Hmm, night soup. Enjoy-y-y.'

'Pack it in.'

'Speak soon, lovely friend. Get better.'

'I will. Lots of love.'

'Enjoy your soup!'

'Yes, all right, very funny. And keep me posted.'

'I will.'

YOU CAN RUN BUT
YOU CAN'T HIDE

I'm in my bedroom in Crouch End. I can't find Inka. I'm really tired and I need to go to sleep. I feel okay until the light bulb blows. Suddenly the room is dark, with only the light coming in from the night-time window illuminating the room. Now I desperately want to get out of here, but I 'know' I can't. I'm stuck on the bed. Then I hear a shuffling in the wardrobe and I know what it is. The feeling of dread is almost overwhelming. I have to open the wardrobe and I really don't want to. Please don't make me, please don't make me.

I approach slowly and painfully and pull the door open. At first I only see dresses, shirts and a threadbare bathrobe in the gloom. Then, wishing I could run, I pull the bathrobe to one side and there is Dan Beck – creepy, stocky little murderer Dan, on his knees, his tie biting into his neck-folds, head cocked painfully to one side, face white like a horrid clown. I want to scream but nothing comes. Just silent air.

Then he wakes up.

Inexplicably he looks at me with concern in those Deputy Dawg eyes. Then he opens his mouth, a cavern of shadows and secrets, like the stone-arched window at the Black Gate, and suddenly bellows, 'RUN.'

Holy mother of Christ. I was not expecting that.

I fall backwards onto the bed and kick the door shut on that huge, scary noise. I'm terrified, but I still can't leave the bed, so I scramble up to the pillows and bury myself under the covers. I lie as still as I can, biting on the duvet, screwing my eyes shut and willing myself to wake up.

Then I hear something. A tap-tap-tapping.

Tap-tap-tap. Tappety-tap-tap.

What is that? Is dead Dan crawling out of the wardrobe to get at me, in his expensive sweater and jeans, reeking of death and craziness? I peep my eyes over the top of the duvet. The wardrobe is still closed. But there's a little boy with a dirty face and an old-fashioned cap standing, tapping a stone against the wardrobe door. *Tap-tap-tap*. He's in shadow, but his eyes are red-hot coals burning in a black lagoon.

I am going to vomit.

My heart is jumping out of my ribcage. I can't tell what expression is on his face, but that only makes it worse. It's like he's pixelated. I try to scream once again, but only silent air escapes me. And I know I'm going to die. I'm going to die alone and no one will help me.

'Frankkkkk. Frrraaaaaaaaank.'

In my head I scream for the only one who can help me, who can unravel this nightmare and make the ghosts go away. But Frank doesn't answer because in this nightmare

Frank's not there – Frank's dead. My friend is dead and gone forever.

I hide under my duvet again, a terrified ball, until two hands, belonging to I don't know who, begin to drag the covers off the bed. And when I scream, it's still silent.

I am alone and scared, and no one is coming to help me.

YOU CAN ORDER
SHOES ONLINE

Thank goodness I'm supposed to look like an absolute sack of shit in this show. My eyes have purple plums under them and my skin is like crumpled paper. This is what happens when you have to be up at six-thirty in the morning and you spend the hours leading up to it shivering in your hotel room, trying not to go back to sleep in case you have another nightmare.

That dream was epic; it was so real. In the back of my head I *knew* I was dreaming, but it didn't matter because I also knew I couldn't escape and, even though it was a dream, the terror was real enough. I'm now scared it was one of my mam's 'portent of doom' dreams. What if something horrible is going to happen to me? Having no one to help you when you're trapped is the loneliest feeling in the world. Plus, it's made me upset about Frank all over again. I woke up crying my bloody heart out.

It's only in the past year, since I started talking to Frank in my head, that I began to get a grip on my grief. Realizing that he is still here – just not *here* – was such a massive help.

I stopped waking up, drowning in tears that my friend had died in a stupid car accident. A pointless end to a funny, talented, handsome lad with everything to live for. And though I've not stopped missing him, I have accepted that life goes on and that Frank's certainly has (he's always off doing mysterious stuff when he's not being deliberately obtuse with me).

But last night's dream made me wake up feeling like I'd been fooling myself. My fear and my loss told me: 'Frank is dead, you've been pretending to talk to him, and eventually everyone you love will die.'

I know. Cheery.

I tried to get back to sleep, but I couldn't. I wanted to talk to Frank, but I was in such a negative place I couldn't hear him; and even if I could have let him through, I would still have wondered if I was making it up. It was only as getting-up time loomed that I was thrown a lifeline, when he suddenly spoke in my head, as clear as crystal.

'If I'm a figment of your imagination, then how do I know there's a man about to knock at the door with breakfast?'

Within one minute there was a knock. I hadn't ordered breakfast. The guy with the tray was very embarrassed, as he was on the wrong floor; and I was mortified because I looked like I'd done three rounds on a ducking stool, with my sweat-matted hair and my bloated cry-baby face. He couldn't apologize enough, but actually, suddenly, I could have kissed him. The hairs on the back of my neck lifted and I told him it was no problem whatsoever. He looked

rather scared of me at that point and ran off to find the real
owner of the breakfast. I fist-pumped the air.

'You said a man would knock and he did, Frank. You
must be "real".'

'Of course I'm real, you fool.'

On the way to work I get the driver to stop at a petrol
station and grab myself a cherry Diet Coke and two
Double Deckers. I convince myself that I need the sugar,
and that the residual fear from my nightmare will burn off
the calories. When I reach the Make-up truck I've already
had a passive-aggressive stand-off with Stepford Kelly, who
is determined that I should freeze to death, dressed as a
low-rent prostitute, and is providing flimsier and flimsier
tops to hurry the process along. When I voiced a polite
complaint, she just gave me a steely smile and said that she
thought my costume was completely 'fitting', then left. I
now look angry as well as knackered. Vicky raises an eyebrow at me.

'Heavy night?'

'Actually, I had an early one.'

'You're kidding me.'

'Nope. Just a night of bad dreams waking me up.'

'Oh dear. Claire, will you shout to Catering to make a
super-strength coffee, please, before this one keels over?'

Claire, a perfectly canny lass with pretty red hair and a
glass eye, smiles and gets off the bus, hand already reaching
towards the vape machine in her bag.

'Come on then, what were the bad dreams about?'
Vicky asks.

While she applies grease to my already mussed-up hair,

I give her a speedy rundown of my life since I started working at the now closed-down Mystery Pot, plus a brief
summary of the scary little boy at the Black Gate. Instead
of being dismissive, Vicky is completely intrigued.

'That's insane! That was *you* who got kidnapped?'

I'm glad I kept my face out of the newspapers and
refused to be named. Can you imagine the pain in the arse
if I'd been all over the tabloids?

'Are you psychic, then?'

'I don't know. I'm not sure what I am.'

'I love all of that stuff. Where am I moving to, do you
reckon?'

'Sorry?'

'Me and my fella, we've been looking for a house. We
still haven't decided where it will be. Do you know?'

I can't believe I just told her about my traumas and all
she wants is for me to be her fortune-teller. I think this is
the pitfall of being a 'sensitive' and telling folks about it. I'll
always be a bit of a sideshow freak. I'm about to tell her to
get lost when I 'see' a road sign in my head. I move past it,
like I'm driving; it says 'Lamesley'. Then I hear Frank.

*'Tell her she's been looking in Low Fell, but this is where
she's going to live. That should shake her up.'*

'Do you really want to play this game with Vicky?'

'I love games! Go on. Just for fun.'

I do as I'm told. If I'm wrong, it won't matter. At least
she'll leave me alone.

'You've been looking in Low Fell, but Lamesley's where
you're going to settle.'

Vicky's eyes boggle.

'*Oh my God.* We *have* been looking in Low Fell, but last night my lad found a place in Lamesley that he wanted to look at. I wasn't into it, until I saw a photo of the house. It's beautiful. He's trying to book us in to see it tonight. I haven't told *anybody*.'

I feel an inordinate amount of satisfaction at this. Frank is awesome – he *knows stuff*!

'Tanz, that's absolutely amazing. You're the real deal. What does my boyfriend look like?'

I've had enough.

'Stop it, please. I'm not in any fit state for fairground tomfoolery.'

Then I hear Frank's voice again, telling me what to say. He's laughing. Sounds like he's having great fun messing with Vicky. He always liked blondes. 'Frank, you're such a flirt.'

'All right. So, your boyfriend has brown wavy hair, rides a motorbike and has a blue leather biker jacket . . . his surname's Jackson. Now, leave me alone.'

Now Vicky doesn't look so much amazed as totally freaked out.

'You've seen him. You must have seen him. That's not possible. And *how could you possibly know his name*?'

'Of course I haven't seen him – how would I see him? He doesn't come on-set, does he?'

'No.'

'Right then. Now, stop it.'

I think Frank would carry on like this for a while longer,

but there's no reason to completely mess with Vicky's head. For me, it feels a bit cheap. She carries on with my horrible hair, not even having to bother with the under-eye shadows that she usually paints on. They're already there, like squashy mauve beacons.

She keeps eyeing me up in the mirror, then looking away again. When she's finished messing, she puts her hand on my shoulder.

'That's really special, your gift. I hope you realize how amazing it is.'

She leans in closer . . .

'Caroline May would give anything to have a proper talent. That's why she's so bloody awful to everyone. Don't let her upset you, right – she just hates getting old. You're the real deal as an actress, and you're younger. It must kill her.'

'That's very nice of you, Vicky. But don't go thinking I'll tell your fortune every day simply because you're being sweet to me.'

She laughs and spanks me on the top of my head with her plastic comb.

As I'm leaving the truck, burning hot industrial-strength coffee in hand, a thought occurs. It doesn't feel like Frank, so I don't know where it comes from. I duck my head back in.

'By the way. Go to the cinema next week. Don't go shopping.'

Again Vicky looks amazed.

'I cancelled our cinema date. I decided to go shoe-shopping instead. A late birthday treat.'

'You can order shoes online. Go to the pictures with your fella. That's an order.'

She shrugs and gives me a big grin.

'All right, you spooky woman.'

I make a silly ghost noise and leave her laughing.

SUPER STEVE

'HELLO?'

Steve speaks really loudly on the phone. It's like he doesn't trust the receiver to do its job, so he tries to shout it right at you, across the miles.

'Hey, Steve, it's Tanz. How are you?'

'Oh, I'm dandy. Me and the kids are watching *Columbo* and having a snack.'

He sniggers. I love that sound – he's like a six-year-old who's just dropped a spider down your trousers. And I can picture him in the living room right now, his dead wife's embroidered cushions propping him up in his armchair and his little gas fire burning. As I've seen him do plenty of times, I can imagine him gumming his Marmite-and-cheese sandwiches as he feeds our two cats little bits of Cheddar that he rolls into balls between his thumb and forefinger. Inka loves cheese.

'Inka's sitting on my knee. She's not so much in a strop now, the little madam. You're a little madam, aren't you? Aren't you, though?'

His voice is so very gentle when he speaks to the animals. Steve truly is a cat man. I feel a pang. I want Inka to be on *my* knee right now, I miss her warm little body vibrating like a furry truck. Sometimes I think she feels so at home in Steve's house that she'll probably go and live there, if I leave her for too long. She'll stay next door and eat mild Cheddar with Steve and Compo. Inka's started to be more tolerant of Steve's old tabby, to the point of actually letting him groom her some days, as they sit together in Steve's yard. It's very cute to watch.

'How are you feeling, Tanz?'

After I got this job, I went round to see Steve and asked if he could take care of Inka for me while I was away. We had a tipple and I told him about hiding in bed. Then he gave me his theory of life. He said that the world had changed so much, and thrown up so many choices, that it was easier to be depressed now than it used to be. Mostly because of all the things we're trying to live up to, and because we don't have to work every hour God sends, to feed ourselves and our families, any more. He said he'd had such a hard working life that, at ninety, he's very happy to sort his plants and look after his cat. Steve thinks we are the poorer for having nothing physical to take up our time in the modern world.

While I wouldn't want to live a life as difficult as he did, I think he has a point.

'I'm feeling better because I have a job, thank you. But you've made me think. I'm not sure acting is very good for my head.'

'I'm not sure modern life is very good for anybody's head.'

Steve's got it sussed, I reckon. He has every episode of *Columbo* available on DVD, plus many, many black-and-white films. He gardens, he cooks nutritious food, he does the crossword, he strokes his cat and he has a dram or two. He doesn't let anything get him down – not even his rattling ninety-year-old bones. He's the polar opposite of my nanna, who is a slave to every single ache and pain and is completely at a loss as to what to talk about, if she's not complaining about something or bitching about celebrities. I think the last 'celebrity' Steve took any interest in was when the Profumo scandal broke. He has no interest in the TV unless he's watching his own DVDs or carefully chosen documentaries and films. I really like his style.

'Do you need anything, Steve? I can post stuff to you. Or send money?'

'What? Why would I want you to send me money? You already gave me cat food, plus you brought that whisky round. Going down very nicely it is, too, thank you very much.'

'That's good to hear.'

'I'll tell you what, though . . .'

'Yes?'

'When you finish the job and you're coming home, could you get a couple of those stottie cakes for me? I love them, I do. I used to have them when we docked in Newcastle, and they're lovely with good sausages and brown sauce. Best breakfast a man can have. I can freeze one and have it later.'

'Of course! It would be my pleasure.'

'Great. Well, listen . . .'

It goes quiet for a minute, then suddenly I hear a distinctive little meow, then another longer one and Steve's laugh.

'What a good girl, eh? I held one of those treats over her head – the ones you left – and put the phone next to her face. Right on cue, she said hello!'

'Aw. Thank you, Steve. You've made my day.'

And he has. Some people are just marvellous.

'That's all right, girl. Speak soon.'

'Speak soon.'

Bless.

PARANORMAL IAIN

I've decided to visit the library. I love Gateshead library. I borrowed my first library book from here – it was an adult one called *The True History of Vlad the Impaler*. I was six. Don't ask how this happened, I don't know myself; my dad was obviously very liberal over my choice of books. I remember reading stories of Vlad impaling people on wooden spikes, and eating his dinner as he watched them sink lower and lower and scream louder and louder until they died, and thinking, *Wow, those ancient people were a bit harsh.*

When I wander in I am hit by that singular library smell, yellowed paper and old carpet, and the wave of nostalgia that comes with it almost knocks me off-balance. It's hardly changed at all and brings back memories of my imposing infant and junior schools, which were next door to each other and have since been razed to the ground and replaced by a one-storey new-build and a primary-coloured playground. It's not that I miss my childhood, it wasn't exactly

51

Little House on the Prairie, but sometimes I wish I could have lived it with a tad more insight and enjoyed myself more. But I'm sure we all wish that.

'*At least you can live your happy childhood now. It's not too late.*'

'I know. And I do mostly act like an immature idiot, don't I, Frank?'

'*Mostly.*'

'Shut up!'

'*You shut up.*'

'How are you?'

'*I'm very well. Worried about you. You've taken playing this not-so-attractive character a bit personally.*'

'It's embarrassing.'

'*It's a job – get on with it. You're brilliant.*'

'I don't want to be brilliant playing an ugly, common old tart. It'll just mean I'll get offered more ugly, common old-tart parts.'

'*Get a grip. Or stop acting.*'

'And do what? I just don't like feeling stupid and doing stupid things.'

'*But you're always doing stupid things anyway. Take that audition, for example.*'

'Oh my God. Do you ever *stop*?'

I can feel Frank's amusement.

I approach the desk, but nobody seems to be manning it. I look around and, apart from a couple of very heavy-footed little boys with inordinately big heads who are darting about, unchecked, as their shell-suited mam chats on her mobile phone whilst slumping on a bean-bag, the place seems to be empty.

I'm sure I can find a book on the Black Gate myself, if I go to the reference bit. As I walk away from the desk I hear a God-awful crash. I spin round in time to see a young man with spiky ginger hair and little round glasses hopping out of the way of a stack of hardback books that he has dropped to the floor. I also think I hear him mutter a strong expletive, but I couldn't swear to it in a court of law.

'Are you okay?'

He stares over at me, trying to focus through his specs, then rolls his eyes.

'Just being a clumsy twat, as usual.'

He glances at the Munsters, who are clomping around making a fort out of cushions. He looks relieved that they haven't heard him say 'twat'. I'm pretty sure they've prob-ably heard worse than that, but that might be a sweeping generalization. I'm good at those.

'I'm always dropping something.'

'You want me to help you pick them up?'

'No, no. You're fine.'

He's a little thing, like a wiry pixie. His voice is much deeper than I'd expect, with a soft Geordie accent. He starts piling the books up again, then suddenly straightens and looks right at me.

'Wait a minute, I know you! Is your name Tanz?'

I'm scared. It's a knee-jerk reaction. Like when you have a police car driving behind you with the blue lights flashing and, even though you've done nothing wrong, you think they've come to arrest you.

'Erm. Yes.'

'You're an actress aren't you? You were in *The Neighbourhood*. I loved that show. You were really funny.'

Another tart role, but at least it was a comedy and my character hadn't given birth multiple times. It was ten years ago, though. How does he remember?

'That was ages ago!'

'You haven't changed.'

'Fibber. Yes, I have.'

'Well, your hair maybe. But please let me shake your hand – you're a brilliant actress.'

Oh my goodness, he thinks I'm good. The only time I really get recognized as an actress these days is in the North-East and it still surprises me, as it's been so long since I did anything of any substance.

He approaches shyly and holds out his hand, a big grin on his face. His eyes are dark. His teeth are off-white and a tad pointy.

'Are you doing anything at the minute?'

I take his paw in mine. It's warm and dry. He has clean nails.

'Oh, well, actually I have a small part in *Pendle Investigates*. Not my finest hour, but it's nice to have some work.'

'Really? That's excellent. It'll be great to see you on the screen again.' He dips his head conspiratorially. 'You'll be the only real northerner in it. That'll make a nice change.'

So he noticed, too. It makes me wonder how many

Geordies sit there watching it, shaking their heads in disbelief.

'You'll get me in trouble, saying things like that . . . erm' – I look at his name badge – 'Iain.'

'Sorry, no offence. I'm just a bit overexcited to have you here. Absolutely zilch ever happens in this place. You've made my morning.'

'Thank you.'

'Anyway, what can I do for you? You looking for something to read "in between scenes"?'

He looks very pleased with his knowledge of 'the business'. It always amuses me that people imbue acting with such otherworldly glamour. Waiting around to go on-set is about as boring as anything you can think of. Someone seems to have informed him of this.

'Actually I'm looking for information on the Black Gate in Newcastle. A local book or some leaflets on the subject would be fantastic. I want to know about its past.'

He shows me his fangs again.

'Well, that's not difficult. Wait a minute while I gather that pile of boring nonsense off the floor, then we can get you what you need. Me and my mates used to go and stand outside the Black Gate when I was a kid, you know. To scare ourselves.'

Bloody hell.

'Really?'

'Oh, yeah. Plenty of spooky tales about that place. Loads of kids used to hang about there.'

'Wow. Did you find any ghosts?'

He raises an eyebrow at me.

'No. But I happen to be interested in the paranormal, so I research that kind of thing.'

Coincidence or what?

'Wow. You have no idea how glad I am that I came in here today.'

'There's no way you're more glad than I am.'

GLADYS AND THE
GHOST WALK

Amongst the pamphlets and books Iain handed me, along with his mobile-phone number (in case I needed to ask him anything else, of course), was a leaflet for a ghost walk in Newcastle. Not an official leaflet, more of a photocopied handwritten piece of paper with a really rubbish ghost-in-a-sheet drawn on it. I rang the number and booked it. And that's why a very nervy Milo and I are now on the quayside, alongside a wide old lady carrying a small plastic bag filled with what looks like all kinds of goodies. Standing a bit apart from us are a young goth lad and his girlfriend who only speak in whispers, have coordinating black-and-blue hair and are seven inches taller apiece, because of extraordinary black wedged boots with rubber soles.

Our host, Llewellyn Bartholomew, is decked out in a red-and-gold jacket and a jaunty fedora and looks as crazy as a coot, with his tailored white beard and his commanding glare. For all we know, he's a crank, but he's only charging us a tenner each for this walk and he's also quite fabulously theatrical. Plus, I'm interested in what he'll say about the Black Gate, so it's worth a go.

Milo links his arm through mine, which is a good indicator that he's not over the stone-throwing incident yet. He looks so tired. I don't like what the writing world is doing to him, but he doesn't want to do anything else with his life, so how can I help him? Right now, I can't.

'Tanz, I'm not sure I'm cut out for this ghost stuff. I had a horrible dream about a little boy with coals for eyes last night. It freaked me out.'

'Whoa. I had a nightmare about him too.'

'Did you?'

'Yes, I bloody did – I'll tell you about it later.'

'OMG. I'm scared, Tanz; he threw the stone at me, and not at you . . . What can it mean?'

'Maybe he doesn't like men. Or he desperately needs the attention of a man. A daddy?'

'You think he wants a father figure? Because, I mean, this isn't *Casper the Friendly Ghost* here, is it? Even if it was possible to mentor a spectre, I wouldn't want one that throws things at me. I'd want one that gives me insights into the unknown – like what Barbra Streisand wears to bed, and whether heaven's full of cake.'

'You don't even like cake.'

'I do; I do like cake. I don't like *fruitcake*. Because fruitcake is like a cow pat full of fucking raisins.'

'You are.'

'You are!'

'Fruitcake.'

'*You're* the fruitcake!'

'*Ahem!*'

Llewellyn has assumed a 'stance'. Superior and hilarious. A seventy-year-old man with a beer belly, a jaunty hat and a cocked knee might be the most splendid thing I've ever seen. I suddenly think I might love Llewellyn; I hear from his suppressed giggle that Milo has found a new hero, too.

'I shall now begin the tour. Follow me.'

Llewellyn does not walk, he stalks. He is the poor man's Laurence Olivier. After ten steps or so he stops dramatically and points up a stone stairway that is narrow, unmistakably old and very steep.

'In 1810 those little doorways were the front doors of very, very poor and, from what we can see, relatively tiny people.'

He steps forward dramatically and points up the stairs.

'If you look on the first level, up there in the gloom, before the stairs go off to the left and up again, you will see the site of a murder. Eliza Dawn, a lady of disrepute, left her own hovel on the next level up – perhaps taken a little too much with drink – and made her way down, shouting after a client who, as it were, took his succour without paying for the goods and ran away. She reached the level that you can see now and shouted after the ungentlemanly gentleman to come back and pay for his pleasure – waking, behind the dark red door we see, a husband, his wife and their newborn infant.'

I look at Milo, who is gripped.

'The husband, John Chalk, was quick to react to the din after his baby son began to cry. Blazing with fury, he leaped from his bed, grabbing a poker from the cooling hearth as he covered the insignificant distance between his bedroom and the front door.'

Llewellyn is acting all of this out as he speaks, one hand gripping an imaginary poker, the other hand an outstretched Nosferatu claw. Milo suddenly nudges me. He has to stop it or I'll laugh.

'As he swung it open, he discovered the neighbour from upstairs, Eliza, drunk and caterwauling curses after the ungentlemanly gentleman; and, without taking a second to think, he swung the poker and, with the power of his fury, smashed her skull and silenced her once and for all. He then kicked her down the stairs, closed the door, wiped the poker and went back to bed.'

He pauses for effect and looks straight into our eyes, one person at a time, hammering home the gravity of such a death and the cruelty of the man who committed it. I have to say, I salute Llewellyn's flair. But I also must admit that I hate loud noises, and being woken up by them is especially irritating, so I have a lot of sympathy for John Chalk. If I'm honest, I wouldn't want a crazy, drunken prostitute screaming her head off outside my front door, either. And while I don't have a poker, I would probably smack her with something else until she stopped.

Milo links his arm through mine again and I can feel a quiver run through him. The story has given him a scary thrill. My sweet, beautiful Milo is just so blinkin' sensitive. Llewellyn, suitably satisfied that he's caught our macabre interest – the old lady is chewing on a toffee with an entertained look on her face, and the goths are gripping each other's hands and staring expectantly up the stairs as if the angry prostitute is going to come tumbling down at any second – carries on, after clearing his throat loudly.

'Now John Chalk, for all his attempts at denying his actions, was swiftly found to be the culprit and was hanged, leaving his wife and child to fend for themselves. This was not a great prospect in times of such poverty. As for Eliza, she was buried in a pauper's grave at the age of twenty, after a horrible life and a violent death. Now, where's the "ghost" in all this? I hear you ask. Well, there have been reports from many a person climbing the steps late at night, after a drink or two, of the sound of a woman's cries, then whimpering on the stairs, up near the doorway there. I would conjecture that Eliza didn't die immediately and these are the sounds of a woman in trauma, bleeding and breathing her last, probably trapped in an endless cycle of not understanding quite what happened, or why she died . . .'

Oh, Llewellyn's good. I loosen the focus of my eyes and glance up the stairs, to see if I can 'see' any kind of shadow. But I can't. All I can feel is a huge, heavy sadness; partly for the girl who died there, and partly for the family who lost so much, all because of one moment of hot anger from a new father who was probably exhausted.

Out of nowhere, I have a flash. Suddenly there's the smell of a dying fire. A damp, peaty scent in the air that wasn't there before. And the stink of rubbish on a tip. Plus shouts. Not scared or drunken ones, but the sounds of men calling to each other, and of wood on metal, like in a shipyard or maybe a factory. For a moment the middle of my forehead feels like it's being sucked down a tunnel and I

61

think I'm going to faint. Then, just like that, it's gone again; everything is back to normal and I have no idea what happened.

Milo leans in and whispers in my ear, 'This is so horrible – I love it!'

'Follow me.' Llewellyn's off again.

I glance over at the old lady, who's still chewing her sweet, and feel discomforted to find her magnified eyes fixed right on my face. I give her a weak little smile and she gives a tiny nod in return. Not knowing what else to do, I grip Milo's arm more tightly and turn to follow in our leader's determined footsteps. Llewellyn strides across the Swing Bridge – that beautiful, low red-and-white bridge that can actually open to let ships pass through – and leads us to Bottle Bank on the other side, near a bunch of clubs and a restaurant. Further up there's a luxury hotel. This side of the bridge is Gateshead and it's certainly getting posher. Llewellyn stands, eyes closed and waiting, until the old lady, huffing and puffing, catches up with the rest of us, eyes looming large behind her thick blue-rimmed spectacles. He waits until she's settled her carrier bag, after grabbing a can of fat cola out of it and popping the ring.

'This part of town looks very different from how it looked in 1854. Then the whole of the quayside was a mass of large warehouses, manufactories and mills right by the water's edge on this side. It was one of the largest ports in the kingdom and was filled with work and bustle. Behind the large buildings and up all of these steep banks – some of the oldest streets in the North-East, I might add – were densely populated tenements, built extremely close together and filled with poor rancid folk, crammed into small rooms, living from hand to mouth. In these tenements cholera was rife and sanitation was rudimentary, to say the least. At one point, two privies served literally hundreds of families in the area, so you can imagine how many people "relieved" themselves in thoroughly unsuitable places. Especially when you add alcohol to the equation.

'And it was on Friday the sixth of October 1854, in this setting, that a fire started in Wilson and Sons' worsted factory. This then led to the fire in Bertram's bonded warehouse nearby, which was huge – seven storeys high – and stored sulphur, nitrate of sulphur and other combustibles . . .'

The old lady tuts and shakes her head, obviously knowing the story well. Llewellyn acknowledges her with a serious nod, then carries on.

'As you may already know, the fire in Bertram's caused such a monumental explosion that it was heard clearly twenty miles away, and spread burning debris of huge proportions all over Newcastle and Gateshead, destroying much of both towns. The fire engines, already deployed on the Gateshead side trying to control the first fire, were buried under rubble and . . .'

Llewellyn looks ominously up the nearest steep bank.

'All of the tenements were utterly destroyed in this, the great fire of Newcastle and Gateshead – killing many people, and getting rid of a cruel, dingy firetrap forever. It was decided afterwards not to re-erect the tenements, but to start afresh. Now as you can imagine, such a concentration of violent death will have turned up plenty of stories, with witnesses stating in the next fifty years or so that they heard children's cries in the night, the sound of screaming women, phantom explosions and men weeping. But a more notable and recent story, which has cropped up many times – usually from people walking down here near dawn, returning from night-shifts or clubs – is of a man dressed strangely, asking for a light. He always tells them not to walk any further as there's been an explosion up ahead, then disappears. Many witnesses, on being shown an example outfit, testify that he does indeed sport the garb of a fireman of the era. One of those who were buried in the rubble perhaps?'

Just as Llewellyn's finishing, I see a heat haze over his shoulder. A disturbance in the air. There seems to be a very tall man standing behind Llewellyn, wearing some kind of waders. The back of my neck prickles. I wonder if he's the ghost of a fisherman who used to fish the Tyne. But that seems unlikely, as the Tyne, until recently, was far too dirty to contain fish.

Then I hear Frank's voice, warm and matter-of-fact.

'That's Sebastian, his uncle. He likes to watch the ghost walks. He goes everywhere with Llewellyn.'

'Really? Should I tell him, Frank?'

'Wait until the end . . .'

Llewellyn strides off again, back across the bridge and up the steep hill towards the Black Gate. Our little old lady is seriously sweating now, but is waddling after us gamely. The two rather sweet goths, who kiss and canoodle between each ghoulish story, march like a pair of skinny giants in their moon-boots, following diligently up the hill. Milo

64

holds my arm a little tighter and slows my gait as we approach the Black Gate.

'I'm scared to go back, Tanz. That little dead hooligan might start lobbing boulders again.'

'It was one stone, Milo. And how do you know he'll single you out this time? Even if he is there, he might choose Llewellyn, or Marilyn Manson over there.'

'That Marilyn Manson would probably like it. I think he got a chubby on when Llewellyn was describing the prostitute bleeding to death.'

'Well, whatever. All I know is that Llewellyn might be able to tell us who that little lad is, or at least tell us if anyone else has seen him.'

'Fine. But one sight of a flying pebble and I'm off.'

'Fair enough.'

Even as we round the corner and approach the trip-trap bridge I've already got a bad feeling. Whatever is hanging about this place doesn't want us back. My skin tingles as the air gets noticeably colder. No one else seems to feel it. We all stop near the arch where I saw the little boy. Milo stands to the other side of me, using me almost as a shield. Or a protector. I wink at him but I'm feeling uneasy.

Llewellyn motions around him, pointing at the building with a flourish.

'The Black Gate. Built between 1247 and 1250, this was the last addition to the castle's defences, and had a portcullis, no less, and a walled tunnel straight into the main castle. The building has changed a lot since then, and very little remains of the medieval layout. Since its original inception it has been remodelled as a rich man's house, then a public house, then a slum dwelling, then a library for the Society of Antiquaries. Now the library has been moved and this wonderful building is open to the public until five o'clock most evenings.'

My eye is drawn to the stone-arched window – how could it not be? I glance at the lady in the glasses who, I find, is also staring at the shadowed space. Just then I feel a weight in my belly, much stronger than before, and the pit of my stomach begins to contract. I hope I won't be sick.

'Obviously a lot of people have passed through this building, many of whom will have died here. And there are many accounts of temperature changes, strange noises in the halls, shadows moving and, sometimes, a little girl dressed in red.'

Milo leans in. 'Like in *Schindler's List*.'

I try to smile, but I feel faint as well as queasy. I glance into the arch again and spot the haze at once by the right-hand edge. When I 'unfocus' my eyes, I can see him: the boy. Inside my head, he's in the same garb as before, but this time his face isn't fuzzy; it's like that of a cunning man, and he has black eyes that burn into you. The black irises look to be rimmed with red, giving the impression of burning coals. The pressure against my diaphragm is almost unbearable and his face is as scary as hell.

Llewellyn looks at me, as he's about to carry on, and stops dead. 'Are you all right, there? You've gone a very strange colour.'

'Erm . . .'

Milo stares at me, then backs off from the arch. 'Oh Christ, is he here?'

Suddenly the goths are all kohl-rimmed eyes and expectation, channelled in my direction.

Llewellyn sounds a tad put out. 'Is *who* here, young lady?'

'It's nothing – it's just . . .'

Right then and there, sweet-faced Marilyn Manson jumps a few inches off the ground and spins towards the building. 'What was that?' He has an unexpectedly manly voice.

'Someone threw something at me.'

Milo shrieks, but at least he doesn't run.

'He did that to me! He threw a rock at my leg.'

'*Who* did?' Llewellyn is sounding distinctly peeved, now.

The old lady with the bag of snacks and the blue-rimmed glasses points a finger at the arch. 'That evil-looking schemer in the corner over there.' She takes a bite of a Snickers and nods.

I'm dumbfounded. 'You see him too?'

'Of course I do. He's not what he seems.'

'What's your name?'

'Gladys.'

'Gladys, how come you can see him and didn't say anything?'

'I see all of them. That poor lass on the stairs; if you go there late enough at night, she's there. And if she'd not died that night, she'd have died another one. She was trouble with a capital T, and she's not really a ghost – that's only an imprint.'

'Oh, wow. Is that why I couldn't sense her?'

'Aye, pet. I've seen her before, but she's only around at the time it happened in the early hours. She's not aware of anything, it's just like a film playin'.'

She's so broad Geordie that I doubt any of my London friends would understand a word she says. She looks at Llewellyn, who is rather unimpressed by this turn of events.

'And that story you were tellin' about the fireman, that's not true, is it? I could see about ten people millin' around there and they weren't firemen at all. It was families from the houses, and a poor lad who was asleep on board one of the boats when the explosion went off. Nice tale, though.'

Llewellyn has the grace to look a little ashamed. The goths are agog with awe, clutching each other's hands for dear life. I am so impressed I have almost forgotten how sick I feel.

'Listen, lass, you want to be careful of that devil. He's gone now, but he doesn't like you pokin' about, does he?'

'No. He's fond of throwing stones as well. Poor Milo's got a bruise, haven't you?'

Milo nods and rolls up his trouser leg.

Llewellyn clears his throat.

'As far as I'm aware, there are no stories of little boys haunting the Black Gate. Are you sure this isn't a case of a vivid imagination in a historical setting?'

Milo rears up at this, offended on my behalf.

'I'll have you know that my friend here is a top-of-the-class, grade-one genuine article psychic medium who got kidnapped by a psychopath and solved a murder case for the police recently – so don't you go questioning her credentials as a ghost-sniffer, right? And you try getting physically attacked by a dead chimneysweep and see how you like it. We are *not* making this up. Ask her.'

He looks to Gladys, who nods sagely, as the two black-garbed teenagers stare at her and then me, with something akin to hero worship. Out of nowhere the girl speaks, in a teeny-tiny, cutesy voice, which suits her red cupid-bow mouth perfectly.

'Did you really solve a murder?'

'Yes, but the police didn't know there'd been a murder until I was kidnapped and the murderer hanged himself.'

Marilyn Manson shakes his head in wonder.

'That was you? A ghost throws a stone at me, and now this. This is the best day of my life.' He and his girlfriend kiss.

'Thank you for the warning, Gladys. I'll be on my guard. There's more to this than meets the eye, I think.'

Gladys stares at the building, chewing thoughtfully, as Llewellyn puffs out his cheeks and shakes his head.

'This is most irregular, you know. We don't usually spend so much time in one place.'

'Sorry, Llewellyn. Your ghost walk is really good – no one's trying to ruin it – but me and Milo had a bit of an experience here already, and now this lad here's had a stone thrown at him by a ghost. It does make things quite spicy, don't you think?'

Llewellyn shrugs, unwilling to give up his superiority just yet.

Gladys approaches me, a dot of chocolate glistening on her chin, and grabs my hand.

'Watch out for that bad one, all right? He's behind all this and he's not exactly friendly.'

A cold chill goes through me. Why can't I see nice ghosts, and give people comforting messages about their nannas and stuff? Milo looks terrified.

'You want to go home, darlin'?'

He nods as the two goth kids strike up a conversation with Gladys, now they realize that she knows her onions about the undead. I turn to Llewellyn and offer him my hand. He takes it a little unwillingly.

'Thank you so much – that was fantastic, but I think we need to go now.'

'But you'll be missing a treat at the Bridge Hotel. A headless waif and a disgruntled porter.'

'I'm sorry about that. I bet it'll be great; we . . . we need to get off home. But . . .' I take Llewellyn's elbow and lead him to one side. 'Just to let you know. A big man in waders called Sebastian is watching your ghost walk. He always does. He really enjoys it.'

Llewellyn's face is a picture.

'Sebastian, you say?'

I nod.

'Great Uncle Sebastian?'

'That's him. He's always with you, apparently.'

Llewellyn stands stock-still for a second or two, looking into my face like I might be having him on. Eventually he speaks again, partly to himself.

'Sebastian was an adventurer. A real credit to the family. And, in later life, a keen fisherman. You really saw him?'

'I did, down by the quayside after you told us about the great fire. He was huddling in, having a whale of a time.'

Llewellyn's theatrical smile takes on a more childlike aspect.

'He was the best uncle in the world. Quite the character.'

'He obviously thinks you're quite the character now. He sticks to you like glue.'

Llewellyn swallows.

'That's very good to know. I'm so glad he enjoys my walks. So very glad.'

I smile my best smile at him.

'Most of the ones around us are good. That's nice, isn't it?'

He nods.

Most of them.

FOLLOWED HOME

'It hit me while I was standing there and it hasn't left yet, Tanz.'

Milo is on his best squashy sofa, clutching a gin-and-tonic bigger than him, with every lamp in the room lit. (He has lots of lamps: a lava lamp, three side lamps, a tall standing lamp and a string of Chinese lantern fairy lights strung around his fireplace.) He simply can't get enough light into this room tonight.

'What does it feel like?'

My drink is mostly tonic. I have work in the morning and I don't want to get drunk and wake up extra-moody. I'm currently curled up on his comfy armchair, which looks like it was made for the giant up the beanstalk (fee-fi-fo-fum). I have spent quite a lot of the last three years dozing in this chair after nights of booze and chat. It's the magic sleep-chair.

'It was like a pressure on the top of my head and against my chest when you said that horrible stone-throwing mutant was there. Then it went away a bit, but not totally.'

Milo takes a large gulp of his drink. The ice clatters and the slice of lime bobs merrily. His eyes look much darker tonight, more of a stormy grey than his usual blue.

'You don't think that violent little bastard has followed me home, do you?'

'I don't know, Milo. I'm so unsure about this stuff. I know Mona was still around when I went home from the shop that time, but she was crying for help. I don't know if she was following me particularly; it was simply that I'd tuned into her, as had Sheila, and she could communicate with us wherever we were.'

'But I'm not a bloody medium. What does he want with me? Ghosts are all very well as a concept, but I don't want a little freaky one with an attitude problem latching on to me. It'll be like my last boyfriend all over again.'

I can't help a little giggle. Milo's last boyfriend was a tad on the short and aggressive side.

'I remember Sheila telling me once that certain earth-bound spooks who should have moved on by now hook into people, because of a similarity or a personality trait that they recognize or want to exploit. The question is: what have you got in common with that boy?'

Milo sighs.

'I don't know. But he better *fuck off* immediately, because I've got enough on my plate right now, without this kind of hassle.'

He leans from the settee and grips my shoulder. He's blinking rather slowly, falling into the grip of the icy, limey gin.

'Tanz, if it does turn out that little sod has followed me,

73

will you be able to exorcise him into next week? I mean, how dare he? I should be able to choose my house-guests, shouldn't I? I don't even like kids. I never have real kids in here, never mind invisible ones with superpowers.'

'If this feeling hasn't left you in the next couple of days, we'll get it sorted, I promise.'

'Thank you.'

'You're welcome. Anyway, I just wanted to say: thank *you* for what you said to Llewellyn about my abilities. You have more faith in me than I do. You are really sweet.'

'You are.'

'*You* are . . .'

When it's time to get into my taxi, Milo is pretty contented. He's pleasantly drunk and drowsy. We hug mightily, then he stands in his front doorway, illuminated by a gazillion-watt light bulb (the brighter the light in the hall, the less likely burglars are to choose your house, he reckons).

'Milo, I think you're going to hear about your script in the next few days. All will be well.'

'Really?'

'Totally.'

'Thank you so much, lovely witch.'

'You're welcome.'

As I clamber onto the back seat of the Nissan (I think it's a Nissan), which has a vanilla tree-thingy hanging from the mirror so that it smells of custard, I glance back to give Milo a last wave. For a second as I look his way, I see a shadow behind him. A tall shadow – not a boy, a grown-up man – and in that instant I think I see the glow of coal-black eyes. Nothing else. Just those eyes. And even though I keep waving, I get a shot of fear. Then, as quickly as I saw it, it goes.

'Frank, who's that standing over Milo? Who is it? Should I stay with him tonight? Is he in danger?'

The cab pulls off, and Frank doesn't answer. Frank only answers when he feels like it, it seems. On the way back to the hotel I begin to wonder if I'm getting paranoid and my nightmares are teaming up with my worry about Milo, to make me think I saw something that I didn't.

My anxiety is calmed by the text I receive from Milo as I'm exiting the lift to go to my room:

Off to the land of nod. Morrrtal drunk with every light on but defo goin to sleep. Thank you for making me feel better. We have the best adventurings. Big love

But as I settle down on the laundered hotel sheets, I can't get rid of the nagging at the back of my mind that something has homed in on me and my best mate, and it isn't finished with us. Not by a long shot.

GELFLING INVASION

I'm in my caravan, my tiny little dressing room with a fan heater and a mini chemical toilet, when I hear one hell of a commotion. It's a woman shouting. Knackered after a fitful night, buzzing from two very hot cups of vile coffee and done up like a dog's dinner in my disgusting costume (*kill me now, please, kill me now*), I amble out of my door, trying to look for all the world like I'm just off for an innocent wander.

As I reach Caroline May's considerably larger accommodation – an American camper van no less, with a double bed in it and a kitchen and all sorts – I hear the kind of tantrum screams that can shatter eardrums at thirty paces. I'm really not sure whether I should knock on the closed door. As it goes, she doesn't acknowledge my presence onset yet, and still calls me Tammy when we're forced to share a scene, and her aloof exchanges with me are painful. Why would she want me to knock at her door now?

I still find it hard not to stare at Caroline, due to her extraordinarily tight and altered face, juxtaposed with those lovely lilac eyes. Every time I look at her I remember a puppet-based movie I used to love called *The Dark Crystal*. There are elfin creatures in it called Gelflings. More and more actresses these days are having 'work' that turns them into Gelflings. Even the young ones. A whole new master race of vain, terrified, neurotic, immobile-faced Gelflings who can only think about looks and their place in the pecking order of Gelfling City. It's an epidemic, and I'm afraid Caroline is now Queen of the Gelflings. She is Mistress Gelfling, *numero uno*. And she is currently screaming at the top of her highly strung lungs.

'DON'T YOU DARE EVEN TRY THAT SHIT WITH ME. YOU WILL NEVER WORK IN THIS TOWN AGAIN. DO YOU READ ME, MISTER?'

I didn't know people actually said things like that; it's a clichéd line from a bad movie, surely? Boy, she's pissed off. As I'm standing, deliberating and pretending not to listen, Vicky sticks her head out of the Make-up bus and motions me in. I'm already 'done', but I obey. When I've scrambled up the wobbly steps and entered, Vicky closes the door behind me.

'Oooohh, dear. Fireworks!'

'What's going on?'

'Turns out the ratings aren't so good on this as they used to be. Looks like Miss Lady doesn't have the same clout any more. And I think the newly weird face is about to make things worse. Anyway she has found out that, in a bid to boost ratings, she is going to have a new "boss" for the last episode of this series, and then the whole of the next.'

'What's wrong with that?'

Vicky sighs and lowers her voice.

'It's Amber Chase.'

'Who?'

'Amber Chase, played her daughter in *Terminus 5* for a few eps? She's a big, grown-up girl now. Just did a massive stint in the West End. Completely gorgeous, funny and a brilliant actress. Caroline is spitting tacks. Looks like her time is nearly up. I can see them edging her out soon enough. Now she's on the phone to the producer, giving it all that.'

Vicky does snapping lobster claws in the air.

'The thing is, she's going to have to suck it up. You see, be an arsehole long enough and it catches up with you. I almost feel sorry for her.'

I try not to laugh. Caroline's simply a terrified Gelfling after all. But that is one hell of a row she's making, and it's not like she's Mrs Charm with anybody on this set, so I'm not sure what she expected.

Just then the door opens and in comes a very beautiful young lass who goes straight up to Claire, who's manning the other Make-up seat, and gives her a hug. I think I recognize her but can't remember where from. Then it hits me; it's Katherine Banner, the Brummie who got my part in this series – the rookie cop. She's petite and smiley, with green eyes and tousled boyish hair, and has not yet succumbed to the Gelfling factor. She grins at me.

'Hello! I'm Katherine! Have you heard *that* out there?'

Vicky pulls a face and nods. Katherine laughs like a drain.

'Someone's not happy!'

She holds out her hand to me.

'Are you Tanz? Vicky says you're amazing. And you're *psychic*. How cool is that? Nice to meet you.'

Everything Katherine says is perky. She's one of life's optimists. I don't always trust perky people, but she seems nice and friendly.

'Thank you, good to meet you, Katherine. Just so you know, I don't always have my hair plastered to my head with grease.'

'I know you don't, you daftie. I've seen you on telly before – you're fab.'

She sits in the chair that Claire has waiting for her. *Bless her.* I'm now thoroughly disarmed and feel bad for being so horrible about Katherine's Geordie accent. She looks again towards the door, as Claire begins to open an expensive foundation and get her brush ready. A lot of indignant noise can still be heard.

'How's Caroline been treating you?'

'Erm . . . well, not that brilliantly actually. She calls me Tammy and ignores me.'

'Oh, she does that. She ignored me for the first year and now she calls me by my full name all of the time. *Katherine Banner, could we do those lines again, please, you were a little fuzzy last time. Chop-chop.*'

Her impression is perfect.

'Ignore her, Tanz, she's an angry old cunt.'

I was so not expecting the c-bomb. I explode with laughter.

'At least it's not her in your scenes today. You've got me and Jamie.'

'Is Jamie okay? I've not really spoken to him, apart from a nod hello.'

'Oh, he's fine . . .' Katherine leans forward conspiratorially. 'Just not the sharpest tool in the box, poor little dimwit.'

This girl. I'm going to wet my pants in a minute. Vicky has her hand over her mouth and Claire is openly snickering. Vicky wags her finger.

'Kath, stop it – you're so naughty. She's right, though, Tanz. He's as thick as four short planks.'

Now Vicky's laughing too. It's suddenly a great comfort to me that the few lines I have today will be addressed to Kath.

I return to my caravan a whole lot happier and slip on a warm costume coat. Inexplicably my character is walking on the moors in this scene, still in her ridiculous sandals with the aforementioned miniskirt and vest, when she finds a dead body. The sun isn't out today and, apart from looking ridiculous (why wouldn't she have a jacket?), there's the small matter of keeping my teeth from chattering while we're shooting the scenes.

As they call me to go to the car that's going to take me to set, I think about Milo and that scary thing looming over him last night. I shake my head to dislodge the thought. Maybe it really was a trick of the light because I was feeling scared. But deep inside, I know it wasn't. I don't see things like that because I'm scared. There was definitely something there. And why wouldn't Frank answer me? What's he up to?

'*I'm here.*'

'Oi! You could at least have made me feel better last night. Seeing that thing behind Milo was horrible.'

'I was busy. Plus, you're doing very well on your own. Though of course if you get stuck, I'll give you a nudge, young Skywalker.'

'Oh, great. Giving it the Obi-Wan Kenobi business now, are you? Well, for your information, it's very scary trying to cope with spooks on your own.'

'You're never on your own, Fool.'

'It's Fool now, is it?'

'You're a very nice fool . . .'

'Plus that nasty little so-and-so at the Black Gate was throwing things.'

'Not big things.'

'Oh, that's all right then.'

I know who the fool is around here, and it isn't me.

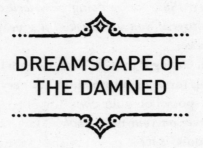

DREAMSCAPE OF
THE DAMNED

Newcastle looks so different, and yet I know fine and dandy where I am. I'm in a pub that is part of the Black Gate. I was studying the Black Gate last night, and this pub is almost definitely the Golden Fleece gin palace. The smell in here is hardcore; it certainly does not live up to its grandiose name. The cigarette smoke is acrid and the beer smell is very strong, but then the smell of sweat and dirt and rancid breath is also overpowering. I can see the people in here, but I don't think they can see me. They're certainly not acknowledging me. Their clothes are a revelation. They are truly scruffy. Maybe I had a picture-postcard impression of poor people from those days, but these people are wearing rags, held together by more rags. And the noise!

I know I'm in a dream because I can remember what I was reading about the Black Gate when it was a slum dwelling. How up to sixty families lived there at one time. I mean the building's not that big, so it must have been horrendous. I know that I'm seeing what I read about the pub. I don't know what they're drinking, but these people are deafeningly sloshed and it's rammed in here. A lot of the women are cross-eyed and gurning. I remember the nickname for gin in those times – 'mother's ruin' – and I can see why. There are people here who are dangerously out of it. I wonder if they've left their kids upstairs or wandering the streets as they drink their time away?

I make my way to the door, a sense of terror overtaking me as I try to escape the oppressive, doomed feeling I suddenly have when I look round at the exhausted faces and hard smiles of these long-dead people. I'm a step away from getting out into the fresh air when a man pushes his way through the throng in front of the door and looks straight at me. He is tall and strongly built. Beneath his chin is a raised scar, like someone tried to cut his throat. His hair is wiry and he has a filthy scarf knotted loosely at his neck. His jacket is threadbare, but he carries himself like he's somebody. His knuckles are raw and he's not handsome. 'Rugged' would be a kind way of describing the rough, dry face and eyes as hard as steel ball-bearings. I'm sure somewhere there's a cobra with kinder eyes than he's got.

As everyone carries on raising holy hell, or slumping against the wall or over the table in a stupor, the rough-faced man smiles a cocky yellow-toothed smile and walks straight at me. I find I'm rooted to the filthy floor as he reaches me and stops, close enough to breathe his whisky-soaked, fetid breath in my face, then produces half a brick from his pocket and smashes me over the head with it.

Just like that.

I wake up yelping in the gloom of the hotel room,

clutching my head, trying to keep my brains in, still hearing the crunch as he smashed my skull. It's 3 a.m. and I'm absolutely shell-shocked that I could dream such a thing. I have never had such a violent dream before in my life. If that's what happens when I read history books about the Black Gate, then I'd better start reading *Grazia* or something instead. I sit up and turn on the bedside lamp. That man in my dream was evil personified; I can still smell his breath and still feel that cold nothingness coming off him, the absolute lack of any human feeling. It makes me shiver to think of him. That ghost of the little boy and the shadow behind Milo have really got to me. But I know I desperately need to sleep if I'm going to put up with playing that idiot tomorrow. I put the TV on, turning the sound to virtual silence, and drink some water. When I lie back down, I try to see only the blue of the TV screen, which is illuminating my eyelids, and count slowly to one hundred. If I don't think about that evil, peg-toothed man, then hopefully I won't dream of him again.

At some point I fall asleep.

I wake up in a dark place. It feels hot, like a furnace, and I can't see a thing. I want to get out of there, but I have no idea where I am. It's pitch-black and burning hot. Then I hear it: breathing. Heavy and close by. I turn and try to crawl away from it but, everywhere I crawl to, the terrifying breaths are with me. Sometimes in front, sometimes to the side, sometimes behind me.

I begin to plead with whoever is following me to leave me alone. But then a man begins to laugh, like it's all a hilarious game to him.

That's when there is a blow to my head. Again. A bone-shattering crunch. I want to scream, but it's too late. I hear the strains of a Gypsy violin. Death-music.

Realizing that I'm again caught in a nightmare – this one cloying and bleakly sad – I fight desperately to open my eyes. Just before I manage it, I see the filthy little boy in the cap. He reaches out his arms. His face is sweet and his eyes are pleading with me. I try to hug him to me, but I wake up before I can touch him.

This time when I open my eyes it's nearly 5 a.m. There is absolutely no way I am going to risk sleeping again before I go to work. I can still feel the vibration of the blow I took to my head in that last dream. Light is filtering in around the hotel curtains. I go to the mini balcony, open the curtains and doors, wrap myself in the duvet and stand out there, breathing in the crisp morning air and letting the flow of the river calm my jangled nerves. Once again I will need caffeine and carbs if I'm going to survive today. I hear a lot of cries downriver. Men loading ships. Ships from more than a century ago.

There's no other explanation for it. I'm going bloody mental. These dreams are going to have me in the loony bin soon; first, Dan the murderer, and now this. All I can do is make a herbal tea, then stay on this balcony until I can muster the energy for a shower. The violence of these dreams has completely rattled me.

I don't like such negativity. I need something nice to happen, and I need to get some proper sleep or I'm going to end up in a right state.

For Christ's sake, Newcastle, leave me alone, will you?

DEATH OF THE GORGON

On the moors the crew, some of whom I travelled with to get here this morning (obviously I didn't mention my horribly disturbed night), are going about their business setting up the shot. Some poor sod is lying on the ground, playing dead. Probably a supporting actor, who'll catch pneumonia from lying there all day and will earn a pittance for his trouble.

Brian, the lovely but extremely overworked director who gave me this job – they shoot these episodes very quickly and the weather doesn't always play ball, so I've had very little chance to say anything but hello – is having a chat with Vicky about some kind of corpse make-up for a morgue scene later on. He turns as I arrive and gives me the thumbs-up. I blow him a kiss and he winks. Vicky sticks her tongue out at me. Kath and Jamie are just arriving in a car together; Kelly is in the front of their car, but no one speaks to her as she gets out. Everyone hates her costume choices, and it's common knowledge now that she's leaving at the end of this series to train in a job that she'll be less shit at.

If what Kath has told me is anything to go by, she and Jamie will have constantly worked on their lines en route. She reckons you have to keep going through them with him, because otherwise he gets them wrong. She affectionately calls him 'the village idiot'. Not to his face, of course; but the way she describes him, he would probably be impervious to it in any case. I wouldn't know, because apart from hello, he doesn't really speak to me. I'm obviously not important enough. Still it can't be denied: he might be a dick, but he still has the most beautiful green eyes ever. And so has Kath, so they must look like a pair of bush-babies onscreen together.

The one person who's missing is Caroline. She usually comes to set in a showy pale-blue Audi but it's not here yet. She has a driver called Dave, who wears a cap. It can't be cheap, having your own driver. Bored and waiting restlessly, I muse on whether she's wangled his wage out of the TV company or whether she stumps up for Dave herself.

Just as I'm thinking this, the Audi sails into view. It's virtually silent, like all very good cars are. Dave parks, then gets out. There's a troubled look on his tanned, leathery face. He stares over at Brian, who's still engrossed in his conversation with Vicky, then his eyes swivel under the cap around the rest of us, desperately – like he's looking for a friend. Not finding one, he gets on with his job and opens the back door for Caroline. When she steps out (well, not steps so much as stumbles), I can see that she has her usual peachy skin, stretched like a drum over peculiarly sharp cheekbones, but her eyes look puffy and she's definitely not 'right'. She's carrying a beautiful, expensive-looking flask with what looks like birds painted on it; she has eyes like murder, and she can't walk in a straight line.

I make towards her car just as Vole (who brings me coffee and is actually called Adrian) also notices something isn't right. He runs to the first assistant, who was talking to the director of photography, who then walks at a pace to intercept Caroline as I reach Dave the driver.

'It's absolutely none of my business, but is she okay?'

Dave looks at me. Thinks before he speaks.

'She's a bit upset. Had a shock yesterday.' He has a strong cockney accent, which makes me think she hires him herself. The Newcastle-based TV company would probably employ someone local.

'She can't walk straight.' Just as I say this, the first assistant reaches Caroline, and she smacks his hand away as he tries to take her arm and guide her to Make-up.

'Ged tha fug off me.'

Oh my God.

Dave gulps, looks helpless.

'It looks like she's gonna kick off. Should I go and get her? I'm only her bloody chauffeur and gofer. This isn't really in my job description.'

I'm hypnotized as Caroline barrels unsteadily towards Brian, who has his back to her. The crew have started to notice now and are looking on in bemusement as she stumbles towards her goal.

'I don't know. Dave, isn't it? Dave, what the hell has she had? Why is she so wankered?'

'When I picked her up, she took a pill – I don't know what it was. She was trying to calm down; she'd been stewing all night and didn't want to come in today. She washed it down with about five shots of vodka out of that flask. She thinks I don't know what's in it, but I do. Then she went bloody weird. I don't know what else I can do to help her. She's losing the plot.'

I pat his shoulder reassuringly.

'She looks very unhappy, Dave. I wouldn't take it personally – you seem nice.'

'Thank you.'

'No bother.'

Just then there's an almighty crack, as Caroline spins Brian round from his conversation and slaps him square in the kisser. He had no idea it was coming, so he yips in fright as well as pain. Vicky nearly falls over with the surprise of it. Kath, who is standing next to her car with Jamie, lets out a cry of amazement, and the crew all stare. Jamie looks befuddled.

'THIZ IZ YOUR FAULT, YOU SHIDBAG!'

Brian backs off from this evil-eyed gorgon, obviously none the wiser as to what's going on. He is holding his face. Caroline must have really hurt him. I like Brian; he's a sweetheart, and I hate violence. I'm also very raw after last night's dream.

'YOU ARE SHID AT YOUR JOB, YOU'VE POIZENED THEM ALL AGAINZT ME AND NOW I'M TAKING THE FLACK. HOWWWWW DARRRE YOU?'

Caroline lifts a fist this time. Ed the grip (the camera-man's lackey), who's standing quite close by, tries to grab her arm, but she pivots slightly and smashes him in the nose. He squeals. He's only twenty.

That's when I see red. That woman has made everybody's life a living hell, and now she's hitting innocent people because she's a nasty Gelfling with no sense of responsibility for her own actions. Without really thinking about it, I break into a run, with Dave hot on my heels, as Caroline turns to Brian and starts flailing her arms. He does his best to keep her at bay, but she's determined to do him damage.

'WHY ME? WHY REPLAZE ME WITH SOME LIDDLE COW WHO FANZIES HERSELF TO DEATH?'

That's when I reach her, and my northernness goes to ten on the Richter scale. I grab her by the hair from behind and kick her ankles from underneath her. I have never done anything like this in my life (apart from the odd girly slap). I detest violence.

'Caroline! Fucking stop it, *this minute.*'

A bunch of hair extensions come out in my hand. Oh, shit. She screams and the flailing hands go to what must now be a bit of a bald patch as she falls to her knees. Christ, I see a court case. She'll do me for assault. Caroline's that sort of woman.

I get on my knees in front of her and hold her arms.

'I'm so sorry, Caroline. I didn't mean to do that, but you can't go around smacking people in the face. You'll get arrested! And what did Brian do? He's a nice man.'

She tries to get her arms free and nearly lands me a wallop, but I wrap myself around her, like I'm giving her the tightest hug, and I whisper in her ear the first thing I think of, 'You're better than this.'

Dave is wheezing like a bagpipe. It wasn't far to run, but he's obviously not fit. He's standing behind Caroline, but he doesn't need to do anything now, because suddenly she's weeping like Medea and not fighting at all. I loosen my arms.

'They're tagin' it all away from me. Tammy, they're tagin' it all away. I've worged my arze off on this, but you can't make a silk purz out of a sow'z ear. I worg so hard but I can't do it on my own . . . *and him*!'

She motions her head towards poor, injured Brian, who seems to have a bust lip, as there's a rather vampiric trickle of blood running down his chin.

'He's never liked me – he's been edgin' me out forever. He doesn' listen. I'm a seazoned pro, I know my craft . . . I know I'm a bitch zometimez, but I know how to act.'

She's weeping what seems to be last night's mascara down her shiny, tight face. God knows what pill Caroline mixed with the drink, but she is mental. I dread to think how excruciating this will be for her later on.

'*Good.*'

'Frank!'

'*She needed a wake-up call.*'

'But this is horrible.'

'*Only in the short term. Loved the move with the hair and ankles, by the way.*'

'That is going to get me in trouble.'

I can't help thinking Frank has a point. Awful as this is,

Caroline brought it on herself. The first assistant – cheerful, practical Nigel – steps forward and bends to help her up.

'Come on, Caroline, we all get a bit tired sometimes. Let's get you back to the car and find you a lovely cup of coffee.'

She's weeping sad tears by now and, limply, lets us help her up.

'The covvee on this set is fuggin' SHIT!'

What a charmer she is. She turns bloodshot eyes in my direction, her voice climbing higher in her desperation.

'It getz us all, Tammy. Age getz us all. And then we're finished. You hear me? Fuggin' dead in the water . . .'

Nigel leads her forlorn, over-slender, slightly stooped body towards Dave's car. I feel like I've been hit in the face with a shovel. I can hear the sobs she's trying to swallow.

It gets us all.

I want to go home. I don't like acting any more.

YOU CAN'T FOOL
YOUR MAM

'Tanz?'

'Hello, Mam.'

On impulse I've popped round to my parents' place. Caroline's breakdown this morning was quite a surprise, but even more shocking was how quickly we whipped through the following scene, leaving me free for the afternoon. Everyone was so unnerved by what they'd witnessed that they became robot-like in their efficiency. James the bush-baby is always robot-like when he acts, of course, so he was exactly the same as always. Poor Brian had a fat lip and didn't mention it again, but it looked very sore.

At one point I whispered to him, 'Are you all right, lovely Brian?'

And he winked and nodded, but with anger in his eyes, and I realized then how much Caroline had blown it.

When I reach the familiar cream bay window, the front garden on a slope overflowing with flowers, bushes dying back but still impressively fulsome, the front door with the wonky number three, the plastic bins out on the street with the peeling flower stickers, I feel relieved. Today everything feels comfortingly the same, instead of exhaustingly the same.

My mam is ironing in the kitchen, looking even shorter than usual. Has she lost weight? I'm not positive, but there definitely looks like there's less flesh in her leggings. Goodness knows where my dad is; probably in his shed, doing whatever secret stuff he gets up to. I peer out into the garden and see a train whizzing along the railway tracks close by, with the hills looming large in the distance. He's definitely not in the greenhouse, so I'm probably right; he's in his precious shed with his precious dog. My little mam's hand flies to her hair. She doesn't like being untidy for visitors.

'Eeeh, hello. You haven't phoned for ages. I thought you'd gone missing.'

'Mam, it's been two days, and I've been working and stuff.'

'All right, I'm just saying. Seeing as you're only staying up the road. I mean, honestly, I don't know why you didn't save your money and stay with me and your dad – we'd love to have you.'

I don't want to tell her that if I stayed with them, my dad would say virtually nothing the whole time I was around, making me feel like a complete imposition on him and the dog; and she would spend each night telling me the plot-lines to every soap she watches, until I actually had a nervous breakdown. So I give her a kiss on the forehead and play my masterstroke instead.

'Mam, they're giving me a posh hotel for free. I wouldn't save any money by coming home. They even *pay for my breakfast*. Eggs with soldiers, and everything. Why would I say no to that?'

'Mind, I don't blame you. I wish someone would make my breakfast every morning – you'd think I was a bloody slave in this house. I never get a minute. Clean, clean, cook and clean. Me mam said, she said when I was pregnant, "Don't get married; stay here. I'll look after the little 'un, you go and get a life." And did I listen? Of course I didn't. You think you know everything when you're young . . .'

This could go on for quite some time.

'Mam, I can't stay long. I only popped round to ask if you and Dad want to come for a Sunday roast at the hotel this weekend – my treat? Save you from cooking. You could have a rest from the washing up.'

She goes quiet for a minute. She likes to moan about the housework, but at the same time I just insulted her function as a woman. I tell you, it's a bloody minefield.

'Tanz, you know your dad likes my cookin' best. And I mean, nobody makes a Sunday dinner quite like I do.'

Up North, of course, dinner means lunch, and my mam nukes vegetables for at least two hours, so she's right – nobody cooks like she does. She stews them like rhubarb and serves them as an unidentifiable mush. Exactly as my dad likes them. Though, it has to be said, she makes a fantastic roast potato.

'All right, Mam, I'll come on Sunday. But I can't stay the whole day. I have lines to learn.'

This is the classic get-out clause, in case things get nasty or awkward.

'Lovely. I'll make treacle puddin' and custard, for afters. I know you've been a bit peaky lately.'

Nothing gets past my mam. She probably 'felt' my last downer setting in before I did.

'Mind, it's a godsend you got this job. Are you enjoying it?'

'It's okay.'

'What about Caroline May?'

'What about her?'

'Well, is she nice?'

'She's a bit of a drama queen actually. But no more than most actresses.'

I have to be careful. If I say too much, the whole of Gateshead will be gossiping and I'll get in trouble.

'Well, at least you're earning some money.'

'I know, Mam. And I get to hang out in the lovely North with my lovely mammy.'

She smiles, then stops rubbing the hot iron over my dad's faded green cardigan and stares at me while she clutches the handle.

'Tanz?'

'Yes, Mam?'

'Have you been messin' around with them ghosts again?'

Lie. Lie, lie, lie. She's very touchy about the ghost thing, even though she's completely psychic herself.

'No. Why?'

'Because I just remembered: I dreamed about a little boy

96

with a dirty face last night. He was crying and scared. It was weird.'

Holy guacamole. How does she do it? I endeavour to maintain an interested but blank expression.

'Really?'

'Yes. And in the dream, every time I saw you, he was standing behind you, pulling at your coat, but you couldn't feel it. It was bloody creepy. Don't you be messin', all right? You've had enough frights.'

'Okay, Mam.'

She gives the cardigan one last press and sighs.

'Fancy a quick cuppa, pet?'

I hate cups of tea. I've always hated tea. She knows this. But she'll probably keep offering me one until I'm old and grey and in my fleecy slippers. This is what my little mam does.

And sometimes the familiar can be what we need the most.

LONELY GIRL

I'm in the City Bar in Gateshead. It's just next to the Tyne Bridge. The Tyne Bridge is my favourite bridge in the world. It looks like Sydney Harbour Bridge, and many people think it was modelled on Sydney Harbour Bridge but it wasn't. The same company built them both, but actually ours was built first. Sadly, we may have got the bridge first, but what we didn't get – and never will – is the lovely Australian weather. Tonight, again, it's blinkin' chilly, and I walked across from the Copthorne hotel swaddled in jeans, jumper, thick coat and trainers. My only concession to glamour is cherry lip gloss, clean hair and sparkly green eyeliner, which is a bugger to get off, but always cheers me up.

After my mam and I had the 'I dreamed about a little boy with a mucky face' conversation, and then a good hour of family bitching over a cup of peppermint tea for me and two giant mugs of builder's tea for my mam, I slipped back to the hotel and had a swim, after unsuccessfully trying to call Milo. At five o'clock I got a bit antsy and realized that

I hadn't spoken to any of my friends but Milo since I'd started on *Pendle Investigates*. I tried a couple of numbers but nobody picked up, so I grabbed myself a gin from the minibar and chugged it down with a full-fat tonic. (I've totally caught the gin bug from Milo.) Then I felt a bit better but wanted more, so I ordered a double from room service. Then I felt lonely again and did exactly the thing I shouldn't.

I called library boy, Iain.

I know, I know. More than a bit of an obvious ego-boost tactic. But it's been a long time since my brief affair with Pat, and a girl has needs. Even though I'm not on TV much any more, Iain's a kind of fan and I suddenly want some male attention. Also he's familiar with the building that I'm researching and with all things paranormal, so he's exactly who I need to speak to. It isn't *just* because he made such a fuss of me when we met at the library.

'*Of course it is.*'

'Give me a break, Frank. I've not had a sniff of attention since Pat left.'

'*Hey, it's up to you. I only want to say, for what it's worth, I think he's a dick.*'

'You call everyone a dick.'

'*He's not made of the same stuff as you.*'

'Good. I'm made of mentalness.'

'*I give up.*'

As I'm at the bar, getting myself a gin-and-slim (the 'slim' makes me feel like I haven't totally given up on my never-ending diet), a tentative hand touches me on the shoulder. And there Iain is. With his flame-red hair, his dark muddy eyes – spectacle-free tonight (probably wearing contacts) – and his friendly little fangs. It's nice that someone looks so happy to see me. I kiss him on the cheek, and his smile beams ever brighter.

'Hiya, Tanz. You look lovely.'

I'm in a frumpy jumper; he's being kind.

'Oh, thank you. I like your *Star Trek* T-shirt.'

The T-shirt is ridiculous, but Iain has nice sinewy arms, so it doesn't look too bad. He's also wearing jeans, and he's only about three inches taller than me. But he smells of nice body spray and he's obviously glad I'm here. That's enough for now.

We sit in the corner. He's bought a pint of some horrible dark, cloudy beer with a strange name like Strangled Goat. It's a badge of honour for certain men, I've noticed, to drink pints of dishwater with stupid names. Iain takes a huge pull on it. Then another. He must be nervous.

'So how's your day been?'

'Oh, interesting, I suppose. An actress had a meltdown on-set and it went downhill from there, basically.'

'Intriguing. Anyone we know?'

He raises an eyebrow. I suddenly remember that I have to be careful. A quick phone call to some cheapo celebrity magazine from an overexcited librarian and I'd be right in the shit.

'No, no. Only a bit-part actress. How about you?'

He shrugs.

'An old man wet himself on the giant beanbag, then walked off and tried to pretend he hadn't. That was pleasant. I had to drag it out the back into the yard and dump it there until we can get the council to take it away. Then a party of kids from a very rough school turned up and ran riot. I'm still deaf in one ear from it!'

'Sounds like fun.'

'I hate working there, but something has to pay the bills.'

'Right. So what do you really want to do?'

'I'm a drummer. But it takes a long time to get anywhere with a band. In the meantime I'll be mopping up old-man piss and dropping piles of books on my feet, until further notice.'

A creative. A drummer, no less. (Good rhythm?) I like musicians. Tonight just got more interesting.

'What's your band called?'

'The Blasted Hymens.'

I spit gin on his T-shirt. He begins to laugh.

'I'm joking. We're actually called Bim Bam Bomb. We're quite good.'

He's funnier than I expected. Dry. He notices my glass is almost empty.

'Top up, fair dame? Then you can tell me what's going on with your ghostly research.'

'Great, thanks. My round next.' I don't mind if I do. After hammering the gin, he's taken on a rosy glow. I usually like men taller and with more of a chin, but he's got something about him.

When he sits back down, Iain hands me my drink and his knee touches mine for just that bit too long.

'So come on, spill the beans. The Black Gate, what's the deal? And how was the ghost walk?'

I usually don't like to go on too much about my 'gift', but drink has loosened my tongue and I tell him about the ghost in the arch throwing stones, and then describe Llewellyn in all of his camp glory. Iain finds all of this very funny. Or he's humouring me. I'm not sure which.

I think the gin he brought me was a large. A very large, the cheeky git. As I carry on, my stories get more expansive and loud, and he laughs longer and more heartily. I don't tell him about the shadow behind Milo, though. That wasn't funny. Plus, it's nobody's business. (Which reminds me, Milo needs to pick up his phone next time I call or he's going to be in trouble with me.)

'Would you like another drink, Tanz?'

'MY ROUND!'

I don't know why I shouted like that. I'm feeling ebullient all of a sudden. I jump up to go to the bar and my head spins. Should have eaten before I came out. I forgot about that. Still, in for a penny, in for a pound.

THE SHADOW MAN

I'm in the pitch-dark.

I can't remember where I am. I feel around me and discover I'm under a bed. An iron bed. I am trying very hard not to make any noise, but I'm so frightened, my breaths are coming in hollow rasps. I think I've wet myself. I'm shaking. There's a nasty smell.

I want my mam.

If I move I am going to be dead. I know it. I try to scooch up further, so I'm against the wall. But I can hear footfalls and it's very hard to do it quietly, and I really, really want my mam. I stop moving but the footfalls have halted. There is a moment of silence. Then, all at once, a pair of eyes, black as death and burning with the fires of hell, are looking straight at me. He's found me under the bed! I try to scream, but only silent air escapes. I scrunch my eyes shut, mouth still soundlessly open, and beg and beg in my head not to be pulled by unseen hands from my hiding place, because I know my fate will be as terrible as the fire in those eyes.

And suddenly I can hear Milo in my head.

'I didn't die terribly, darlin'. It only hurt a bit. Only as much as a smash to the skull. Only a smash . . . but I can still talk to you. We can still have great chats, can't we, Tanz? Can't we?'

And suddenly I'm standing in the dark and there, in the distance, are Milo and Frank, waving goodbye, leaving me behind and closing a door behind them. And it's just me. In the pitch-black.

Alone.

I wake up drenched in tears.

I can't remember where I am.

SHAKY HAND

I'm gasping like a beached haddock. It's very dark and I think I'm alone. Then, surprisingly, a shaky hand snakes around my back and a voice in the half-light says, 'Shhh, it's all right, shhh . . .' in a tired and slightly alarmed way.

It's only then that I am smacked in the face by the memory of the night that preceded the saddest nightmare from Sad Nightmare Land, ever. I resist the temptation to groan aloud. Why on earth did I drink so much gin last night? And why was I so stinkingly drunk so quickly? Oh, actually, it's probably because I only had a packet of dry-roasted peanuts for dinner.

Rule 1: You must eat first, if you're going to drink.

Last night Iain stuck to that murky beer, and my stories of my spooky life got less and less guarded as the drink took more of a hold. He seemed to be loving it and told me a few of his own, frankly less impressive stories (temperature drops and strange sounds), involving electrical gadgets, beepy boxes, gauges and measuring-thingies. He treats the paranormal as a science, which is interesting in its own way, I suppose.

As I lie in this unfamiliar bed, I remind myself that Milo isn't actually dead and it was only a dream. I still feel bereft, though. I wipe my tears on the pillow. It smells of cheap washing powder. The pillows at the hotel don't smell of anything. My pillows in London smell divine. I want Inka to be here, wrapped around my head and purring, my fluffy little comfort machine. I want Sheila. She knows how to put scary things into perspective. And maybe, just a little bit, I miss the cuddles of a gorgeous young Irishman, who knew a million times better than this man how to hold a woman.

'*Oh dear.*'

'I know. I'm a slag.'

'*No, you're not. He is.*'

'It was horrible, Frank.'

'*I told you he wasn't made of the same stuff as you.*'

'You sure did. And my head hurts.'

'*That's what happens after two gallons of gin.*'

I don't like Iain's hand on my back; it's like a dying sparrow. Cold and lightweight. A proper man would wrap his arms around a woman in distress, surely, or am I expecting life to be a romantic movie? I move so that he knows I'm awake and pull the duvet tighter around me. Oh Christ, I can't believe I'm completely naked. How embarrassing.

After the final killer gin, I realized I needed to go back to the hotel immediately and drink some water and eat a cheese toastie from room service. But Iain said he had some sexy coffee that would 'sort me out', and he could play me some of his band's music and it was only two minutes' walk away. This sounded like a fabulous idea at the time, so I agreed and we went back to his little one-bed place with the *Star Trek* and Pink Floyd posters, and the drum kit in the living room, which he can only play on a Sunday when 'downstairs are out'. While I drank coffee and tried not to hurl, he played me this CD of his very thumpy, jazzy ambient music, which I quite liked, then leaned forward on his navy settee and gave me a wet kiss.

Next thing I knew, I was naked in his bed, he was thrusting away like a little piston and I wasn't sure what I was doing there. Even in my sozzled state, it felt ridiculous. Then I blacked out. Not long after, it seemed, I was having that bloody awful night-terror.

I look at Iain in the half-light of dawn. He's facing me, eyes drooping, about to drop off again.

'I had a bad dream.'

He is so close to falling back to sleep that his voice is a wisp.

'Are you okay?'

'Yes, thanks.'

'Good . . .'

I think he's nodded off when he adds, very quietly, 'I've set my alarm for seven. I'm afraid I'm meeting my girl-friend for breakfast at half-past and I need a shower. Hope that's okay . . .'

And then he's gone. Warmly wrapped in the arms of Morpheus. Or pretending he is. And I'm crawling stealthily out of my side of his double divan, at 5 a.m., pulling on discarded clothes and creeping out of the house into the chilly, cleansing air, wondering how I could have slept with such a prick. Such an under-performing prick. With a girlfriend.

Well done, Tanz. Round of applause.

I'm a twit.

BLOOD AND MENTHOL

I don't want to go back to my hotel yet. I want to wander around in the growing light and feel the stillness of the collective unconscious, before the chatter of the day starts invading the air around me.

I know. Deep.

As I cross the still and quiet Tyne Bridge I look towards the Millennium Bridge, that lovely arc that lights up in a myriad of colours at night, reminding me of the chakra points inside my own body. (I read about them one day in Mystery Pot when I was bored and actually found it all quite fascinating.)

I have a pain in my tummy.

I know it's not from the sex, as he wasn't exactly the most hugely endowed man I've ever met; it's the shame, the gin and, I think, my period coming. My period always brings a dose of hormones that would kill a bull elephant. At its worst, it's basically a fortnight of unpredictable manic depression, starting the week before I bleed. I would not like to be a friend of mine when I'm in Hormone Beast mode. I can get quite crazed.

I stop and look down towards the water, then run my eyes over the lovely buildings lining the Newcastle side of the quay. My eyes 'unfocus' as I think about the insecurity I've been feeling recently, and how it has actually been breeding more insecurity and how I have to stop it *right now*. I mean, if I'd not been feeling so bad about myself, would I have behaved how I did last night? As it was, Iain and I talked and got on okay, he was sweet enough and he had quite a nice, wiry body. Plus of course, I *love* redheads.

But.

But I didn't want him. There wasn't a connection. I completely ignored this fact – why, oh why? – and instead I talked and talked, and let him laugh at my stories and tell me how pretty I was, and all of that shit. And for all the flattery and the drink, the sex felt alien and I knew it wasn't right . . . And now, lo and behold, he has a girlfriend!

There's a sound in the silence. Women's shrieking cries. It could be the remnants of a hen party, but probably not at this time in the morning. Such harsh voices and a distinct smell of fish, coming from the opposite quayside. It stops my train of thought and I wonder what's going on. I don't know about any fish markets around here; the only one I know about is in South Shields. I hear laughing – well, cackling – and I smell a rubbish tip, like the other night on the ghost walk. Maybe there are some dicky drains. The air feels different, weightier somehow. I hear a ship's horn. Where the hell is that coming from? The back of my neck crackles as I feel someone brush past me. I get a snippet of musky scent, but there's no one there.

Then it hits me. Oh my goodness, is old Newcastle *haunting* me?

At this early hour, with the sun only just up, I get the strongest feeling of nostalgia and, strangely, of things being exactly as they should. Like Newcastle isn't haunting me, I'm haunting it. Invading its past. I think I'm tuning into a past time, and I think I did the same the other night on the ghost walk when I heard and smelled those strange things. This is a brand-new thing for me and the prickle of excitement is stronger than the accompanying prickle of fear. Why now? Why this now?

As I think it, I sense the feeling leaving me. And suddenly the sound of traffic beginning to move about the city in the chilly early-morning sun, and the smell of fumes and river, replaces the other things I could hear and smell. Now I'm simply 'here' and it's a different kind of beautiful.

Newcastle is so peaceful right now, I allow my legs and my subconscious to take me where I need to be. I congratulate myself on wearing comfortable clothes last night. And even bringing a warm jacket. For once I've done something sensible. Though I'm not sure that my golden trainers can ever truly be classed as sensible. Unless you live in Dollywood.

As I approach the little turning that will lead me to the Black Gate, I let the negativity of last night wash over me and try to get it in order in my brain. Okay, so I slept with a total idiot. I let it happen because I needed attention. He's a shit, and that's the last I'll see of him. End of. And I had another horrible dream. This is becoming the norm now and I need to sort it out. In my opinion, someone or something is trying to contact me, or scare me or mess with me. I need to be proactive and find out why. My clues are the ghost of a little boy, who sometimes has the face of an evil leprechaun and sometimes looks sweet and lost; and the man with the scar on his neck who tried to smash in my head in my dreams. What do they want from me? I need to do some research, and plenty of it. I also need to look into Newcastle Quayside in the past. The fish, the smell of rubbish, the cackling – look it all up. No more scaredy-pants. It's time to sort this out.

I reach the low wall in front of the Black Gate, by the bus stop, and marvel at its height and scale. It's such a strange, ugly-beautiful building, plonked next to the New Castle but so different from it. I pull out a tiny Vogue menthol cigarette. I bought them because I was going for a drink and I thought they were cute. Now I really fancy some minty smoke.

As soon as I light up, I feel a dampness that probably means I just started to bleed. Timing! Well, at least my jeans are black.

I ignore it and continue to smoke. As the dinky cigarette comes towards its end, I feel a need to stand up and walk towards the side of the building. The other side. The opposite side from the arch that's so far yielded a staring spectral child and a couple of unwanted missiles.

I don't feel any fear, partly because I'm too tired to, what with last night's shenanigans, and partly because I can feel Frank with me. Mentally I hold his hand. Physically I draw the last half-lungful from my tiny, minty cigarette and do a quick 'protection' so that nothing can latch on to me.

This side of the building is where one of the doors used to be when it was a tenement, apparently. There was a pub attached to it then – the one, I suspect, that I saw in my dream. That time in its history seems to want to come and get me. I make my way down, underneath the trip-trap bridge, and as I stand there next to the blank stone wall, I feel a pressure on my chest and wonder if this is a significant spot.

I look up and one of the higher windows catches my attention the most. When I 'unfocus' my eyes and concentrate on the bricks slightly to the left of it, I get the impression of a face at the glass. A woman's face. I take a deep breath and tell myself I'm not allowed to run away or cry. I try to link into her, but it's not easy. There's no real detail – only an unkempt, unhappy woman, blank-eyed with alcohol; a woman who never had enough money or love, and who hardly knew how to function any more. Before I can attempt to ask her anything, she's gone. But then I feel something else. A pressure from lower down, accompanied by a deep fear. I breathe and concentrate on the wall in front of me. Then I 'see' him. It's the little boy. Not a boy with a cruel face. This is the face that begged for help just before I awoke this morning, the eyes soft and pleading; no burning-coal stare or evil presence. He takes me by surprise, not because of my fear, but because of his. It's so stifling and overwhelming, I really wish I could cuddle him. He seems so vulnerable and alone.

As I listen with my 'inner ear' I hear chatter and singing,

arguing and brash laughter. A piano maybe. It's the pub again. The gin palace from my dream. Then I hear the distant sound of a horse on cobbles, hooves slipping, pulling some kind of weight.

'Frank, why can I hear a horse?'

'Horse-drawn trams. Look them up.'

'Huh?'

'Very popular at the time. Went electric around 1900.'

'Wow.'

'I know. And if you look up the fish market, there was one on the quayside in the late 1800s.'

'How do you know this stuff?'

'Did it as a school project while you did yours on British mammals.'

I laugh.

'Really?'

Then suddenly Frank's gone. And he's not the only one. The little boy has disappeared, too. All that's left is an all-pervading sense of desperate sadness and the feeling in my heart that I need to help that child. Though right this second, before any of that big stuff, I need a shower and a tampon.

I turn in the direction of my hotel.

Positive Mental Attitude. That's how I intend to live from now on. Or, as Frank would say . . .

'Chin up, moody Mildred.'

VEGETABLE SOUP

I don't know why my mam sets the table in the kitchen, because there's a little TV that's always on in there, so we might as well have our food on trays on our knees in the living room in front of the big TV (which is what they do every other day). But rules are rules, and on Sunday you sit at the little table.

My first thought when my mam puts lunch in front of us is how hilariously big my dad's portion is. He has about eight scoops of mashed potato plus a pile of roasties, what looks like half a chicken, a swamp of vegetables only semi-identifiable by colour as they've pretty much disintegrated into a soup, three Yorkshire puddings and a jug of gravy all to himself. This is another Sunday-lunch ritual. The man of the house has to have enough food in his belly to render him legally disabled for the rest of the day. My own plate could feed a family of four, but I know better than to complain, because then I will be given the third degree about whether I've become anorexic.

We all have cold lemonade with our lunch today, which

I find strangely comforting, as we had lemonade with our Sunday lunch when I was a kid. In those days we had a delivery man with an open-backed lorry, which was full of bottles of many different kinds of pop. We called him the pop-man and my cousin Dale and I would squabble over what flavour was best. I liked cherryade, he liked pine-appleade, but neither of us ever said no to cream soda.

I think about this now, as Dad finishes his mountain of food. After he places his knife and fork on his plate he nods at me.

'You look well.'

'Thanks, Dad.'

'I'm off.' And he scoots down to his shed. Which, I've decided, is probably the centre of operations for MI5 or a small undercover space station.

My mam will take him a cup of tea in half an hour. It's all like clockwork. I remember seeing all this going on when I was little and finding it so depressing. Even when I was wee, I didn't get why they liked mugs of tea so much, and why the rules about meal times were always so rigid, and why they always argued when we went to bed, and why married life seemed so tiring. I swore to myself, aged about seven, that I would never, ever settle down and/or have children. I would not be tied to cleaning the house like my mam, or doing jobs that I hated like my dad. I was going to be an adventurer. I was going to act and sing and write and travel, and experience everything there was to offer and not let a man 'ruin it'.

It's only now, when I look at them so many years later, that I think: who am I to judge? People are what they are and, whatever has gone on, my parents seem to need each other. And even though I still think the domestic life will never be for me, I wonder why, if the single life is so much better, I sometimes get so depressed. Maybe I'm just a melancholic little drama queen.

I stand with my virtually empty plate and take it to the kitchen sink. My belly is rammed.

'Mam, do you think it's weird that I haven't settled down?'

'Well, Tanz, you've never really been one to follow the "usual" path, have you?' She sighs.

I scrape the last of the vegetable mush off my plate into the plastic bin in the cupboard, as my mam runs the hot tap. Somehow my dad's managed to avoid the dishes, as usual. For all of her complaints, my mam doesn't let him do anything. He hoovers the sitting-room carpet now and then, and that's it really.

'No. But I nearly did with Blake.'

'Oh, that freeloader. He was due the boot long before he got it. He said some horrible things to you.'

She's right, he did. But I loved Blake, and it still stings that I was such a fool, letting a man live off me for so long. I thought he was a tortured artist. My stupidly romantic mind wouldn't accept that he was merely a nasty, immature swine.

My mam clatters the plates into the sink.

'Haven't you met anyone since, who makes you go all fluttery?'

Oh, bless her.

'I sort of did, but he went off travelling.'

'That's a shame. What about up here? No one on the series any good?'

'God, no. The crew are mostly married and I don't fancy them anyway. Then there's that young lad actor, Jamie Brown, with the green eyes. He's not for me.'

'Oh no, stay away from the young 'uns. They're a nightmare.'

'How do you know? You met Dad when you were fifteen.'

'Hey, that doesn't mean I haven't had any interest since.'

I find it virtually impossible to think of my mam in sexual terms, so this freaks me out.

'When I used to go clubbin' with my mate Karen, they were like bees round a honey pot!'

'*Mam!*'

'They'll tell you anything to get you into the bedroom, mind. It's the hormones, you see. They're drippin' with hormones. No good for a proper relationship.'

I'm half amused, half horrified. *Dripping?*

'I got asked out the other day by a librarian.'

'Now there's a good, steady job. And you've got to be quite clever to work with books, I'd imagine. What did you say?'

'I went for a drink with him.'

'Eeh, well done, pet. Was he *nice*?'

When my mam uses *nice* with the intonation she just did, it means handsome. She'll nod at Jon Bon Jovi if he's on TV and say, 'Now, he's *nice*.'

'He's a cute little redhead and he plays the drums.'

'Well, it takes all sorts.'

I don't know what she means by this, but I plough on.

'Yes, we talked for a long time, then he . . . erm – he gave me a kiss, then told me he had a girlfriend.'

'He *what*?' Mam gives a scathing sniff, and her mouth sets in a line.

'I know. I felt so stupid.'

'You see what I mean? I bet he was a young 'un. They're like rats up a drainpipe, if you give them half a chance. Why should you feel a fool because he didn't give you all the information? You're not at fault. He's the dirty liar.'

I can't help thinking there might be a bit of history firing up that righteous indignation, but I daren't ask. My mam describing her saucy past adventures might be the end of me.

'Thanks, Mam. I felt terrible. I mean, what if I'd *slept* with him?'

'Oooh, you don't want to be sleepin' with anyone that quickly. Give yourself time to find out they're not a pig first. If they're nice, they'll wait a bit.'

In her own way, my mam is a sage. She mightn't have much of a clue about what goes on out there, apart from what she sees them shouting about on the soaps, but she understands the basics all right.

'Mam, I'm wondering if I should just become a nun.'

'Nuns aren't allowed to drink.'

'Well, that's that plan scuppered.'

We laugh.

'Tanz, I've never been a big one for compliments, but you're a lovely-looking girl and you've got ages yet. And as for children . . .' She hands me a pan she's washed, then goes back to the next one. 'I mean, I don't want to put a dampener on it, but it's bloody hard work being a mam. Only do it if you really want to. You don't have to make me a grandma if you don't want to.'

'Mam, I can't even look after myself, let alone a child, so there's not even a thought of it.'

She stops what she's doing and looks straight at me.

'You'd be a lovely mam, and don't you forget it. All I mean is: don't do it until you've done all the other things you want to do that involve leaving the house on your own. You'll not be able to leave the house alone again, without worrying. Not even when your child's over thirty.'

She's only semi-joking, I can tell.

'Mam, even at my age I'm too scared to think of having kids. I could never have done what you did so young. You did good.'

'I didn't do anything. That's the trouble. Now, pass me that basting tray.'

Only once in a while do I realize what it must have been like to be my mam. And she did do good.

WHO'D HAVE THUNK IT?

Milo wouldn't come to lunch at my little mam's yesterday. He'd finally deigned to pick up the phone, after worrying me sick, but he said no. Apparently he's writing something and 'on a roll'. Obviously I'm glad for him, but he sounded very subdued.

I'm in the car going to work. My driver is on mute and it's school-run time, so I think I'm going to be late for Make-up. Less time with greasy hair, though, so I'm not complaining.

I was surprised at how great I felt after having lunch at my parents' yesterday. Dad put in another appearance at the table when my mam served up the treacle pudding and custard, which was heaven on a plate. I came away content and full of food, and actually managed to sleep without some horrendous dream of doom last night, which is a great relief. On a less positive note, today I have to say the worst line yet: 'Wey it wasna me, Mister, I were with me fella in tha chicken coop.'

I'm starting to think some of these writers are taking the

actual piss and know how terrible their scripts are. Poor Brian, the director, having to make sense of this piffle when his own writing is actually good. I wonder how his fat lip is today? And, dread of dread, I wonder how Caroline will be with me, after I pulled out a handful of her hair the other day. The Positive Mental Attitude might be sorely tested if she's being crackers again.

As we pull into the car park and I get my bumble-bee umbrella ready (it's just starting to drizzle), I spot Vole opening up his own umbrella (an enormous dark-green dome) and a hunched figure in a huge, navy Costume-department coat and dark glasses stepping out of her own car and straight under the ready-made shelter.

Caroline.

And when I look more closely at her ridiculously sleek automobile, I see a skinny man in his sixties is in the driving seat, wearing the same cap, but most definitely not Dave. Oh dear. What's that about? My heart starts beating a little faster as I step onto the tarmac under my own tiny yellow-and-black rain shelter and try to get across the car park without her seeing me.

I've only taken three steps when I hear a voice, clear as a bell – the Queen's bell – coming from the giant umbrella's direction.

'Tanz!'

I wonder if I can pretend I didn't hear it and scurry off? I almost decide to do exactly that, when the tiny, honey-blonde crazy woman whose legs I kicked out from under her darts towards me from beneath the big umbrella. I stop and stand still, because I don't know what else to do. She looks quite demented. When she reaches me, she stands there and looks into my face. Which is very disconcerting, because she's wearing dark glasses and it's raining.

'Do you want to get under my bumble-bee? You'll get soaked.'

'No, thank you, I have a hood.'

She pulls it up further, then stands some more.

'Erm, Caroline, I'm really sorry about what happened.'

'What, you mean when I was totally humiliated in front of the cast and crew and my hair was ruined?'

Oh Christ.

'I'm so sorry. I just couldn't watch you lashing out like that. It was too painful to look at.'

'Yes . . . well, unfortunately I had an allergic reaction to my medication, which is why I was behaving in such a strange manner.'

She takes off her sunglasses. Her eyes are red. She looks very upset. I can't help feeling a twinge of sympathy.

'Oh. That explains it.'

'I was going to sue you.'

Bile rises into my neck when she says this. What the hell would she get out of me? Twenty quid, my new coffee machine (bought on a whim when I got this job) and my cat? That's about the sum total of what I possess. Oh, and a car worth less than a pair of roller skates.

'But then I had a long conversation with Brian. He explained that he hadn't been stabbing me in the back, as I thought he had, and that if I'd managed to land another hand on him, he'd have been suing me; plus, I'd have been "let go" immediately. So I guess your violent outburst may have had a more positive effect than you intended.'

'I didn't intend anything, I just wanted you to stop battering people. You've got some right hook on you – I'll give you that. I've seen lads in bar brawls in Gateshead who wouldn't take you on.'

Caroline seems surprised at this turn of the conversation.

'Where I grew up in Liverpool, you learned to fight as soon as you could.'

'Liverpool? That's one hell of a strange Scouse accent you've got there.'

'Unless I wanted to spend my life playing scrubbers, I had to lose the accent.'

'You know what, I'd argue with you on that point, but I'm about to go and dress up as a scrubber and practise my slag-walk, so you probably did the right thing.'

'They really do make your hair look terrible. It's not so bad without the grease. A little dry maybe.'

'Yes, well, I haven't had the money for expensive hairdressers for quite some time now. That's what happens when you play scrubbers.'

'No offence.'

No offence? That's a bit like an apology, isn't it?

'None taken.'

Surprising me again, Caroline's eyes well up.

'Dave, my driver, resigned. He's gone. After ten years – kaput. This whole business has been awful. I hope we can all just get on with our jobs and the backbiting can stop.'

Hmm. As far as I know, there's only one backbiter

around here, but I'm not going to rock the boat by saying anything. I nod and make an 'understanding' face.

'Yes. I agree, it's much better when people get on with each other. I hope you're feeling better after your allergic reaction, Caroline. I'll see you on-set.'

I run to the Make-up bus, as relieved as I've ever been in my life that I'm not getting prosecuted, but also disturbed by Caroline's uncomfortable attempts at not being a bitch. I can't wait to tell Vicky actually, but when I get on the bus she's not there; it's another girl called Lisa, who I've never met before. She's tall and rangy, with dark hair in a ponytail and perfect skin. Like she's been drinking bottled water and eating broccoli since she was born. Claire is at her mirror, setting up cosmetics for her next actor. She gives a little smile.

'Hello, Tanz. Vicky's on her way in – she's been delayed. Lisa's come in to make up a bunch of supporting artists, but she'll start your hair, and Vicky'll take over as soon as she gets here.'

'Right.'

I don't like changes in routine, they mess with my head. Plus, this Lisa isn't even second-in-command; she only came in to make up the *extras*. My ego is not happy about this and begins to mutter and growl in my head. I try to quash the stream of gripes by talking out loud.

'Is she okay?'

'Oh, she's fine.'

And that's all Claire says, leaving my ego to snivel and rage. And to add insult to injury, Lisa puts too much

Vaseline in my hair and overdoes it with the eye-bags. I tell her as nicely as possible, but I start to get more and more mad.

Why isn't Vicky here? Why isn't Vicky here? I'm all unseated now.

Just as I'm getting to ultimate mind-blow stage, Vicky rushes in. Her cheeks are flushed and she looks weird. She fixes on me straight away.

'Too much purple on the eyes, Lisa. Here, you can go and see to the nightclub crowd now, thank you. And, Claire, could you go and check on Caroline and make sure she's ready to come over, while I do this?'

They both do as they're told. The minute we're alone, Vicky rounds on me.

'Why did you tell me to go to the pictures with Con instead of shopping?'

'Sorry? Who's Con?'

'My boyfriend, Con. You said: don't buy shoes, go to the cinema. That's what you said.'

'All right, all right, if that's what I said. I don't always remember this stuff.'

'His house blew up.'

'You what?'

'While we were at the cinema and he was moaning about how rubbish the film was, and saying how he could have been at home watching the football. There was a gas leak on the street and three houses copped it. Including his.'

She begins to shake. She's probably in shock.

'If I'd not cancelled the shopping and said, "Let's go on our date instead", he'd have been in his house when it blew up. He might even be dead. Oh God, this stuff is serious, I can't even believe it. What you said saved him, Tanz.'

She emits a few little frightened staccato sobs. Poor Vicky. I stand up and hug her and inevitably I start feeling emotional, too.

'How is Con?'

'Gutted about his place, but glad he wasn't in it. Thank you, Tanz – really, thank you. I could have lost my man. My sweet man.'

We hug for a bit, then her sobs subside.

'Is he insured?'

'You're so *practical*! Yes, he's insured. We can still get our new place together.'

'So there you go then, all's well.'

'How can you be so calm? He was out of the house because of you.'

'Yeah, but who's to say something else wouldn't have got him out of the house, if I didn't? It mustn't have been his time.'

'That's not the point. It *was* you! You did it! Oh, *shit*, I've got mascara on your top.'

'Fuck it. Kelly can use baby-wipes to get it off. It's a piece of cheap crap anyway.'

Kelly gave me a different top today. A shiny sateen nightmare, in light copper. The wrong shade. A brassy, unflattering mess. I'm glad Vicky got mascara on it. Given the chance, I'd burn it in a skip.

'By the way, Con wants to meet you. Just to say thanks.'

I immediately feel shy and odd.

'No-o-o. Really. It's fine.'

'You have no choice, Tanz. He wants to say hello.'

'Bloody hell, I don't even remember telling you to go to the cinema. Really.'

'Again that's not the point, is it? Whether you remember or not *isn't the point*.'

HELL FOR LEATHER

If the police were around looking for trouble earlier tonight, I'd have been in it up to my neck. I didn't find out I had the day off tomorrow until 6 p.m., after a schedule rejig, and I thought, *Right, that's it, I'm going to see my girl.*

I threw some dirty washing into a carrier bag, jumped into my bean-tin car and stopped off at the best chippie in Gateshead, immediately smothering my big bag of chips in salt and vinegar. As soon as they were on my knee, open and steaming, I drove for half an hour on the south-bound motorway, filling my face with hot, oily-potato fingers. With my diet already in tatters and grease stains from the chip-shop paper on my jeans, I then stopped at a service station, filled up with petrol and bought some supplies. I learned long ago that the easiest way to stay wired enough to drive for four hours is to consume a hideous, poisonous energy-drink accompanied by a bag of Skittles. The effect is usually instantaneous. So I bought both and had them for dessert. Within fifteen minutes I was hanging upside-down from the ceiling, singing show tunes backwards. I was *flying*.

I didn't allow the car to go less than ninety, apart from through those damnable 50 mph zones with their closed-down roadworks and invisible workforces. As I drove, I plugged in the far less trendy, but much more comfortable long wire with earbuds, so I could speak hands-free, then made some calls. Apart from telling my neighbour Steve that I was on my way, I also called Milo. But the conversation was weird.

'Hi, Milo, you feeling any better?'

'I'm fine, babes, only a bit knackered.'

'Really, what've you been up to?'

'Tippety-tap-tapping.'

'Brilliant. What are you writing?'

'Oh, just some bits.'

'Bits of what?'

'You know – stuff. Anyway I need to go to bed.'

'Bed? It's seven o'clock.'

'I know. But I was up all night last night.' (He yawns very loudly.)

'Were you? What were you up to?'

'Working. Listen, Tanz, I'm exhausted, so I'll speak to you tomorrow.'

'Okay. Love you.'

'Yeah. Bye.'

I mean, it sounded like Milo, but it didn't *sound* like him at all. He never has early nights. If he stays up all night working, he usually then goes to bed till the afternoon and then starts all over again. I wondered if it could be the drink, but he didn't sound drunk or particularly like he had a hangover, either. There was just zero banter.

If I'm honest with myself, what he really sounded like was someone who didn't want to talk to me. Me! His favouritest buddy. Well, one of them. I'll go and see him the minute I drive back North again tomorrow. No more phone calls, no more Mrs Nice Guy. I need to know what's going on.

As I floored it, firing on two thousand cylinders from a nuclear-powered sugar rush, watching the lights, cranes and smoke-stacks whizz by, I considered my afternoon on-set. A scene with Caroline – until now a thing of dread – took on a whole new meaning as she attempted not to stumble over her lines (which she still did several times) or look any of the crew in the eye between shots. Even James, of the emerald eyes and flirtatious bent, kept his distance from her, as if afraid that her bizarre director-punching, job-contract-shortening behaviour might be catching.

In our scene Caroline was doing most of the talking, grilling my character, whilst I only had to mutter a few semi-intelligible sentences, as usual. But the fight seemed to have gone out of her, and as the DOP waited for the right light – and Kelly, the plain-Jane costume pain, tugged at skirts and adjusted collars – I willed and willed Caroline with my whole being to keep it together.

At one point, during a short break, she actually followed me to the awning they'd set up in case it started to drizzle again, and we stood side-by-side, looking out over the fields, Caroline with her warm water and lemon, me with my dishwater coffee. Then she spoke to me. Voluntarily.

'I don't seem to be able to get my words out today.'

'Yeah, well, they're information lines, aren't they? Attempting to learn lines that simply explain the plot is like trying to remember every syllable of a really boring shopping list.'

She shot me a sidelong glance then, and I saw her vulnerability.

'That's exactly what it's like.'

I decided to take a chance and attempt a proper conversation.

'Have you heard from Dave?'

At the mention of her driver, Caroline stiffened then shook her head. When we went back to the scene, she started getting her lines right and said very little to me again. Much as I think people reap what they sow, I couldn't help feeling bad for her. How does anyone turn that sour?

At that thought, my phone suddenly trilled in the car and made me jump in my seat. I was far too buzzy for that kind of surprise. A number I didn't know flashed up. I considered not answering, but then I'd have to listen to a message – or not get a message and spend all night wondering who it had been.

The 'hello' was jaunty, male and confident. At first I was nonplussed, then I quickly twigged. He must have kept my number after I called him, enquiring about the ghost walk.

'Tanz, Llewellyn here. How are you, after our little brush with that stone-throwing scamp the other night?'

I take note of the 'our'. I'm guessing he's done an about-face and is telling all and sundry about 'our' ghostly

132

encounter at the Black Gate, because it makes a fabulous addition to the ghost-walk stories.

'I'm fine, thank you. Just on the road to London, so if you hear any background noise it's me crashing the car at speed.'

There's a bark of laughter down the phone.

'Oh dear. Please don't kill yourself on my account. I wanted to ask a quick question.'

'Okay. Shoot.'

'I've had a request from one of our fellow adventurers, asking if they can have your telephone number. I'm aware this is most irregular, but I promised I'd ask. It's Gladys. The lady with the spectacles, who also saw your little ghost friend. I would have said flat-out no, but she was most insistent.'

'Oh, interesting. Do you know why she wants to call me?'

'Not in detail. She said she had something to tell you, and if you're happier taking her number, then I can give it to you.'

'I don't think she's dangerous, do you?'

'I think you're more dangerous than her.'

Another bark of laughter. Is he flirting or taking the mickey? I can't tell.

'You're probably right, Llewellyn. Seeing as I'm driving and can't write hers down, tell Gladys I am very happy for her to have my number, as long as she doesn't wear it out!'

'I shall. And I shall also look out for you on the television. I'm sure you thought I didn't notice, but I recognized you straight away and, after utilizing Google, it turns out you're about to star in *Pendle Investigates*. I'm sure my Uncle Sebastian will be on the sofa with me as we watch you in your glory. How very exciting.'

'I'm afraid you might be slightly less excited when you see the part I'm playing. And you may have to shield Great-Uncle Sebastian's eyes from the eye-wateringly short skirt they've put me in.'

'Oh, now there's something to look forward to.'

Is Llewellyn *straight*?

'Naughty. Listen, I'd better go, as my phone's running out of battery. I need it to call the emergency services if I roll the car over.'

'You are funny. Hope to see you back on my walk soon. You never did get to visit the Bridge Hotel.'

'I'll look forward to it.'

'Marvellous.'

'Bye-bye.'

'Goodbye.'

That was in the first hour and a half of my drive. There were three more hours after that. Loud music helped a lot. Gladys didn't ring. I actually started to feel the comedown from the poison drink/Skittles combo in the last half-hour of the journey, so the end came just before I fell asleep doing ninety and ended up on the central reservation.

Bless Steve. He'd popped round to my flat and put on the lamps and the heating. I came back to a warm flat and, joy of joys, Inka waiting on the sofa. There was a note on my side table:

*Tanz, Inka knew something was up when
I came in here and lit the lamps. I suspect
she'll be waiting for you when you get in.
Have a nice sleep. Hope to see you in the
morning.*

   Steve x

He is such a sweetie. Not only that, but he's left a few slices of bread, some cheese and a cup of milk in my fridge. There's already coffee in there for my cafetière in the morning and two bottles of wine I bought before I left, all cold and inviting. I wonder if I should have a glass as a nightcap.

Don't mind if I do.

Inka stands at my feet as I pour and lightly claws the bottom of my leg. I pick her up, all black and fluffy and in love, and she puts two paws on my shoulder and rubs her face against my hair as I bring the glass to the living room and kiss her whiskers. As she purrs, she makes the tiniest of humming sounds and I actually feel like I could sob. I thought she would be in a huff because I'd been away, and would at least have shit on my bed or run off after five minutes back to Steve's, to teach me a lesson. But no, it looks like she's missed me. I sit down gently and hug her into my chest. After a few minutes of serious feline cuddles I place her on my lap and sip my wine. I don't care how knackered I am tomorrow, when I have to drive all the way back. This moment of peace is worth it.

'*Enjoy it while you can.*'

'What's that, Frank?'

'*You've got some very interesting times coming up.*'

'What's that supposed to mean?'

'*It means, cuddle your cat and get some sleep, my little witchy friend. Life's about to get busy.*'

'Are you going to explain yourself?'

I know, as I'm asking it, that Frank isn't going to explain himself.

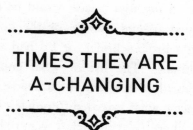

TIMES THEY ARE A-CHANGING

I cannot believe how comfy I am when I wake up. At first I think my sleep was dreamless, as I observe the soft light sneaking in around the edges of my rather shabby blinds and burrow even harder into my duvet den. Inka, sensing I'm awake, nestles even more tightly into my neck and begins to rumble contentedly like a distant combine-harvester.

I sink my hand into her fur as I suddenly recall that no, it wasn't a totally dreamless night. At some point I found myself in some kind of cabin with no front to it, which was awash with sunlight and looked out onto the bluest of oceans. I was in a hammock and beside me was a white shimmering lady who radiated a rainbow of light. She was like an iridescent light bulb, in a long transparent gown with ever-changing colours glowing from her core. She had a hand on my shoulder and, as I looked into the aquamarine water, she fed strength and warmth into me. I presumed she was some kind of healing being, or maybe she was simply an angel. Whatever this dream-being was, I now feel a darned sight more relaxed than I've felt for weeks, as I lie here all warm and protected. I thought running back to snatch a night in my own space would be risky. What if Inka had stayed around Steve's, or the house had been freezing, with a broken boiler, or I'd had another nerve-jangling nightmare? The list of what could have gone wrong is endless; but this time the universe has been kind and this is exactly what I needed to quieten my mind.

I check my cherub alarm clock. I went to bed just before 1 a.m. and it's now half-past nine. I can't believe I've slept for eight and a half hours solid. I could happily do at least another two but, knowing how short time is, I slip out of bed, put on my giant teddy-bear dressing gown and go to the bathroom to turn on the shower to get it hot. Inka follows me, emitting insistent 'I want some breakfast' mewls. As quickly as I can, I patter across the cold kitchen lino, empty a posh tin of cat food that I was given as a sample into her dish and fill her empty water bowl. Then I run back to my super-blaster shower (I bought a new shower head, it's the Rolls-Royce of bathroom fittings) and soap myself from top to toe with grapefruit shower gel and condition my hair with this ridiculously expensive product that I was given in a sachet when I went into Boots. It smells really nice and, once I've shaved my armpits, put my dressing gown back on and wrapped a towel around my head, I again consider chilling out for a couple of hours, putting on the TV, opening some chocolates and curling up with my feline friend. Inka is currently licking her lips and staring at me. She's obviously now in love with the extortionate but tiny tin of cat food she just walloped down, which probably had cat cocaine in it, and is attempting to hypnotize me into giving her another fix.

But the tin is finished and I can't hang around. I have an important visit to make.

RAINBOW LADY

'Oh my *God*, Sheila, you should be in hospital.'

'I don't like hospitals.'

I called round at ten-thirty with two big coffees. Not unfeasibly early, in my book. Sheila answered the door in a fuchsia silk kimono and flip-flops, with her hair in a messy bun and only two of her usual huge selection of knuckleduster gemstone rings on. I have never seen her with no make-up. She would actually look really cute without slap, if her face wasn't the colour of curdled milk. She's lost weight that she didn't need to lose and she's smoking a fag. I despair. Even when she's this ill, she's got a ciggie on the go. Her beautiful eyes look so tired. I hand her the coffee and she lies back against a bunch of opulent cushions. She was watching a Sherlock Holmes film when I came in; she's got them all on DVD. It's on pause now.

'Where's Troy?'

'College, I think. I don't see him all of the time, you know, he's simply my friend.'

She's wheezing.

'I don't care if you're just friends or not, woman. I'd rather know he was with you all of the time, so you have company. You've got me scared, Sheila, I'm not going to lie. Why didn't you tell me it had got this bad?'

'It's that cough that everyone's been getting. It's lingering a bit because of the smoking. And before you start, I'm on eight a day now, which isn't bad at all, and I've ordered one of those vape-thingies, to see if I can get the nicotine from that instead. But I don't know if I'll like it, if there's no smoke.'

I pull a chair nearer the bed and hold back from stroking her hand. Sheila doesn't like sympathy and I'm scared she'll give me a slap.

'Sheila, go and get tested. Make sure you're not getting pneumonia or something. It's been weeks now. You're right, it might be a bug, but it's good to be on the safe side. You look so bloody tired.'

'That's just the coughing in the night keeping me awake. It's got better since I built up my pillows.'

She has to take sips of breath between phrases. She puts her fag out in the ashtray. It has a painting of a seahorse on it. I feel like bouncing it off the wall. I hate that the smoke is making her more ill.

'Anyway, it's mostly because I've not been hungry that I look so drawn. And I'm *not dying*, if that's what you're worried about. My lot would tell me if I was on my last legs. I simply need to rest and eat the food Troy cooks.'

She smiles at me.

'Tanz, he's a lovely man. We have a laugh. But it's not a

relationship. It's not got a name, what we're doing, but friendship's the closest, so that's what it is, okay?'

I wouldn't dare try and figure Sheila out. I'm merely glad she's got Troy right now, and happy that he cheers her up. I wish I could do something for her. I didn't realize I'd missed her so much.

'Anyway . . .'

She stops for a second to stifle a wet cough.

'Enough of that. I want the juicy gossip about the Black Gate. And what about work? Enjoying it any better?'

The cough gets out anyway. It sounds terrible. I look into those tired, pretty eyes and see that her eyelids are drooping. I figure she would probably have dozed off in front of the telly if I'd not shown up. I decide then and there I should make things short and sweet. This isn't the time to discuss anything.

'Not a huge amount to tell about the Black Gate, I'm afraid. There's definitely a little boy there, but I'll have to investigate more and let you know when I've read up about it. As for work, it's not so terrible now. The director's a sweetheart and the cast are nice, mostly. But listen, I've got to shoot off soon or I'll get caught in the traffic on the way back.'

She suddenly lifts her head, which has started to nod. Her coffee is virtually untouched beside her. She puts her hand on my arm.

'You're going back today?'

'Yes, can I bring you anything before I leave?'

'Oh no. I've got everything, lovely. I'm so sorry I'm

falling asleep. I had some Night Nurse this morning. I know it sounds strange, but it helps me rest . . .'

Her voice is trailing off.

'I won't be away much longer, Sheila. I really hope you feel better soon.'

'Thank you. And watch out for the man with the scar on his neck . . .'

'Sorry?'

Her voice is almost gone as she passes into slumber.

'He's a devil, that one.'

And she's asleep.

As I move towards the front door I glance back at Sheila one last time, to make sure she's comfortable. There's a fearfulness in me, seeing her lying there, all waxy and thin. I really wish I could do something to help. As I think this, I catch a movement from the corner of my eye. Disconcerted, I look straight towards the table where I saw it and glimpse a long, transparent garment and a tiny flash of rainbow light to the right-hand side of a vase of lilies.

That's when I know I can relax a little. Whatever happens, Sheila is being watched over; protected by the glowing rainbow-healing lady. Now I'm sure she'll be safe until I return to London. And if anything gets worse, I'll 'feel' it.

WHAT A HEADACHE!

As soon as I get on the M1 my head begins to throb. Not a headache in the classic sense, but a banging in the middle of my forehead.

Whilst I was at Steve's, having a cup of mint tea and a last hug with Inka, I'd felt fine, if a tad upset that I had to leave my girl again. We'd had a great old chat about the healing effects of animals, and I'd given him a hand-made lemon drizzle cake that I'd picked up in a high-class bakery on Crouch End high street. He loves a bit of cake, does Steve.

But now my head has a taut feeling and I have this irrational urge not to go back up North. Obviously I don't have a choice in the matter as I haven't finished my job yet. Surely I can't be reacting like this because I don't want to leave Inka? I decide to ask Frank what's going on and am relieved when he actually replies.

'*Change is scary.*'

'Huh?'

'*You've gone up a notch. We know these things*

subconsciously long before they happen. But it's much easier to stay the same, so you're trying to avoid what's coming. You can't. At least I've told you now, so you can relax.'

'Shit! Is something horrible going to happen?'

'Stop thinking the worst.'

'No.'

'Suit yourself.'

I hear Frank laugh. I can't join in, with this bad head.

'Am I basically being a subconscious wuss?'

'Something like that.'

'Okay then, guru Frank, I will attempt to man up.'

'Good girl.'

And that's when Gladys calls. On the phone her voice sounds like warm Geordie honey.

'I think I might have something that can help you.'

Even though I want to see Milo asap, I decide on the spot that I must take a detour to Gladys's house before I get to Gateshead. I know in my gut that I have to see her.

My headache diminishes, but doesn't disappear.

DON'T JUDGE A BOOK

I am in the tiniest cottage in the world. And it is *rammed*. Not with knick-knacks and ornaments and crocheted coasters. No. It is filled to the brim with crystals. Pieces of rock, little and big, all different colours, some transparent, others dark and heavy. Everywhere a normal old lady would have porcelain shepherdesses and clowns and animal figurines, Gladys has crystals, plants and little vases with wilting garden-picked flowers in them. Some of the crystals are quite breathtakingly beautiful. Others not so much. A lot of them are dusty; you can see she's not a houseworky type of woman. And the place smells of flowers, old newspapers and cooked sausages.

The chair I'm sitting in is a little threadbare but comfortable, and Gladys is wedged into a matching one. When she opened her front door I gave her a quick hug (I'm an actress – we can't help it) and she smelled of a really sexy, musky perfume, which is perfectly at odds with how I perceived her on our ghost walk. I don't think she's as old as I first thought, either. The short grey hair, Cornish-pasty loafers and thick lenses gave me the wrong impression.

She has made us both a camomile tea in these lovely china cups, and has piled up enough treats on a flowery cake-stand on the glass coffee table to feed six tea-partying chimps. Close up, I realize that behind the thick specs she has large, incredibly expressive mocha eyes. On the wall is a huge framed black-and-white photograph of Gladys as a bride, still in glasses, but with a long sixties hair-do, a slim figure and a beautiful smile. Beside her, an adoring look on his face, stands the groom, a man who might be Spanish or French: dark hair, dark eyes, good bone-structure and, frankly, far too good-looking to be purely English. Gladys glances up at the photo and chuckles.

'Giancarlo, my husband. Died twenty years ago. Was still that handsome when he passed. Used to drive the buses.'

'Oh, Gladys. I'm sorry.'

'Don't you worry, pet, I still talk to him. To be honest, he's nicer now than when he was alive. He could be a right misery-guts. He had a bad back and it used to drive him barmy. I didn't know I was a healer then, so I couldn't help. What a shame, eh? Anyway he doesn't have that problem now.'

I'm tongue-tied for a moment. I usually only talk to Sheila about this stuff.

'You're a healer?'

'Aye. Didn't I tell you?'

'No. That's amazing.'

'Oh, I'm used to it these days. It comes as naturally as

sleep. Not that I can always sleep, like. But you know what I mean.'

'How did you find out you could heal?'

'I went into a tarot-reading place on Westgate Road after Carlo died. I was looking for some kind of comfort. Life hadn't always been easy . . .'

She doesn't elaborate, but a look of pure unguarded grief crosses her features, for a second or two.

'Turned out the tarot reader's friend had just popped in for a chat. The minute she sees me, she says, "You've got the gift", and I'm sayin', "What gift?" and she says, "You're a natural healer, like me. A medium 'n' all. Come and see me and I can set you on the path."'

'Wow.'

'I know. I didn't believe her really, but I was at such a low ebb I thought, *Well, what can it hurt?* Turns out it was one of the best things that ever happened to me. Don't think I had the right attitude before that. Didn't think I had anything left to live for. But you can't be like that. If you don't know your purpose, it's because you haven't found it yet, or you're looking at your life the wrong way.'

'That's a good way to see it.'

Gladys looks at me over her specs.

'It's the *only* way. Nowadays I do a few healings every week. I don't charge a lot – nobody's got much around here – but it helps them and I feel great afterwards. Of course you're healing yourself while you're healing others, so it's a two-way street.'

'Really?'

'Oh aye. Too right.'

All at once there's that wide-open feeling in the front of my forehead and I get a little dizzy. This lady obviously has the 'gift' times twenty. She's *powerful*.

Gladys lives on the edge of a very depressing estate in Blyth, where the young people are zombie-like and the ghost of a dead coal-mining industry bears down on the town, in the shape of large slag heaps looming on the horizon. But it seems to have no effect on her at all. This house feels safe, cheerful and peaceful. It's the modern-day version of a witch's cottage. I'd go as far as to say it feels magical.

'Thanks for comin' over, Tanz. I bet you think I'm a right oddball. Which is fine, because I am odd.'

I smile at her and blow on my tea.

She takes a sip of hers and eats half a French fancy with one bite.

'You know, since Carlo died, I don't bother with fellas any more. I've got my books, my crystals and my food. He liked slim lasses, so I was always careful what I ate, but now – now I can do what I like. It's great!'

I can't help grinning as she eats the other half of her cake. She looks so contented. I know it can't be healthy eating so much sugar, but there's something very impressive about someone who decides they don't give a fuck what anyone thinks of them any more, and wears what feels comfortable and enjoys themselves.

I take a Bakewell slice and have a nibble. It's simply delicious.

'Good for you, Gladys. The world's too full of people

who care more what other people think of them than what they think of themselves.'

'Amen to that!'

She takes a gulp of tea. I look around at all of the stones.

'I can't believe your crystal collection. I've never seen so many in one room.'

'I know; it's a bit crackers really, and I don't get round to cleaning them as much as I should, cos it would take all day, but they're lovely company. They're all alive, you know. All got their own light and personality.'

'Wow.'

'Oh aye, lovely things they are. And they help me when I do me healings.'

'Really?'

'Oh, most definitely.'

She licks icing off her thumb and moves on to a macaroon.

'So why did you want me to come over?'

'Wey, when we went on that ghost walk, I could tell you were a "sensitive". I got a bit of a headache when I stood next to you, as it goes.'

'Did you?'

'Oh aye – strong light you've got shinin' there. That's why they're attracted to you, you know. Them lot. The good ones want to say hello, and the not-so-good ones . . . well, they feel threatened by someone like you. That's why they try to give you trouble, the buggers.'

I get a little shiver. No mean feat in a room as over-warm as this one.

'Gladys, I'm scared of all that stuff. The bad ones . . .'

'Well, you shouldn't be. They can put on a bit of a show, but they can't hurt you if you keep in mind that light wins over dark. It always does. Jus' don't let them make you depressed. They're very good at gettin' in your head and turnin' the dimmer-switch down if you let them.'

'Wow. That's interesting. I get a bit depressed sometimes anyway, so that's good to know.'

'Yes, that's something the dark tries to exploit. I could see in your eyes the other night that you get bashed this way and that by life. They don't call people with the gift "sensitives" for nothing. I was wondering if I could help you out with that. Then last night I got this feeling – really strong it was – that I had to get your phone number. So I called the Bard and he sorted it out.'

'The *Bard*? What a great name for him.'

'Yes, some of his stories might be iffy, but he's certainly got the right sense of drama for his job. That's why I like going on his walk. Anyway, if you want me to, I can show you some special signs you can make with your hands and visualize with your mind, to help you heal. And I'm going to tune you in. After a while you'll be able to heal other people. But first you need to do some healing on yourself. Then things won't get so sticky.'

Speaking of sticky, Gladys wipes her sugary hands on her comfortable polyester trousers, then levers herself out of her seat. I tense up slightly as she shuffles around the back of me and puts her hands on the wings of the armchair. Next thing I know, her palms are on my back and they are *extremely* warm and tingly. I gasp.

'Hot, aren't they?'

'What's going on? That's *amazing*!'

I can feel the energy pulsating through her palms. The warmth and the love are incredible.

It's hard not to remember the dream from last night about the angelic healing lady with the rainbow coming from inside. Maybe Gladys is the same as her, but hiding it within the folds of a meaty northern body.

She shifts position behind me.

'You're very open, so you're easy to give healing to. I'll give you twenty minutes of this, then I'll tune you in. By the time you leave here today you'll be capable of strengthening yourself up when you sense any bad feelings threatening, and of protecting yourself against the darkness when you need to. Plus, you'll be on the road to healing others. Can't say fairer than that, eh?'

'No. You bloody can't. That's incredible! Thank you.'

'You're very welcome, pet.'

I close my eyes, enjoying the heat and the tingles.

'Gladys?'

'Yeah.'

'I'm glad I went on that ghost walk and met you.'

'Me, too. I nearly cancelled, because I was feeling a bit under the weather. I almost stayed in and read a book in bed.'

'Wow. No such thing as a coincidence then?'

'Definitely not, pet.'

VOLCANO PALMS

Oh, come on.

I've been tapping on Milo's red front door for five minutes and no one's answering. I've tried his mobile and he's not answering that, either. Milo just doesn't do this. The only reason I can think of for his absence, and his ignored phone, is that he's at a work meeting, but it's nearly seven o'clock in the evening, so it's pretty doubtful.

In a fit of pique I ignore my usual paranoia about pissing people's neighbours off and I bang on his front door, loud, hard and continuously for a whole minute. My knuckles are red by the time I've finished and I have to lick them, then blow on them. Again no one comes. I'm about to abort my mission when I hear a sound from the top of his stairs.

He was in all along!

Another few seconds and there he is, opening the door, hair mussed up from sleep and wearing the shorts and crappy T-shirt of the depressed. I can see it from a mile off.

The scrunched-up eyes, the heavy expression, the holes in his top. Milo doesn't wear shit things, not even for bed.

'Milo, what the hell? Get upstairs now – we need to talk.'

Sullen and heavy-footed, he thumps back upstairs. His voice is thick and slow with sleep.

'Tanz, sorry – I've been busy. And to be honest, I don't really want any visitors right now.'

'I'm not "visitors". What are you on about?'

I close the front door and follow him up.

When we walk into the living room I actually have to stop and orientate myself. By Milo's standards, this place is a catastrophe. Empty pizza boxes, empty gin bottles and an overflowing ashtray. Plus, there's a stain on his carpet. Milo doesn't do mess. He hasn't even opened a window to let out the smoke fug (which is basically a crime worse than matricide in his books) and he doesn't *ever* ignore my calls. *What's going on?*

'Tanz, I need to go back to bed.'

He's just standing there. His eyes are glazed over like he's already asleep. I adopt my bossiest I-mean-business voice.

'Sit down, Milo, I'm making you a coffee.'

I've brought some expensive ground espresso beans for the cafetière I got him last Christmas. I also have really good dark-chocolate biscuits and red wine in my bag. I'm not happy with how much gin he's been chucking down his neck recently, hypocritical as that may be, so I've brought some Merlot, which is much better for him because he can't drink it in such ridiculous quantities.

Milo doesn't argue with me; he simply pulls some jogging bottoms off the floor and drags them on over his shorts. I didn't even think he owned a pair of jogging bottoms. He *hates* leisurewear.

'*Ha-ha. He'll never live this down.*'

'Frank! What the hell's going on here? I feel like I've walked into *The Twilight Zone*.'

'*You're going to have to do your stuff, Tanz. I can't sort this one.*'

Milo looks like he's nodding off again in his chair. There is such a weird feeling in this flat. Nothing like I've ever experienced before. This is a home-from-home for me, but right now it feels like I'm an unwelcome interloper. I fight my unease and chuck on the kettle.

By the time I've filled two large steaming mugs with strong coffee and opened up the expensive choccy biccies, Milo is not looking with it at all.

'Milo. Why are you sleeping all of the time? This isn't you.'

His voice is small and underpowered.

'I was trying to write all last night and I ended up watching some films. It made me really tired today, that's all . . .'

'What films?'

'Creepy things. Horror films. I can't remember.'

'Milo, you hate horror films.'

He sips his coffee, glances at me, sips again.

'Maybe you don't know me as well as you think you do.'

'What? I know you inside-out, you loon . . . There are bits of *Dirty Dancing* that scare you.'

There's something wrong with his eyes. At first I can't work out what it is. Then it hits me. They look darker, almost as dark as coals.

'Things change.'

He looks almost *spiteful* as he says this. Milo is not spiteful.

I nearly spill my coffee. I thrust a biscuit at him and he bites it in an animalistic way that I've never seen before. I want to smash the rest of the box over his head. I'm suddenly very frightened. But I'm going to defeat my fear because *light wins over dark*. That's what Gladys said, and that's also what Sheila said when I first started with this crazy stuff.

I take a big gulp of Colombian blend and let the caffeine kick in at the back of my neck. Despite the kick, I am also finding my centre of calm with my breath. I know it's a contradiction, but it works for me.

'Frank, I think I know what's going on here. Fuck it, I'm going in.'

'Good girl. I'm right here . . .'

I walk round the back of Milo's chair. He is now gulping at his coffee and eating biscuits like they're going out of fashion. Like he's another person.

I tune into the protection that Gladys taught me and plug into the energies of the sun and the earth, like she said. Then, feeling my palms beginning to tingle, I place one on Milo's shoulder and the other on the back of his neck. There's no way I'm powerful enough to do this alone; I'm only a beginner. But I know someone who's an expert. She's iridescent and beautiful and she can help me rock this shit.

I think of the beautiful healing rainbow lady from my dream and ask for her help. Almost at once I feel her presence. She's so calm. And, just as I thought, she's one powerful mamma.

'Holy crap. My palms are suddenly like lava.'

'I always told you you were hot.'

'Not now, Frank.'

I know Gladys said I was only to concentrate on healing myself at first, but this is an emergency and I've got some red-hot help.

Milo actually screams and tries to jump up, at the touch of my furnace hands, which gives me a fright, but I quickly push him back down in his seat and begin to talk authoritatively and calmly, directly into his earhole.

'Milo, this is going to heal you. Your sadness and tiredness are going to lift and you're going to get back your mojo. It doesn't matter whether you got an email from the TV people or not. You have to write the next thing, because you have to write to feel alive and it will make you happy again. Whatever's been making you feel bad this week is not part of you. It's come from outside, and now it's going to leave.'

Milo twitches. I know 'he' can hear me. I remain businesslike as I address the 'other'.

'You're leaving. Because if you don't, you're going to know about it. Get out of here now or you will face the consequences. I'm not scared of you, and I will get rid of you. Do you hear me? *I will properly get rid of you for good, then you'll be nowhere.'*

I mean it. All at once I am righteously indignant at this

dark spectre who is messing with my best friend. And it helps to focus the power that I am channelling. I don't feel a single shred of fear or doubt as I say these things, because I will not tolerate his behaviour and I will find his weakness.

As I concentrate on sending 'good' energy through my palms, I see a shadow dart away from Milo. It's not a normal shadow, more of a greyish-black haze, and it has a pulsating quality to it. Still keeping my hands on my friend, I face my third eye to the unwanted smudge and say, 'I don't know who you are, but *how dare you!*'

I hear his voice. I *hear* with my 'inner ear'. It's like a nasty snake. 'You'll not get rid of me that easily, you sneaky little bitch. Just you see. I'm going nowhere till you take your nose out of my business.'

I have no idea what 'business' he means, but I won't be spoken to like that.

'You don't scare me and I'm not interested in your business. Get out.'

'No.'

His voice is hard and stubborn. It only makes me more determined. There's something deep inside me that tells me I'm more powerful than he is. Fuck him!

'You're not going to make my friend ill in his own house any more. You're pathetic. *Get out.*'

The shadow remains. I sense the rainbow lady's healing energy being beamed through my forehead like a laser, and imagine blowing him away like a water cannon clearing up dog mess.

'You're a ridiculous parasite. I find you funny. All you

did was make my friend more miserable because he was already sad. But I'm going to help him be happy from today, so you've had it – there's nothing for you to grab onto. You are pointless and powerless. Bye-bye, you nobody . . .'

For a moment nothing happens, then the shadow wavers. I see it flicker and I hear a whooshing roar. Not loud, but elongated and low. Like a growl. The shadow weakens, then putters out. Before it can come back, I 'see' a huge protection around the house, like a silvery-blue skin, and then watch all the negativity being shot out through the roof and the protection sealing the last hole against it coming back in. My hands are still on Milo's neck and back. Again I feel the heat in my palms. I'm so grateful to Gladys for sharing such a wonderful gift, and for the rainbow lady's help (though I suspect I'm going to get a telling-off for doing too much too soon). The moment the shadow has been banished, I feel the rainbow lady fading and I thank her from the bottom of my heart for her help. I see a cascade of tiny blue flashes out of the corner of my eye, then she's gone.

Just then I'm distracted by a splashy wallop as Milo's coffee cup hits the carpet. He snaps his head round to look me in the face, and his voice is thunderously scandalized as he cries out, 'Oh my God, Tanz. Why the hell am I wearing tracksuit bottoms?'

My boy is back. Praise the Lord!

OUT WITH THE BAD

The light is fading over the river and I have my curtains open as wide as possible to watch the water flowing by. Milo is sitting up on the firm hotel bed, with a glass of red wine in his hand. There are two beds in this room. I think they only had twins left when they booked me in, but that's a good thing, because Milo can have a sleepover in his own queen-sized cot.

I have one palm on his back and the other on the top of his head. I am going to keep filling him with positive, sparkly energy until there is absolutely no room for any bad thoughts. Now it's just me doing the healing, but my palms are surprisingly hot, which makes me wonder if the rainbow lady 'charged up' my healing energy.

'So he was in my house?'

'Yes, he was, and he was sapping all the joy out of you. Not that you've been helping matters, what with the continuous gin you've been throwing down your neck. Buy more tonic, please – that stuff's lethal, you know. It's a depressant.'

'I know, but it's easy to drink and it's got less calories than wine.'

'Yes, but it also gets you drunk quicker and makes me worry about you.'

'Aw, don't worry about me, I'm tip-top. Especially with you to look after me. Anyway, my mam's drunk gin all her life and it's not done her any harm.'

That's a moot point, but I won't say so to Milo; he loves his mam. The truth is, she's a sweetheart but she does like a snifter in her morning tea, so by mid-afternoon it's very hard to get a coherent sentence out of her.

'I know, but you're a writer; you have to pace yourself.'

Milo obviously doesn't want to discuss this, as he shrugs his shoulders and changes the subject.

'Has that bastard gone out of my house, Tanz? I can't go back if he's still in there.'

'Too right he's gone. He did his worst, but it wasn't nearly enough to mess with us, eh, Milo? We're far too strong for that cheeky swine.'

'But, Tanz, I can hardly remember the past three days. That's bad.'

'Best not to think about it, eh? You'll be much better now. Bet you're writing again by tomorrow.'

He smiles and toasts me with his wine.

'This is so freaky. Your hands feel like two cups of tea against my back. What did that Gladys do to you? She's like the Blyth messiah.'

'I know. She's amazing.'

I daren't tell him quite how ill that spook could have

made him. I can still feel reverberations of his malice when I think about him. That voice. At least now I know I've got to stay on my guard, because there's no predicting what else he can do. I'm quite positive it's him messing with my dreams, and I'm also sure that the little boy is something to do with him, but they're not one and the same person. (It has occurred to me that if I leave the Black Gate thing well alone from now on, I might be able to put this whole matter behind me, but I have the feeling that's not how things work and it won't be as simple as that.)

I managed to persuade Milo to come to the hotel tonight by telling him I wanted company and that it was easier to use my new healing skills by the river. But the real truth is that I wanted his flat to stand empty overnight. I didn't want that 'thing' to get the chance to come back, which it might have done if Milo had started mulling over the past few days. Thinking about spooks too much can accidentally make them return.

The question still remains: what exactly was that horrible 'man' trying to do? Induce a worse depression? Make Milo suicidal? The thought makes me feel sick. That ghost must have been a very vindictive person when he was alive. In my dream he was violent and cruel. The thought of his nasty face and vile yellow teeth still makes me shudder.

'I'm probably going to need to try to clear him completely, Frank. He tried to hurt Milo and I know I haven't seen the last of him.'

'*Well, keep yourself protected – he's not the nicest.*'

'I know he's not.'

'*He's no match for you, though. He left pretty quickly after you told him to go.*'

'He's not gone far, though; I can still sense his energy.'

'*Well, it's far enough for now.*'

I can tell Milo is getting antsy. He's beginning to squirm.

'Tanz, how much longer do I need these volcano hands on my back?'

He's not the greatest one for being touched anyway, so this prolonged hands-on treatment is probably annoying the hell out of him.

'It's been more than twenty minutes, so I think you're done now.'

'Great, thank you! Now you can have a glass of vino with me. Doesn't it look lovely out there?'

'It's gorgeous.'

I pour a small glass of red.

Milo's cheeks have a glow now, instead of that weird pallor he had when I knocked on his door. He's definitely looking less peaky. And his red-wine smile says he's not been overly affected by the past few days. Haunted or not, he's definitely over the worst.

'Thank you so much for that. I feel like a new man.'

'I bet you do, you naughty boy.'

'Oh God, chance would be a fine thing. I'll make do with this vino for the minute . . .'

He goes to the mini balcony and pulls the door behind him, so he doesn't set off the smoke alarms. I am so relieved that he's now in his best black jeans instead of those hideous sweat-pants. He said his mam got them for his Christmas present last year and he'd thrown them into the back of the wardrobe, never to see the light of day again. He said that at first, when he 'came to', he thought I'd put them on him as some kind of joke. I mean, how could I put hideous jogging pants on Milo, without him noticing? Why would anyone do something so dastardly anyway?

I've already ordered Milo to stay here tonight and go home in the morning. That way, nothing bad can get at him – I'll bloody make sure of it.

And when I go to bed I shall have to do some healing on myself, because I wasn't really supposed to be healing other people yet. Not that I had any choice. It does occur to me, as I look back on what just happened, that every-thing I said to Milo about his life and his work could equally apply to me. And it reminds me of what Gladys said – about healing other people also helping the healer.

I watch Milo return and pour the last of the bottle of wine into his glass, before sinking back against the bedpost, his gaze caught by reflections on the river. He smiles to himself as I sip my wine, and I silently offer up thanks that he's my mate again.

I'd be in a right state if I didn't have Milo.

NO ONE CAN SAVE ME

'Holy Jesus.'

I hear a shivering boy's voice, quiet and insistent.

'Holy Jesus.'

I can't see anything, I can just hear hooves and smell horse shit and poverty. The dirt of the unkempt and the forgotten. I can also smell food. It's freezing – freezing cold, snowy cold, and I can smell some kind of savoury food. Stew or maybe soup . . . Children are crying, men are arguing, women are gossiping. I can't make out single words, only the thrum and echo of many voices in a concentrated place. Suddenly I hear a commotion. A fight has broken out and women are screaming. Men are bellowing and laughing. One man lets out an injured howl. Then it fades away.

Now I can smell something awful and I can hear running water. I'm still freezing cold and I'm near a large body of flowing water. Someone's teeth are chattering – I can hear them. It's a child, sobbing and repeating the words, 'Holy Jesus, Holy Jesus, Holy Jesus.'

And suddenly, in the pitch-black, I see those hideous eyes, right there in front of me, taunting me. I recoil, but I know wherever I move they'll follow. I'm trapped in the dark with this hideous being and there's nowhere to go.

This time, though, I'm aware enough to remind myself that I'm in a dream. I will not hand my power over. I am not a lost little boy. I'm Tanz, I'm a big girl and I can wake up whenever I want to. *This is a dream, this is a dream, this is a dream.*

The eyes look cruelly amused.

'It doesn't matter if it's only a dream, you whore. I'm still going to smash your head in and then you won't wake up at all . . . not on that side, you won't. You'll be here forever and it'll just be me and you.'

Wake up, wake up, wake up . . .

And before he can bash my skull into a thousand splinters, I'm awake in a hotel room at 5 a.m., with Milo snoring quietly in the other bed and the sounds of the river gently swooshing through the open window. I am shaking like a spider plant in a monsoon, and the bed is soaked with sweat. This truly is the limit. It takes a while to breathe myself off the nervous-breakdown ledge before I can consult with Frank. That coal-eyed bastard is going to have me dead or in a loony bin, if I don't sort him out.

'Right, let's cut to the chase. Is he going to kill me, Frank?'

'No one's going to kill you.'

'Is he going to try?'

'I don't know. Maybe he's just mouthy.'

'Great. Thanks for nothing.'

'I don't have all the answers, I'm sorry. But he has got a big mouth.'

'He's really rattling me.'

'That's what he wants.'

'That doesn't stop me being terrified. It's making me really worry about going to sleep.'

'I'll send you a lovely dream next time, I promise. I won't let him in.'

'Thank you.'

Milo shifts on his bed. I hold my breath, but he opens an eye anyway.

'Hello, cheeky!'

'Hello, sleepyhead. Sorry to wake you up.'

'You didn't. I wanted to wake up and say hello. It was my plan.'

I nod. Not quite ready to laugh yet. Milo's tone changes.

'Are you okay, Tanz?'

'Fine. I just . . . I had another nightmare. I'll have a glass of water and try and get back to sleep.'

He looks very concerned.

'Fuck that.'

He creeps over to the minibar in his best smoking jacket, the one he brought specially, and pours us both a drink.

'One won't hurt.'

As I lie here with a G&T in my hand, my shaking subsiding, I'm very thankful that Milo is with me. Nobody likes to wake up alone after a nightmare, unless of course they wake up next to fangy Iain, who's worse than a night-mare. The gin is helping to soothe me, but drinking alcohol at fuck-off-o'clock in the morning, because my dreams are constantly haunted, *cannot* be a good thing.

'What did you dream about?'

Milo has got back into bed, and all I can see is his head, his hand and his glass. He's a terrible influence.

'Oh, being haunted and murdered and stuff. Can't remember it properly. It was a jumble of horribleness and fear.'

Milo's face is a picture. He's terrified of anything remotely nightmarish. Predictably, he changes the subject.

'Well, have your gin and imagine being on a beach with some filthy Latino – but don't get too excited in your sleep or I'll be traumatized for life.'

'Oi, don't put your Latino night-fantasies on me.'

'Not my fantasy. I hate beaches. That would be *my* worst nightmare: getting my white body out in the sun-shine in front of some Adonis, then quickly turning into a boiled crab in front of his eyes. I've got enough issues, as it is. The only fantasies I have at the minute involve my bank balance and a new laptop made of platinum.'

'Milo, am I ever going to get rid of these nightmares?'

He thinks.

'If this is anything to do with that "thing" that was hanging around my house, then yes, you are. You got rid of him once. You'll do it again.'

'Right.'

'He's a bastard ghost, made of ectoplasm and hot air.

He's no match for you – a real-life, flesh-and-blood ghost-buster.'

'Okay.'

'Love you.'

'Love you, too.'

MY OLD NANNA

My nanna is very old and very pissed off that she's still alive. I've decided to visit her before work (I start at noon today), because she wakes up at six every morning and it drives her nuts that she spends so many hours alone. Milo woke up at 8 a.m. and went downstairs to eat my free breakfast with a spring in his step. He really did look better and he wanted to go home and work, which is great.

On the way here I stopped and got a giant soya cappuccino for me and a huge cheese scone for my nanna, who absolutely loves them. I reckon when you're ninety you can eat as many scones as you like, and this is a mighty cheesy monster. I don't feel like eating right now, but I've recovered my composure since my early-morning frighteners, mostly because of that tot of gin and the marvellous company of my Milo.

When Nanna opens the front door she is momentarily confused. I didn't tell her I was coming, so in her head I'm not supposed to be here, right now, in Gateshead, so she doesn't recognize me and just stares. I smile widely at her downy grey perm and the large pink cardigan that hangs down to her swollen knees, and suddenly light dawns and she lets out a loud granny yelp and opens her arms.

'Tannnnnnnnnniaaaaa.'

Only my nanna gets to call me Tania. *Nobody* else.

She has the most piercing old-lady voice you'll ever hear and the sharpest mind. Nothing has dimmed my nanna's mind but, like many people as they age, her tolerance level for almost everything has shrunk (as has she, bless her) and distorted. I'm one of the only people in her life who doesn't get on her nerves. And that's simply because I don't see her often enough to annoy her, and she loves the TV and I've been on it, so I've got a free pass to do almost whatever I like.

I hug her, inhaling her lovely, pastel nanna smell and we walk into her pristine little living room. It couldn't be more different from Gladys's place, which is a shrine to ordered chaos. My nanna has stuff – proper old-lady stuff – like ornaments from the sixties and seventies and lots of family photos, but everything has its place and everything is as clean as a whistle. My nanna hates dust and she makes sure that there isn't a speck of it in the house. She does this by making the rest of the family clean it for her. She doesn't actually lift a finger herself, and never has. She detests housework almost as much as she detests swearing (I've had a few near-misses there, but because she's a bit deaf I don't think she's ever noticed). Whoever comes to visit does 'jobs', except for me. I'm not expected to do anything but sit and gossip.

'Eeh, pet, this scone is enormous. I'll never finish it.'

Once her cup of tea is stewed enough, she will demolish that thing in two minutes flat. We both know it, but we don't go on about it.

'Nanna, you look well. How're your feet?'

'Awful, just awful. I can't walk more than four steps without having to sit down. Slave to the bunions . . .'

'Ah, sorry. I didn't realize they were so bad.'

'Well, they are, but not as bad as my shoulder, so I have to be thankful for that.'

I feel so sad for old people when they only have illness to talk about. I mean, what else can you discuss if you don't go anywhere? I know other elderly people who have full lives, but not my nanna. She likes staying in.

'Mind, did you see that Daniella Willis in the paper? Going on about her marriage break-up again. Eeh, it's all she talks about. She gets her money's worth out of two months of living with that fella. I mean that's not even a marriage, is it? Sixty years – now that's a marriage. And she's terrible on that thing; what is it? Oh yes, *The Melroses*. I cannot stand her.'

Yes, Nanna likes staying in and watching the TV. My nanna watches television all the time. She religiously tunes into random, terrible shows, then dissects them and describes them at length. I don't mind it, because I live in London so I don't have to put up with it that much, but it drives my parents to distraction. My dad's not so affected because he doesn't listen to a word anyone says to him, but my mam tries at least to *seem* attentive and it sends her mental. Really, though, considering how much my mam talks about the soaps, it totally is a case of pot and kettle.

It's while my nanna is describing a very wooden crying scene with an actor who 'pulls far too many faces' that my phone buzzes and I discreetly check it, in case Milo has been told off for having my hotel breakfast, or work suddenly wants me in earlier. But, to my consternation, it's neither of these; it's Iain. Little Library Iain, who I so embarrassingly bumped bodies with recently. I didn't think he'd have the brass neck to get in touch, after his behaviour.

Hello, Tanz. Was a bit scared to text. I didn't really handle the whole 'I've got a girlfriend' thing very well. Can I see you again and explain?

I really can't see what there is to explain. I still suspect he was buying me treble gins, for a start. And I'm too mortified to meet up with him. I mean, he's seen my naked body and he didn't deserve the honour, the little creep. What a fool I am. I can't think what to text back, so I press 'delete' and decide that ignoring him forever is probably the best way.

I pick the conversation back up, and my nanna has suddenly started talking about her past.

'Your grandad wouldn't have been ungentlemanly like that. I remember once he danced with this woman at a do at the electric works. From Langley Lane, she was, had a brother in the forces. Looked like one of them monkeys with the big noses – you know, the ones that hang down their faces?'

Oh my God. 'Proboscis?'

'Proboscis, that's it! And he smiled at her and never once did he let on that she looked like a strange monkey. He danced that lass off her feet, he did. He was a gentleman, Tania. A true gent.'

Now I've heard several stories about grandad's exploits at the electric works and, if I remember rightly, he almost definitely didn't think that woman looked like a proboscis monkey. Her name was Gloria, she went to the same school as my nanna, but was much more into 'socializing' and Grandad probably did a lot more than dance with her, but I would never, ever dare say that to my nanna, who has now eulogized him to the status of demigod.

As she chatters away, I go to the little sofa she's sitting on, plonk myself beside her and place a hand on her shoulder and a hand on her arm, just to see what will happen. After about three seconds she gives a yip of surprise and tries to get away from me.

'Eeh, you've put hot stones on me – they're *burning*!'

This sets me off giggling. I have no idea where she thinks I would have hidden hot stones about my person. My nanna is staring at me with big round eyes, so I bite down the laughter and show her my hands.

'Nanna, where would I get hot rocks from?'

'I don't know. Was that your hands? It was *never* your palms, was it?'

I hold them out and she feels my cool palms. Then I take them and put them on her body again, feeling the heat permeate her cardigan. This time she doesn't struggle away, but shakes her head.

'Well, I've felt some strange things in my time, but that beats them all into a cocked hat! What on earth is happening?'

'I've got hot hands, Nanna. They might help your shoulder.'

'They feel like the hot-water bottle I put on my neck sometimes. They're toasty.'

'If I leave them on there for twenty minutes, they should do some good. If you fancy it?'

'Eeh, that's the damnedest thing. I wouldn't have believed it, if I hadn't felt it for myself. What are you like, our Tania? Full of surprises!'

If my parents could see this interaction now, they'd both vomit. But sometimes you just get on with someone because you can avoid the negatives. And that's how it is with me and my nanna. I only see her once a month max, and she doesn't try to get me to do stuff for her every hour of the day. They, unfortunately, aren't quite so lucky.

I hope the healing helps. It can't be all that much fun being really old and on your own, with bunions.

SUICIDE SOLUTION

On the way to work I get a call from Adrian, or Vole as I still affectionately know him behind his back. It's very weird. He says I'm going to do different scenes now, as Caroline is 'indisposed'. The way he says it . . . I can hear the dot-dot-dot after it. And I'm lucky these new scenes are non-speaking for me or I'd be in a lot of trouble. This bloody job.

When I climb the Make-up bus's squeaky stairs to get my hair greased and my face ruined, I find Vicky on her own, looking rather despondent. When she sees me, her eyebrows shoot up and she closes the door behind me, checking over my shoulder for who knows what.

'What's the matter? Con okay?'

'Con's fine. Staying at mine actually. And driving me nuts, bless him.'

'Oooh dear.'

'No, it's fine. I'm just glad he's alive. I can take a bit of aggro.'

She checks through the little bus window again.

'Vicky, what's the matter?'

'I'm checking no one's listening. I don't want to lose my job.'

'Eh?'

'I have to tell you something. It's Caroline. They said I hadn't to tell a soul, but you're different.'

'That's me. "Mrs Different".'

'She tried to kill herself last night.'

'*What?*'

'Yep. The producers are going mad. We've not even wrapped yet and she's trying to top herself.'

'How very caring of them.'

'I know. But they don't think about human stuff, do they? They think about shooting costs and losing the light and scenes not getting finished.'

'Fucking hell. How did she do it? Please don't say she tried to hang herself?'

I'm haunted by the thought of hanging. What a terrible way to die. I will never get the means of creepy Dan's demise out of my brain; it's branded there forever.

'God, no. Pills and vodka apparently. They're going to say it was an accident, but it wasn't. And it's going to be billed as a "mystery illness" to most of the crew and cast.

'Bloody hell.'

'The worst thing is they had no one but her driver to contact about it. And he's only worked for Caroline for a few days. She divorced acrimoniously, she has no kids and both her parents are dead. I mean, it really is a sad state of affairs when you've alienated everyone to such a degree. She has her personal hairdresser who's a friend, but he's over in America right now, styling some awful daytime show, so she really is alone. The cleaner came back to her apartment last night because she forgot her purse. If she hadn't walked in and found her, Caroline would be kaput.'

'The measure of a successful life. No family, no mates and found by the cleaner . . . Wow, even when you're a bitch, it must be awful to feel so low that you want to chuck in the towel and actually have no one you love to identify your body afterwards.'

If I'm honest, my thoughts of topping myself have always been accompanied by a fear of the pain and a worry at how much it would upset my family. Caroline doesn't seem to have that to tie her to the planet. It amazes me that she's been so objectionable that she has absolutely no one there for her. It's like she's *decided* to make life harder and lonelier than it already is.

'She needs someone to put her straight,' Vicky says.

'Er, why are you looking at me like that?'

'Caroline might just listen to you.'

'*Eh?* Why would she listen to me? I pulled a thatch of plastic hair out of her head a week ago.'

'It was real hair actually; she wouldn't have fake hair – far too cheap.'

'Whatever. I removed it with my bare hands. She wanted to sue me. She'll probably throw something at me if I show up at hospital.'

'No, she won't. And so far she's probably only seen a "concerned" producer and the hospital staff. Go on, you'll be finished here by teatime. She's in a private place about five minutes' drive away. She spoke to you the other day during your scene together. That constitutes friendship in her world.'

'Until I asked a nosy question. Then she clammed up like a moody mussel.'

'Oh, go on, Tanz. People shouldn't be that isolated. Even if it is their own fault.'

'Why don't you go and see her?'

'I will, but I'm working until eight tonight. Then I've got to get back and help Con with some paperwork. It's all getting a bit much for him at the minute – it's the shock, plus he's not sleeping too well.'

'Neither am I!'

'But the first day after you try to kill yourself, Tanz . . . I think it's probably important, don't you?'

I sigh. She's absolutely right.

'I'm sorry to put this on you, Tanz, but Caroline opened up to you the tiniest bit the other day. She actually approached you. That's more than she's done with most of us in years. I told you – you're special. People connect with you.'

'All right, all right. I'll go later on. If she throws anything or goes for my throat, though, that's your fault and I expect compensation.'

'Fine. Oh, and before I forget, Con still wants to meet you, to say thanks. He says he'll come over as soon as he's got his paperwork sorted.'

'I've told you, I didn't do anything.'

Vicky shakes her head.

'Tanz, what are you like?'

I'm like a shy loud-mouth who doesn't want any fuss.

'Just meet Con, will you – he'll not bite.'

'How do you know, Frank? Thanks for sending me Gladys by the way.'

'I didn't send anyone. I'm not a flippin' wizard. You found each other.'

'I wish I could give you a hug.'

'Tanz, you are so greedy for cuddles.'

I hear him laugh. It is always comforting to hear Frank's laugh.

'Frank?'

'Yessss?'

'I'm really scared of going to see Caroline. Why me?'

'You know why.'

I don't.

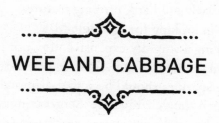

WEE AND CABBAGE

I have always hated hospitals. They smell of wee and cabbage, or they used to, plus there's never been a nice reason for me entering a single one of them, nor will there ever be. Illness, decay, accidents, broken bits. Some may argue that the birth of a child is a positive reason for going to hospital, but seeing as I will never give birth – and watching someone else give birth would make me gip – this doesn't apply to me.

This hospital is a bit different from the ones I've been in before: the one to watch my grandad fade away; the one when I snapped my toe on a radiator in London; and the big one in Newcastle when I dropped the gigantic glass salad bowl on my bare foot and it wouldn't stop bleeding. (My poor feet. Always in the wars.) This one is more a 'hospice', I reckon. It smells of school dinners and flowery air fresheners. They probably have those plug-in things that spray every five minutes, rendering the air as cheap and fake as my best sunglasses.

When I get to the reception desk, after feeding the

parking meter about twelve quid for a forty-five-minute stay, there's a nurse there who looks like a sergeant major. All straight back and hard, probing features.

'Hello, I'm looking for Caroline May.'

I'm carrying a stupidly expensive, tiny pot plant from a swishy florist's on the quayside. It has a sparkly blue ribbon. The sparkles should be actual diamonds, considering how much they charged me. Sergeant nursey stares at me, looks at her computer screen and stares again.

'And you are?'

'Oh. I'm Tanz.'

'No, I mean, are you family? Friend?'

'Erm, we're working together on a show. She's a . . . friend.'

'You're an actress?'

'Yes.'

Her face relaxes. I wouldn't have had her down as a star-fucker.

'What will I have seen you in?'

The dreaded question. I name a few shows. Soon her demeanour is warming up nicely.

'What an interesting job you have.'

'Yes, I suppose, sometimes.'

I don't want to tell her that often I feel inferior and stupid, that TV acting is mostly waiting in your caravan/ dressing room unless you're a star with loads of lines, and if you're an actress who happens to be older than thirty-five you're classed as 'ancient', because her demeanour might suddenly cool down again.

'Well, Tanz, Caroline is down the corridor and to your

right, in room six. She's been a bit groggy today because we gave her some medication to help calm her down.'

She lowers her voice and looks around her.

'I'm not sure she was very pleased that she woke up at all. She certainly wasn't happy to see us.'

Oh dear. They've probably had the sharp end of Caroline's tongue already. Even almost dead, she seems capable of reducing people to quivering jellies. I nod, in as concerned a way as I can.

'Oh, she's probably very stressed. She doesn't mean it.'

'I thought so. She's so lovely in her interviews on telly.'

I work hard on not rolling my eyes.

'So I just walk down there then?'

'Yes, that's right. If I'm not here when you leave, ring the bell so I can sign you out.'

'Thank you.'

I have to take a deep breath as I wander down the smooth, sterile corridor. Even as I approach the door there's a horrid energy coming from Caroline's room. It's still and dark, this feeling, with a twist of despair in the middle.

I knock very gently but she doesn't reply. I take a last steadying breath and enter. The blinds are half closed, but they are white so there's still light in the room. It's small but tastefully decorated, with a TV that's currently switched off. It has little touches that make it more luxurious than you'd expect in a hospital, with watercolour prints on the wall and a nice lamp. Caroline herself is in a single bed with her back to me. She isn't moving. For a moment I have this horrible thought that she's dead.

'Caroline?'

She stirs. Slowly she moves onto her back, tightened against the bed by the sheets, eyes half closed, then turns her head towards me. When recognition dawns, she closes her eyes again and lays her head back on the pillow. Her voice is exhausted and defeated.

'What are you doing here?'

I walk forward with the plant, towards the sterile-looking cream chair next to her and the tiny bedside cabinet, feeling like a buffoon. She doesn't need a plant, she needs to be left alone. This is just another humiliation for her.

'I brought you a plant. I have no idea why – I'm sure you don't need a begonia with a stupid metallic ribbon on it.'

She doesn't reply or look at me. I try again.

'I came to see if you're all right.'

There's another silence. I put the plant down on the cabinet and sit on the chair, wishing I could run right out of the door again.

'I don't even know you.'

Caroline doesn't sound angry, she sounds beaten.

'It doesn't matter. I still wanted to see you.'

I know her arm is under the sheet – her tiny, malnourished-through-years-of-diets-and-exercise-but-still-good-at-punching arm – and I reach out and lightly lay my palm on it. She doesn't pull away. She doesn't move at all.

'Why didn't I die?'

Now there's a question.

'I'm not sure. I don't know how many pills you took or how much vodka you had. I'm just sorry you felt rotten enough to attempt it in the first place.'

Her face contorts and scrunches up in an effort not to cry. Despite, or maybe because of, the Botox and the hair extensions and the skin-peels and the facials, she looks ancient lying there, like a smooth, dying alien, all the life and spirit gone out of her. Her voice is now a whisper.

'I took *all* of the pills. I drank *all* of the vodka and still . . . I'm here.'

'You're stronger than you look. And it wasn't your time to go yet. You may think you wanted to die, but your body and soul had other ideas.'

Tears now stream down the sides of Caroline's face. She doesn't check them or move, or do anything.

'I couldn't even get that right . . .'

I move my hand and feel down her arm until I locate her fingers, wrapped in the cotton sheet. I envelop them as best I can with my own.

'Everyone feels lost sometimes, Caroline.'

Her eyes open again and she turns her wet face fully towards mine.

'I don't want to be here any more.'

'It's only a show – you'll get another show. Or you'll stay in this one and work well with the new actress. There's no need to die because of it.'

'It's not the show – it's . . . Last night I realized . . . how I've spent my time chasing something not worth having. And now I'm old and ugly, with no one and nothing, there's no use me being here. People don't like me and mostly I don't like them, and I've contributed nothing except stupid lines in stupid TV shows. I've completely wasted my life.'

'You love acting. You're good at it. It's true you don't have to be . . . well, quite so harsh to people. But you can change that in an instant. You can go back on-set and smile and say hello. You don't have to be anyone's best friend, simply be pleasant. Next thing you know, they'll be pleasant back.'

'I *don't* love acting. I don't think I love anything any more. I loved my husband, and he slept with half of Surrey. I just . . . don't have the energy.'

She now begins to weep openly, helpless and unguarded, lying here in a hospital room, with a bit-part actress sitting next to her whose name she keeps getting wrong. I claw at the sheets until I can get at Caroline's hand properly with both of mine and I hold it tight. For all of her being a cow, she's a human being in pain and I can't bear it. I squeeze until she begins to squeeze back, albeit weakly.

'Please, Caroline, hang on in there. You can be whoever you want. You're not old, you're just not twenty-five any more. Maybe it's good to start enjoying things now, instead of clinging to the past. This could be the time for you to fly.'

'I don't know how to enjoy myself any more.'

Her eyes are pleading with mine. I don't feel I have anything to offer her; I'm as lost as she is, half the time.

'Sometimes sitting in the back yard with a coffee listening to the birds is the happiest I get. I don't know how to help you, Caroline, because many of my good times are peppered with lows. You've got to go back to bed and not get up until you feel better. Or go for a walk in the woods, or be nice to someone on the street because they look sad. It's simple stuff and it doesn't make everything amazing – it only lightens the heaviness a bit.'

'I'm not like you. I like champagne and Soho House and the finer things, and being treated like a princess. Simple things have never pleased me.'

'Rubbish. What about the sea?'

'What about it?'

'The sea is so good for the soul. Don't you like walking on the beach? Putting some flat shoes on and buying an ice-cream? Looking out to sea and listening to the breakers and realizing there are bigger things in the world than yourself?'

'Last time I did that I was in Antibes and I certainly didn't eat ice-cream.'

A tiny spark of life. Infinitesimal, but there.

'Well, there are plenty of beaches close to here and they are just as nice as Antibes probably, only not as warm. Will they let you out?'

'Sorry?'

'Will they let you out, right now?'

I've decided on something. It's naughty and I'll get into trouble, but hey-ho.

'I'm not in prison. I'm supposed to be in for observation for another twenty-four hours. But I couldn't go out, even if I wanted to, I feel too weak.'

'I can help. What were you wearing when they brought you in?'

Caroline's starting to look a little alarmed now and, dare I say it, the tiniest bit interested?

'My nightdress. But the driver brought some stuff today. I don't know what. It's not really his job, plus he's new. He's not Dave.'

A quiver in her voice again. She needs Dave.

There's a sports bag in the corner and I open it. Inside is an expensive cashmere sweater – a lovely powder-blue thing it is – some equally expensive-looking exercise pants and some trainers. There's also a dusky pink, strappy silk top, a silk skirt and kitten heels. And at the bottom some underwear and a baseball cap. I have no idea where this man thought she was going, but it looks like she's packed for the gym, then a fancy restaurant. There's no dressing gown, pyjamas or coat. Luckily it's mild today.

'Get the jumper, pants and trainers on. And the baseball cap.'

'I can't, I'm too tired.'

'Come on.'

I help her to sit upright on the bed. She's woozy but not immobile. I pass her the vest and jumper. Caroline lifts the vest, but drops it again. She's so listless, I help her pull them on. Then I pull up her joggers and tie her shoelaces. Last but no means least, I put the baseball cap on her and pull her sweaty hair out of the back of it in a ponytail. I'm not sure of the etiquette of taking a person out of hospital who's had their stomach pumped in the last twenty hours, but I have the strongest feeling I must do this. As a last resort, I open my bag and take out some juicy strawberry lip gloss and smear some on her lips. Caroline doesn't resist any of this, and I wonder if she's too knackered to fight.

'Can you walk?'

'I don't know. I'm so fuzzy.'

'Just a sec.'

I leave her sitting forlornly on the side of the bed. In the corridor is a wheelchair. It's close by, so I reckon they've moved her in it already. I edge it through the door and help her climb in.

'Right. Come on!'

'Where are we going?'

'You'll see.'

'Are you kidnapping me?'

'Yes.'

The reception desk is empty. I wonder if I should tell the nurse we're going out for an hour. I decide against it and wheel Caroline's tiny frame as fast as I can and get her into my passenger seat, sharpish. Then I put the folded wheelchair in the boot. I spot three cans of fat Coke in there that I forgot to take out. I drink fat Coke when I have a hangover, so I keep them stocked up in my fridge. For some reason, these ones didn't make it into my kitchen. As I'm doing up Caroline's seatbelt, I'm very aware that I'll probably get into lots of trouble, but sod it. My heart's going like the clappers, but that's what life's about, isn't it? Risk.

When she's secured and looking at me like I'm mad, I pop the ring on a can of Coke and pass it to her.

'Just for a bit of energy.'

'I don't like Coke.'

'Today it's medicinal. Have a sip. The sugar will help. By

the way, sorry about my car; it's so old it's made of clay and bark.'

She glances at me sideways like I'm insane.

I drive off with a belly full of lead. This woman tried to commit suicide yesterday. She is at real risk of trying it again and this might not help at all. And if she does manage to die, I'll probably get the blame for taking her away from hospital when she needed it most.

But she won't be at rest in hospital and I don't think being there will help. I know that when your thoughts are desperate, lying down and thinking is the worst thing possible. Lying down is for sleeping and nesting and avoiding. But when your thoughts are whirling and getting darker and darker, sleep won't help. You need fresh air. You need nature. You need life.

I'm gratified to see Caroline lifting the can to her lips as I edge out into the traffic, which will take us through Jesmond, and lead us, twenty minutes later, into Tynemouth. She is still puffy from crying, but at least she's looking around a little and sipping the drink.

'What's your real name?'

'Sorry?'

'Tanz isn't a name. What is it really?'

'Tania. But if you use it, I'll kill you. Oops, no, sorry . . .'

She gives me a funny look that almost turns into a smile.

'That's okay. I wish you would.'

'Don't say that.'

'I don't see why it's such a bad thing to decide you've had enough and don't want to be alive any more.'

She's so matter-of-fact about it that I don't really know

how to reply. I have to gather myself before I come up with a response that is shaky at best, but as truthful as I can be.

'I think we're supposed to stick it out here because things get better after they go shit. If we die before our time, we miss the next good bit. I'm not religious, but I think there's something about staying here until your time's up. Even if you think you don't want to. I have to believe that or I'd have taken a stack of pills myself by now.'

'Would you?'

She has another sip of the Coke.

'You better believe it. I can be a right misery when the mood takes me. But life's also got quite delightful bits.'

She stares at her knees as we wait for the traffic lights to change. When she speaks it's barely loud enough to hear.

'What's the most delightful thing you've done recently?'

I wasn't expecting that. I have a think, then wonder if I should tell her what springs to mind. I mean, the truth gets me in trouble sometimes. In this case I decide it's best to spill, because it's easier than thinking up something less delightful.

'I had a fantastic night of passion with a gorgeous young Irishman about seven months ago. We'd been seeing each other for a while, just casually, then he was going away travelling and we had our last night together and it was mind-blowing. Probably because he was leaving, so I wouldn't have to get to the "washing his dirty Y-fronts" stage.'

Her eyebrows shoot up. Well, they move as much as the Botox will allow, suddenly making her resemble Jack Nicholson as The Joker.

'Do you miss him?'

'Sometimes. But I told him not to ring me and to have the time of his life – much less painful.'

Caroline nods. I can't believe that my last delightful moment was more than half a year ago. That's pathetic. I need to get a grip.

'What about you?'

'What about me?' she asks.

This is not the woman I first met on-set. This is a broken porcelain doll.

'What was the last delightful thing that happened to you?'

She sits and thinks. It takes a while.

'About three months ago I went to a party in Tuscany thrown by a famous socialite – Victoria Bligh-Cortez. Have you heard of her?'

I shake my head. Caroline looks a tad disappointed.

'She's married to a billionaire shipping magnate. My friend Dominic is a stylist and he'd done her hair for a few big parties, so he was invited and I went as his plus one. When we got there I was the least rich and famous person in the marquee, and virtually no one said a word to me. Dominic was schmoozing and I didn't want to cramp his style, so I went out into the warm night air and sat in a chair overlooking the olive groves, in my grey silk shift dress with my violet Martini. I felt like the biggest outsider in the world, but I also felt the tiniest bit exhilarated that I was sitting there at all, listening to the crickets, in Italy, with a classy cocktail in my hand. Just then a waiter came out. He must have been the head guy, because he wasn't a boy; he looked to be in his forties and was very, very handsome. He asked if I was all right, sitting out there alone, and offered to get me a pashmina. I told him I was fine, then he swooped over, kissed my hand and said I was the most beautiful woman at the party. Then he went back inside.

'That made me sad, because it reminded me of the days when most men thought I was the prettiest girl in the room and everyone wanted me, when now they barely notice me at all. But also it delighted me, because he actually cared whether I was cold or not. I was not totally forgotten. We left soon after that, because Dominic got too drunk too quickly and could hardly speak. But that moment was wonderful.'

Wow! Her best time was a kissed hand from a charmer at a poncy party in Tuscany. No wonder she's depressed. I'm hard pushed to work out which one of us is more tragic.

'Did you find out who he was, afterwards?'

'I did. And he was married. And for once I did the decent thing and left well alone. Mostly because in the old days, if I'd wanted him, I would have got him. In this case he was maybe just being kind.'

Another tear trickles down her cheek.

'Caroline, you are absolutely gorgeous. He obviously thought you were attractive or he would have left you to shiver outside.'

'You think?'

'Of course. And yes, he was married, but he could still have thought you were the most beautiful woman in the room. At least you were honourable and didn't snatch him away from his probably not-quite-so-beautiful but sweet wife!'

She smiles grimly at this.

'I used to be such a cow, I couldn't care less if a man had a wife or girlfriend. If I wanted them, I took them. My ex-husband was with someone when he met me. He left her within the month. And married me within six.'

'How long were you together?'

'Two years.'

'And he cheated?'

'More than once.'

'What a dick! You married a dick. I bet he was good-looking.'

'He was the most handsome man I'd ever seen.'

'Christ, well, that makes it worse. He obviously fancied himself something chronic. Don't marry a dick next time.'

'You can't say things like that!'

'I just did. Look over there.'

I point over the trees and buildings at the horizon.

'The sea.'

'Yup.'

Soon we're driving along Tynemouth coast. The sea is tumultuous and angry – white surf and grey water. I love it. Caroline looks spent. When we reach the parking spaces by the old priory, I'm lucky enough to find a free spot. They're almost always full, but this one is perfect. I'm telling you, there's no such thing as a coincidence.

'Do you want me to push you in the wheelchair?'

'No, I'll walk. As long as it isn't far.'

'It isn't, trust me.'

It's gusty here, but not too cold. I take off my jacket and, as I help Caroline out of the car, I make her slip into it. She looks like she might protest, but I don't let her. I link her arm.

'Come on.'

Twenty steps and we're in the takeaway part of the most famous fish-and-chip shop in the North-East. I get two portions of chips with lots of salt and a cup of gravy. Caroline sits on a little plastic seat while I order. Soon we are walking down to the front, arm-in-arm. Within a very short time we are on a bench overlooking the beach. On our knees we both have an open cardboard box with chips and gravy and little wooden forks. I eat mine with gusto; she picks up one chip at a time, takes little nibbles and pokes at the gravy with her tongue. But at least she tries to eat, and she smiles as the seagulls start to circle. They make strange baby-screeches for the next ten minutes, waiting for the right moment to swoop and steal our chips as we watch the waves lick at the sand. Out on the horizon the sun goes red, orange and pink over the choppy water.

'I used to eat gravy and chips when I was little. It was our treat.'

'Good memories?'

'Not really. But they taste much better than I remember.'

'Good.'

'I'm so tired.'

'Sorry.'

'No, don't be, it was nice of you to bring me here. Nice of you to make the effort. That sunset is going to be spectacular.'

'I love sunsets. And sunrises. I need to watch sunrises more often.'

'That's what I should have done.'

'You still can.'

'I don't know if I want to. I just want to be asleep for good.'

Part of me wants to punch her. My Frank would have appreciated this life that she's given up on. But I know it isn't that simple. A lot of people seem to have very exhausted souls.

'Caroline. Like I said, life's not easy. It's shit, it's cruel, it's nasty and sometimes it's amazing. And would you look at that!'

Like I planned it, like it's a film where everything ends happily ever after, the clouds open and there, beaming down like angel rays, are streams of pink-and-orange light straight from the heavens into the sea. It's gorgeous. It's perfect. I glance her way and she's watching intently. Then she looks at me.

'I know what you're trying to do. Yes, it's really beautiful. And thank you for bringing me here. But it's not changing my mind.'

She pats my hand, very lightly. She's obviously not a warm woman, so it's quite an honour. Now that she's had a few chips and a Coke, her face looks less ravaged. She almost looks normal, with the rosy glow of the setting sun on her skin and reflected in those extraordinary eyes. Now I can see the natural prettiness that turned men to jelly. It's just a fucking shame that I probably won't be able to persuade her to live.

Why do these things fall on me? Why should I be even thinking about this? I'm not exactly the most balanced of people. Dammit, I can even understand her wish to fall asleep, but you have to keep on keeping on. I'll bet loads of people get sick of being a grown-up.

I look at the time on my phone and get a fright. At least there are no missed calls from the police. Yet.

'Caroline, I'd better get you back. I'm probably already in deep poo.'

'Oh, okay.'

I'm sure I detect a little reluctance there. Could it be that she's enjoying this?

'We can stay a while longer if you like?'

'Oh no, that's fine. I'm tired. But I'll have another couple of chips first.'

I knew it. I don't smile or show any reaction. I watch the horizon. Then I can't resist a tiny nudge of her arm with my elbow. Caroline nudges me ever so slightly back. That's all I needed. I am jubilant. I want her to live. I really do.

What's that about?

MONSTER AT THE GATE

I 'm too wound up to settle down for the night and it's
only eight o'clock, so I've decided to have a walk.

Leaving Caroline at that place was flippin' traumatic. She obviously didn't want to stay there, and they
were very angry with me for taking her out. They hadn't
told anybody she'd gone because they were too scared of
getting in trouble, I reckon, but I think I'm now probably
banned from there forever, so it's lucky she's coming out
tomorrow. I have no idea if she'll make it back on-set this
week, but fingers crossed.

Before I left her, I passed Caroline her phone – one of
the few useful things her new driver actually packed – and
I told her to call Dave. Just to let him know what had happened. And maybe to say sorry. She gave me a 'look' but
then, to my surprise, she also gave me a self-conscious hug.
Wonders will never cease.

So now I'm going to have a quick shower, change my
jeans and go for a gin-and-slim. Or two. Purely to soothe
my head. Seeing someone in distress like that serves to

remind me that really wanting to commit suicide is different from when I get upset and think I want to die. I don't really, I just want the world to leave me alone for a bit.

As I wander languidly through the hotel reception, which is a big, beautiful open-plan space with huge arrangements of fragrant pink-and-white lilies and a calming, eye-catching view of my beloved River Tyne, I consider the joyful possibility of a great big bowl of hummus with several warm pitta breads to accompany my gins, from a gastropub up on Pink Lane. I sometimes forget how much I love hummus. My ultimate comfort food, after chips.

It's only as I'm approaching the lift that I suddenly notice a little ginger man with sinewy drummer's arms and a green T-shirt moving fast to intercept me. He must have been lounging on one of the sofas where people read newspapers and drink coffee. I feel panic rising in my throat and momentarily think of running for it, but that would only make me look insane and I'd rather not convince the staff here that I'm a nutter, especially when I'm staying for a while yet.

'Tanz.'

I sigh and stop.

'What do you want, Iain?'

'To apologize.'

'What for?'

'For probably making you feel cheap.'

'Just come out with it, why don't you.'

'Look, I was a bit star-struck the other night, and I think it made me really clumsy and stupid.'

'Shagging someone when you already have a girlfriend

is definitely clumsy and stupid, as well as out of order, but I'm not sure being star-struck can be blamed for that.'

'Actually . . .'

'My God, you only slept with me because I'm off the telly?'

'No. I mean, well, I did recognize you, and I used to have a massive crush on you when I was younger, but it wasn't only that.'

'And is that why my gins were so bloody strong?'

He looks cornered.

'Are you saying I got you pissed on purpose?'

'Yes.'

'I didn't hear you complaining then.'

'Oh, you little shit.'

'Tanz, I don't mean it like that. I just think it was more mutual than you're saying it was . . .'

I look around me. The reception-desk girl is cocking an eye in our direction. I don't want her overhearing this stuff – it's humiliating.

I hiss at him, 'Bar. Now!'

We walk through the double doors into the lounge. I lead him to the most hidden corner I can. I'm really pissed off that he's delayed my hummus consumption.

'One drink, Iain. Then I'm going out.'

Despite my instinct to send him on his way, I don't want him yelling my private stuff in front of the hotel staff, so I sit with a G&T in front of me and he nurses some cloudy nonsense called 'Brewer's Droop' or something.

'Tanz, I said it all wrong out there. Look, I fancy you because you're interesting and lovely, and my girlfriend isn't really into, you know, paranormal stuff. Or sex. She wants a practical life. We do it with the lights off . . .'

I shake my head as I listen to his excuses.

'I'm making this worse, aren't I?'

'Yes. Don't give me your woes about your girlfriend, please. Nothing you say will stop me being annoyed with you, Iain. What you did was outrageous. If I'd known you were with someone, I would never have . . .'

'I know. It was naughty. But you're so—'

'Stop, right now.' I've developed quite an aversion to those fangs of his. I don't know how I even snogged him. What was I thinking? 'I only hope you didn't tell her. That would be very bad.'

'Of course I didn't. She'd disembowel me.'

'Oh well, that's just fabulous.'

'No, I don't mean literally – she's actually quite reserved. But she doesn't like to be crossed.'

'Frank, next time I'm about to snog an idiot, stop me.'

'*I did try.*'

'There's no need to be smug.'

'. . . Listen, I know I messed up, I'm sorry. But I hope my latest research on the Black Gate can help make things up to you.'

Okay, so this catches my interest *slightly*.

'What research? I've already done research.'

'What – about the little boy and what he was wearing, and the pub noise and all of that?'

'Yeah, I know about that stuff already, but carry on.'

'Okay, erm, I looked it up and when the Black Gate was a tenement in the 1800s it actually did have a pub built into it. A bit of a gin palace, by all accounts. From what I read, loads of kids were neglected at that time, there were several ladies who sold their favours to get money for booze, and the whole place was rife with drunkenness and crime.'

I'm not going to tell him that I saw it for myself in a dream.

'I know all of that. What I actually need to know is if there was anything specific about anyone who died there?'

He grins. Fangy-fang-fang.

'Yes. I found a few things.'

Iain pulls a little notebook out of his back pocket.

'A lady called Maura was one of the barmaids at the Black Gate. She lived in the building and fell down the stairs one night and broke her neck. Then there was an old couple who died within two weeks of each other, of TB. Then there was a lady called Reena, a prostitute. She fell whilst drunk, banged her head and accidentally landed in the fire; burned a lot of her room down apparently. Then there were several children who also died of TB; one little girl who was poisoned by her mum and—'

'IAIN!'

He is halted mid-flow by a loud, bland voice from the entrance to the bar.

I peek over his shoulder as he turns his head in fear. There I spy a familiar, pleasantly pretty, passive-aggressive face atop a shirt with little flowers for buttons and a roomy pair of Marks and Sparks slacks. She comes closer, glaring in disbelief at me, then striding right up to him.

'What are you doing here?' His voice is reedy and scared.

Her brow creases. 'I think that's my question for you, Iain.'

I go into survival mode immediately. I refuse even to get involved. I should be mortified, but when you're this far in the shit, being brazen is the key.

'Hello, Kelly, what a surprise. Am I missing something?'

'You tell me. You're the one having a cosy date with my fiancé.'

Iain winces. I laugh. What else can I do?

She looks at Iain, who seems to have turned into a show-room dummy.

I pipe up, 'We're not on a bloody date, woman. Iain, Kelly is my Wardrobe lady.'

'He already *knows* that!'

I can't believe this.

'Have a drink, Kelly. He's drinking that weirdo dish-water, I'm on G&T – what do you fancy?'

Why isn't he saying anything, the fucking wimp? He *must* have known that Kelly was working with me; how creepy. She ignores me and looks at him, probably as frustrated as I am by his silence.

'A lime-and-soda, please, Iain. I've got the car.'

This breaks his spell and he stands. 'Kelly, I'm confused. What's going on – what brought you here?'

'You seem to have forgotten that my friend Susanne works on the desk here, you clown. She called to tell me she'd spotted you lurking in the lobby. Then, as I'm driving over here, she calls again and says you've met up with an actress from the show I'm working on. Your teenage *crush* no less.'

I feign the most innocent of innocence.

'Oh my *God*, Iain, is that true? I was your *crush*?'

His shrug and pathetic laugh are rubbish. I don't think improvisation is his forte.

'Well, Kelly, I'm afraid you haven't found a tryst here at all. I met your fiancé' – I pronounce it very clearly in his face – 'at the library when I was researching the Black Gate. He's come here tonight to give me some information on the place. Look, there, it's in his notepad.'

She glances over it. Narrows her eyes at him.

'How come you didn't tell me about this, Iain?'

She says 'Iain' a lot. She's like a prison warder.

'I mean, I see you nearly every day. And I work with Tanz. Why the big secret?'

'Yeah, Iain, why the big secret? Didn't you know I was working with Kelly?'

I can't resist a dig; he's such a loser.

'Here, let me get your drink, then I'll explain.' He runs off to the bar and I reach over and drag the nearest chair to the table right by me and pat the seat. Kelly sits.

'I'm really sorry about this. I don't know why he didn't tell you. Or me. I'm simply interested in the history of the Black Gate; I'm not after your fella. I've already got one, and that's enough. You'd need to be a bloody masochist to want two.'

I'm better at improvisation than he is, but I don't know if Kelly's buying it. She smiles her pleasantest don't-fuck-with-me smile and seems to decide to play along.

'Well, I feel a bit stupid now. I'm sorry, too.'

'Don't worry. I know what it's like. Relationships are mental.'

She shoots a look at Iain, who's still at the bar, with a rattled expression on his face.

'Since I told him I'd decided to retrain as a primary-school teacher he's been regressing. He thinks he's a rock star, but his band is going nowhere.'

'Yeah, well, musicians – they need their music, don't they? Whether they're good or not.'

'Fair enough, but he's not good, and he needs to have a proper job to support himself.'

I'm glad she's training to be a teacher. I'd rather she was inflicted on young children than on me. She's far too straight to be creative and is the worst Wardrobe woman in the universe.

Iain comes back to the table with the drink. I adopt a teasing tone that belies the fact I'd like to kick him uber-hard in the knee.

'Well, Iain, I had no idea I was your teenage fantasy.'

'That's why I didn't say anything, Kelly – honest. I thought you'd jump to the wrong conclusion.'

'Is that why you never tell me anything at all then, is it?'

Oh dear. I don't want to be here for this.

'I do tell you stuff. I just don't want to have to check in every five minutes.'

'You used to like checking in every five minutes.'

Oh, man. This is all I need. I try to intercede.

'So, how long have you two known each other?'

Kelly smiles bitterly at me.

'Ten years. We met in sixth form.'

'Wow.'

Iain looks at his pint.

'Yeah, wow.'

She glares at him.

'What's that supposed to mean?'

'You know what, guys, maybe I should leave you to it.'

Kelly shakes her head.

'Iain's going to explain what that "Yeah, wow" actually meant, in front of his new friend.'

I wish she would stop sniping at me. I don't fucking care about any of this, if I'm honest. He caused it all. And she's a bloody freak.

Iain sighs and takes a deep breath. He's probably going to say something he'll regret.

'It means ten years is a long time, and things change.'

He looks desperately at me, like I'm some sort of mediator. I don't know why he's dragging me into it like I'm his next bird. I'm not. He pushes on, digging his own grave.

'Kelly works in TV, which is creative. Like I'm a musician and creative. But now she's jacking it in, and she's going to teach kids and be a normal person with a normal job, and we won't get each other at all any more. She's already said she wants me to give up the music, to concentrate on a "proper" job – i.e. the sodding library – and move in together and start a family. But I'm not sure how that will happen when she doesn't like sex.'

'*Iain!*'

Oof! He shouldn't have mentioned their sex life. Her lips have gone pale and tight with rage.

'Plus, I don't even like kids. I recently decided I don't

want them. But I didn't know how to say it. So now I am.
I don't want kids, Kelly. Not now, not soon. I won't even
consider it till I'm forty, and probably not even then. They
get on my tits.'

Oh, boy. I need to escape. He should never have done
this with an audience.

Kelly jumps up out of her seat.

'You absolute liar. You told me you wanted to get married and have kids! Are you showing off in front of Tanz?'

'I said that when I was seventeen, so you'd finally let
me get in your knickers. That was years ago. I bought the
ring because you wouldn't shut up about it. I've not even
been able to broach the subject recently, seeing as you've
been so focused on school catchment areas and wedding
magazines.'

Right then and there is when the lime-and-soda goes in
his face.

Iain falls back in his seat and makes that gasping noise a
child makes after jumping in a too-cold swimming pool.

'I'm so glad that we've not moved in together yet and
you've still got your pathetic little flat, Iain, because I don't
have to spend the rest of tonight packing up your stuff. Sod
you! I don't want you in my life any more, if that's the way
you're going to be. Bye, Tanz, you can have him.'

Why the hell would I want this soaked, stricken little
weakling, currently mopping limey soda out of his hair and
eyes with a napkin? He jumps up as she leaves, then sits
down again.

'Aren't you going to catch her up?'

'No.'

'Why not?'

'We don't like each other any more.'

'Right.'

The barman is staring at us, as are a bunch of men in suits sitting around a table next to the quayside windows. I think of an excuse, fast.

'Look, I need to go upstairs and call my cat-sitter and stuff, then I'm meeting my best mate. I hope you get things sorted with your girlfriend . . .'

'But she's not my girlfriend any more. I'm single. I could come up to your room for a bit if you like? In fact please, please can I come up? I feel so upset.'

Oh gosh – begging. The sexiest thing a man can do.

'Sorry, I really can't help, I'm so busy. It's horrid you're upset, but at least everything is out in the open now.'

'I know, but . . .'

He makes puppy-dog eyes. It's almost comical, but mostly pathetic.

'Good night, Iain.'

This is why I *hate* relationships. Look what they do to people.

'Yes, okay. Good night.'

Boy, he does a cracking line in sad and dejected. I can't be arsed with it. I bolt for the lifts.

If I go outside later and Iain's still waiting there like some sad fucking whelp, I will call the police. That's a fact.

When I reach my room a great weariness overtakes me and I lie down on my back for five minutes, to relax my mind.

God, that was excruciating. And how am I going to face

Kelly at work? Still, one good thing has come out of it – I will not be copping off with anyone else simply because I'm feeling lonely. It only makes things worse.

As my eyelids begin to droop, I whisper out loud to Frank, 'Next time I'll listen to your advice.'

'I'll believe that when I see it.'

When I open my eyes again, to my surprise it's seven hours later, I'm still in my clothes and there have been no dreams. The birds are singing the dawn chorus and it's lovely. After a visit to the loo and lulled by the birdsong, my lids begin to droop once more. But just before I fall back into the peaceful darkness, I see George, the little urchin boy, with fat tears rolling down his mucky cheeks. And in that instant I know for sure that the past won't stop prodding me until I help free that poor soul who's chosen to haunt me.

My little mam's going to have a fit when she finds out I'm messing with ghosts again.

ANGELS COME IN
FUNNY PACKAGES

Another day, another old lady's residence. This time I'm back in the Crystal Grotto de Gladys, with a china cake stand of French fancies perched on the table in front of me and a cup of instant coffee in my hand. Somehow I don't mind instant coffee at Gladys's house. Along with the 1970s buffet selection and Gladys's Nana Mouskouri style, it all seems to fit together.

She is drinking what looks like sludge, but is actually herbal Chinese tea that helps with her bowel movements. At this very second she is looking at me in a very concerned way through her jam-jar specs over the rim of her dainty cup as she blows on the liquid.

'You've got a lot on your plate right now.'

'I'm okay.'

'No, you're not. Your energy's buggered. There's a lot of responsibility on you, with very little peace. It's too much.'

She takes a cautious slurp.

'No, really, I don't mind helping people out and I don't mind the ghost stuff – it's interesting. But I'm not sure how to help Caroline. I just want her to have a nice time. It's playing on my mind. Everyone deserves some happiness, don't they?'

'Tanz, we get what we ask for. And we get back what we give. You must know that.'

'She needs to learn to be nicer.'

'It's not your job to help her be nice.'

'No, it's not. But I've seen a glimmer of a good side. I know she can do it.'

Gladys takes another glug of sludge.

'It's up to her. But you mustn't take it personally. You mustn't take anything personally. You've done your best. Here, have a Viennese whirl, they're blinkin' marvellous.'

And they are – they taste of my childhood. I have a nibble; I promise myself I won't finish it, I'll just gnaw a teensy bit off.

'Anyway, lass, what's happening with that evil sod from the Black Gate? Not bothering you any more, is he?'

'Erm, actually I've had quite a few nightmares. They're about a man with a scar on his neck coming to murder me, and the little boy George crying for help.'

'Oh dear.'

'I know. I got the nasty spook out of Milo's house, but at a cost. He was making it really difficult for me to sleep, but then I've had one or two dreamless nights recently, so it's not all of the time. I haven't been to the Black Gate for a while, so I don't know what his problem is.'

'Sounds like he's fixed on you. You're a threat. I wonder why? You probably know how to get rid of him for good and he doesn't want to go. Typical man – when they're scared they get aggressive.'

'That's the thing. I haven't a clue how to get rid of him, but if I'm ever going to sleep properly again, I think I'm going to have to. Plus, the little boy: he's so sad and scared. I'm obviously missing something here. Do you think he might be the bad one's son?'

'I'm not sure. But my gut feeling is no. What do you reckon you're going to do? And don't say nothing, as you're a stubborn sod and no mistake. I know you'll have some plan cooked up already.'

'I'm going to the Black Gate late at night, when all the drinkers and clubbers have gone home. Probably midweek, when the town's much emptier. I'm going to talk to the man on his own territory.'

Gladys picks up a Wagon Wheel, pulls off the wrapper and bites off half.

'He'll not make things easy for you, mind, pet.'

'I'm sure he won't.'

'Are you going on your own?'

'I'll have to. I can't ask Milo and risk him getting an unwelcome guest again.'

'Why don't I come with you?'

'Don't be daft – it'll be really late.'

'So? I don't need much sleep anyway, and I've got my little car. I can drive to you, then listen to Gene Pitney on the way home.'

She has an orange three-wheeler. It's hilarious. And she

plays tapes in it, she told me. She only brings it out for special occasions apparently, so I'm honoured. I'll put money on Gladys never driving faster than 15 mph.

'I don't want to inconvenience you.'

Her eyes glint.

'You're not. It'll be an adventure. When should we do it?'

Sooner rather than later, I reckon. I'm scared, even talking about it.

'How about tomorrow night?'

'Deal. Give me a ring in the afternoon and we'll finalize everything.'

'Okay.'

I can't help feeling relieved. I seem to be doing a lot of stuff on my own at the minute and none of it is that pleasant.

'Right. Now tell me about this ginger lad. He sounds like a right milksop.'

I settle back in my seat. Gladys is such a tonic. I only hope she won't regret getting involved with me. I seem to attract only the most extreme situations these days, and she's like my angel in jam-jar specs. I don't want to scare her. I look down at my plate and I've finished the Viennese whirl. I didn't even notice.

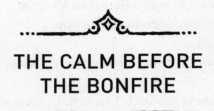

THE CALM BEFORE
THE BONFIRE

The difference in Milo is so fantastic. He's made us an immense pan of pesto pasta and has broken out the red wine. He's also beaming because he's written half of a new play and, *best of all*, he's had an email from the BBC and they want a meeting with him in a fortnight. They like his work and they want to meet for a 'chat'.

'I don't know how you did it, Tanz, but you cleared the bad stuff! You're a doll.'

'You are. It's great to see you productive again. Come here, let me give you a little top-up before we eat.'

He approaches with his goldfish bowl of Merlot and I guide him onto the kitchen seat in front of me. He sits obediently while I lay my palms on him.

'I still can't believe how hot they get.'

'It's funny, isn't it? I'm still not used to it myself. I thought I'd give you another dose, just to make sure you keep feeling better.'

'Are you even supposed to be doing this? Didn't you

say you were meant to do it only on yourself the first week?'

'I have been, every night. It's okay, I think I'd get a bad feeling if I wasn't supposed to help you.'

'And you said you weren't a witch. I always knew, didn't I?'

'Yup. Oh, hold on. Have you got a sore knee?'

'*Yes!* I banged it last night and it's been aching today. How did you know?'

'I'm not sure. It suddenly came to me that it wasn't right.'

'Wow! You see, you're doing readings while you heal. That's bloody brilliant. That's a good USP, actually. You should have that put on business cards. "Heat, Healing and Hot Tips from Beyond".'

'Stop it.'

'Really, Tanz. If you hate acting so much, why not give in to fate and make a living from readings and healings and ghost-busts. You're brilliant at it.'

'I can't. I'm still embarrassed enough telling people I do these things, so how could I possibly make a business out of it? Plus, I'd feel weird taking money from people.'

'Are you kidding? People pay over a hundred quid an hour for therapy. If you charge a quid a minute, you'll still be cheaper than that. And you're good at it. It's not like you're a fraud.'

'Hmm. Anyway, I don't hate acting – I hate shit acting jobs. There is a difference.'

'Yeah, but they all seem to be shit acting jobs, unless you're Judi Dench or twenty years old. When my plays make it big, you can be in them, and be a healer the rest of the time. Good plan?'

He's possibly right. But I truly can't imagine ever having the brass balls to go around telling people I'm some kind of Geordie guru-woman, healing the sick and leading the non-rested dead to the light. It's just too cringeworthy for words. I give his neck a tiny rub to signal we're done and Milo stands and begins to fill bowls with steaming tagliatelle.

'Thanks, Tanz. I feel all snuggly and warm. How about you? How was work today?'

He pushes my plate in front of me.

'Work was okay. Vicky's boyfriend, Con, came in to thank me because he wasn't in his house when it blew up. It was suitably mortifying, but he seems canny and he really loves Vicky, which is good to see. As soon as he left, she asked me if they were fated to be together; and you see, this is the thing: if you sell yourself as a reader or what-ever, people start using you as their life barometer for everything. You're never truly off-duty and it's a bloody big responsibility. I mean, how am I supposed to know these things? I don't know enough about their relationship to tell Vicky they'll be together forever. What does that mean anyway?'

'Go with your gut. Or just say, "He seems really nice." You don't have to give her all the answers. Especially if she's not paying you.'

'I suppose.'

'And how's Caroline?'

I filled him in on the phone last night. I know he won't tell anyone.

'She's out of hospital and back at her apartment. And *get this*: her driver, Dave, has agreed to come back and work for her again. Caroline rang him and apologized last night and he returned today. She's certainly perked up a bit. I only hope he keeps a close eye on what she's up to.'

'Look at that – she does a Marilyn Monroe, and now she's your best pal.'

'Stop it!'

I fork the pasta into my face, painfully aware that my eating habits have been appalling recently. Biscuits when I'd usually have apples, stodgy pasta when I'd usually eat fish, hummus and salad; I know it won't be long before everything I own is too tight for me. But I can't seem to help myself.

'You can't say "does a Marilyn"! Caroline nearly died.'

'I know. But she didn't die, and she did pick a star's way out, didn't she?'

'I suppose so.'

Milo stops talking to chew a forkful of pasta and then washes it down with his Merlot, before exclaiming, 'Oh my God, I almost forgot: what about that *Kelly*? What was she like today? Any itching powder in your vest?'

'No-o-o! Actually she kept out of my way. Then she eventually apologized and said she didn't mean to play out her relationship problems in front of a cast member. But she looked even colder in the eye than usual, and her face was blotchy. I'm amazed to say it, but I think she actually loves that limp fool. I reckon they'll end up back together.'

'Jesus, Tanz. Imagine being trapped in that mess. Be glad you only—'

'*No.* Don't say it. I don't want to be reminded of having relations with that loser.'

'Don't be so hard on yourself. You were rebounding.'

'No, I wasn't.'

He cocks his eye at me.

'Stop lying.'

'That was *ages* ago. He's been gone months and months.'

'Are you missing him? Have you been upset and not saying?'

'No.'

He shakes his head at me.

'I don't believe you. I know you liked Pat. And I know you didn't get back to him because he was having a whale of a time and you were depressed.'

Even hearing Pat's name makes me sad. He was so honest and lovely. Not a fibbing little chancer like Iain.

'Milo, I think I need to make some proper decisions about my life. Pat didn't create the hole, he just filled it for a while. I bet if he'd stuck around I'd have gone off him sharpish.'

'Hmm.'

He eats a forkful with a flourish and follows it with another mouthful of wine.

'If you say so.'

KITTEN

The kitten is tiny, black and white and very thin. I'm in the back lane of a slum. I've been reading about slum housing in the olden days, so it's not a surprise that I'm dreaming about it. It smells of rotting food and urine, and the ground is slimed with dirt.

The baby cat lays its head in my palm and I see it has only one eye. The left eye is sealed up, the socket seemingly empty. The right eye is the most perfect bright green. It's a scrubby little thing, scruffier than any stray I've ever seen before, but so alive, so loving. I caress the tiny head and it mewls its pleasure. Then, through discarded rubbish and splintered pieces of wood, I follow the little mite as it searches for scraps of food and careless mice. After it's found a few bits and pieces to chew on, I scoop the kitten up for a cuddle, glorying in the warmth of its skinny body as it snuggles into my neck and purrs loudly.

Out of nowhere a shadow appears. Suddenly apprehensive, I turn my back to the shadow and try to make off. But I'm not quick enough, and suddenly booze, sweat and terror fill my nostrils as a pair of coarse hands reach over me and wrestle my friend out of my hands. My heart snaps with a tiny cracking noise, like my kitten's neck as the hands twist the head one way and the body another. The carcass is thrown away carelessly.

I scream with horror until a fist makes me shut up. Then I scream inside instead.

ANGEL OF THE NORTH

I arrive at work like a bloody zombie. Always fine with the Make-up department, as it then has less to do. But not so great when you actually have lines to say. Well, I say 'lines', but as I may have mentioned several times before, even in the 'good' episode, my character is an illiterate, ignorant commoner who's only there to show how backwards we are 'oop North'.

Last night's dream has made me rather scared about tonight's visit to the Black Gate. Possibly one of the worst things you can show me is a cat being murdered. (The 'bad one' has gone from a description to a name; in my head he is now the Bad One.) Has the Bad One picked up on the fact that I love cats and exploited it? Does that mean he can pick up on other stuff and use it against me? That really scares me. What's even weirder is that Claire, our second-in-command make-up girl, has a glass eye. I have no idea if that's got any relevance to me dreaming about a one-eyed kitten. I mean, is it just a coincidence or is that nasty spook stringing bits of my life together and throwing it back at me in vicious nightmares?

As soon as I get to set, Brian the director approaches me, now with merely a small scab on his mouth, and asks if I'm okay. I think at first he's asking because I look so knackered, but he's staring at me meaningfully, and it occurs to me that Caroline being temporarily kidnapped from the hospice may have leaked out. I say I'm fine, but it's difficult to know what I should say and what I should keep to myself. God knows why all this secrecy is going on. Surely everyone on-set knows what's happened?

As I'm sitting in a wobbly canvas chair, ready to do my bit, Katherine Banner arrives, looking like the movie star she'll probably be soon, pulls up another canvas death-trap and sits by me.

'I heard what happened.'

'What's that?'

'You going to see Caroline.'

'Who did you hear that from?'

'Bloody hell. Vicky's lovely, but she's not exactly Mrs Discretion. Mind you, even she didn't know you took Caroline out for a drive. Adrian told me that. *I think he might have a thing for me.*'

The last bit is mouthed in a stage whisper. I think just about every man Katherine Banner ever meets probably *has a thing for her.*

'So I'm talk of the set, am I? I simply thought Caroline might need some fresh air. It was stifling in there.'

'I think it was really lovely of you. I mean, what with

her being a total cow and everything, it can't have been fun.'

'It was all right. We had a chat.'

'Why did she do it?'

Katherine's eyes are a bit too bright with anticipation. Vicky asked me a similar question this morning, and I know it's hard not to be curious when someone does something as major as trying to commit suicide, but I really don't think it's my place to be telling people Caroline's business at such a difficult time.

'She didn't say. You know, she's a private woman. She didn't talk that much – it was mostly me waffling on. She simply needed to get away from the nurses and into the normal world for a minute.'

'Did you get in trouble?'

'No, just a telling-off from the head matron-type woman. What could they say? She wasn't a prisoner.'

Katherine seems a bit disappointed with the information I've provided. She has one more poke.

'So, do you think they'll sack her or what?'

I'm not sure why she thinks I'd be privy to that kind of information.

'Well, there's only a week or so left, and the new woman arrives in the script soon, so they can easily eject Caroline by the next series if they really want to. Who knows . . .'

I'm surprised by how protective I feel about Caroline. It's simply because I've seen her so vulnerable. I have to keep reminding myself that she's been horrible to everyone on this set for ages.

Just then Vole comes over, all goo-goo-eyed over Katherine.

'Hey, girls. Change of plan. Can we have Katherine first for a little set-up shot, then we'll call you in about twenty minutes, Tanz?'

As he speaks, his attention is caught by something behind me. I swing my head round and there, sitting at the edge of the field, is Caroline's car. Pretty sharpish, Dave emerges from the driver's side and motions in my direction.

'Tanz!'

I wave at him.

'Hiya, Dave.'

Katherine, Vole, the crew and Brian all stop what they're doing, before pretending to busy themselves again, though I can see them shooting sly glances my way while I tiptoe in my crap sandals over the grass to the posh Audi. Dave comes to the nearest back passenger door and opens it for me to get in. As I clamber onto the leather seat, I smile at Caroline, who is wrapped in a thick gold-and-blue pashmina. Her hair is combed but not lacquered into submission, which is a much better look, and she's only wearing a bare minimum of make-up. She looks tired but certainly not as deathly, or as desperate, as the other day.

'Caroline!'

I can't help it. I wrap her tiny frame in my meaty Geordie arm and kiss her on her bony face. She doesn't hit me or push me off, which is better than I expected. But she tenses up.

'Are you trying to finish me off, Tania?'

'Unless you want me to start calling you Nanna in public, you'd better get used to calling me Tanz.'

'Nanna?'

'Yes. Only my nanna calls me Tania. Or do you prefer Grandma?'

'No, I bloody don't. Just try it.'

Her voice is still not up to par, but it has a little of its cut-glass haughtiness back.

'So, have you got a scene today?'

'Oh no. Two more days of rest, they said. Probably furiously writing me out of the next series as we speak.'

'Stop it!' Dave spins his tanned podgy head round and shakes it at Caroline. 'I told her: stop with the negative. She's going to behave from now on, and she's not going to get sacked.' He gives a sly smile and winks. 'Wouldn't look good in the press, would it? Sacking someone because they got depressed and tried to top themselves.'

She taps his shoulder, not without affection.

'Dave! We're certainly not going to start threatening people . . .'

He smiles at her.

'Yet.'

I only realize then how much Caroline seems to adore Dave. His resignation must have been the last straw for her. I smile at him.

'Nice to have you back, Dave. The new one was a bit ratty-looking for my liking.'

He chortles.

'Tanz, I went home and realized I could listen to the wife nagging night and day, plus my four daughters asking for money around the clock, or I could give this battle-axe another chance. Blimey, talk about a rock and a hard place.'

Caroline actually titters. I can't believe it.

'So why have I been invited into your deluxe car, Caroline? Not that it's not lovely to see you looking better.'

She reaches behind her, then hands me a little box. She looks like an awkward child as she does so.

'I wanted to say thank you. You arrived in my room at a very . . .' – her eyes are welling up, but she manages to keep control and breathes deeply – 'a very fortuitous moment. And I enjoyed Tynemouth very much.'

Dave laughs again.

'Can you believe she made me take her there last night, just to get some bloody chips and watch the sea?'

I cast a shocked eye at Caroline. 'Did you?'

She nods.

'I think the air is good for me.'

I can't help smiling at her.

'Of course it is!' I actually couldn't be prouder. I'm holding the box, not sure what to do. 'Should I open it?'

'When we're gone. I'm sure they'll need you on-set soon.'

'Yes, they probably will. Should we maybe have lunch or dinner soon? I do healings, you know. I could put my hot little hands on your back.'

She titters.

'Yes, I heard you had a "gift". How about Friday, after

work? We could all go to that lovely little fish restaurant we saw last night, Dave? On me? I might even buy a bottle of champagne for us.'

Dave narrows his eyes at her.

'It'll be fizzy apple juice for you, for the time being. Alcohol's a bloody depressant, innit? Can't have that.'

I like how caring he's being. It's so sweet.

'Sounds fabulous to me. Look, you didn't have to, but thank you so much for the prezzie. And I'm really glad to see you out and about. Please call me on Friday to sort out what time and all that. You've got my number, haven't you?'

She nods.

'I'll look forward to it.'

She gives me a stilted little hug and I pat Dave on the back of his shoulder. As I'm getting out of the car, Caroline pipes up again. 'Oh, I forgot to tell you: your plant with the shiny ribbon is thriving!'

'That's good to know.'

As I wave them off, then make my way back to the canvas chair, the crew pretend not to be interested. Brian nods to me and Katherine looks over curiously, but the camera is about to roll, so she has to stay put. I'm glad the plant is thriving. It's like a sign.

Back at my canvas seat, I sit the little red velvet box on my palm, then open it. Nestling in black silk is a white-gold chain with the most exquisite angel charm on it. As I examine it, I notice there's a stone set where the angel's heart would be. I can't be positive, but I think that beautiful, glistening tiny thing may be a diamond. I've never owned a diamond before.

I am speechless.

And that doesn't happen very often.

THE KICK-OFF

There's an hour to kill before I meet Gladys at the Black Gate and I decide to visit the Literary and Philosophical Society, more locally known as the Lit & Phil, not five minutes' walk from the Black Gate and very close to Newcastle Central Station. It's a library with high, vaulted glass ceilings and a downstairs bit that contains books up to three hundred years old. The first time I entered it I nearly had a cow – it's so grand and beautiful.

After hearing out-of-place noises on the quayside and 'feeling' things I don't understand, as well as dreaming things that seem to come out of a Charles Dickens novel, I've decided to have a perusal of some proper Newcastle history books. Considering I'm from the North-East, my knowledge is woefully lacking and most of my facts came from my grandparents over the years.

What I find is quite a revelation. For one thing, I was given to believe that the only fish quay was the one still in existence in North Shields, but – just as Frank told me – the books say that in the 1800s and early 1900s there was a fish market in a building between the Tyne and Swing Bridges, which is now a nightclub. There the fishwives were renowned for their sharp voices, cruel tongues and sudden gang violence towards anyone threatening one of their own (in many cases, abusive and drunken husbands). I recall the shrieks and cries early in the morning as I shame-walked my humiliated self out of fangy Iain's flat.

I also read of barrel-makers and sailors, and factories and general industry on the quayside, which would explain the shouts and cries, and bashes and bangs, I've caught several times with my 'extra ear', especially on the ghost walk that night. I read of the streams that used to flow down the Chares into the Tyne, and the people boozing and scraping a living in cholera-infested tenements, before and after the great fire; of the rich merchants, the beautiful old buildings that still rub shoulders with the newer ones, the almshouses where the homeless used to shelter, the seven bridges built with such precision and care; of the bustle and the life of people who died many, many years before I was even a twinkle in my dad's eye. Most telling of all, I read about the rubbish tip that the children used to play on and plunder, just beyond the bottom of Broad Chare, now faced by the law court, which is backed by the Jurys Inn. And now I know why I could smell rubbish and decay. And now I'm also truly sure that Newcastle itself has been speaking to me.

The Newcastle of the past has been desperate to disclose a secret, but has not managed, as yet, to explain itself very well.

STRONGER AS A TEAM

I've donned comfy jeans, trainers, a hoodie and a small rucksack for tonight. I don't know how long I'm going to be there; it may only be minutes, but I have a Diet Coke and some snacks, just in case.

I'm blindly following my gut on this one, as I don't even know what I'm planning to do when I get there. For now, I'll simply arrive and wait. The way my stomach feels right now, something is definitely afoot and I need to keep my nerve.

As I approach the trip-trap bridge I get that rush of saliva that occurs when you're going to be sick. It catches me off-guard, but I manage to stop myself from gagging by halting and bending at the waist for a moment.

'Are you all right, love?'

Through the darkness, over the bridge, I can see a squat shape standing by the arch where little George was throwing stones. Boy, am I glad to see her.

'Gladys! I'm okay, just suddenly felt sick.'

'Yes, it'll be that bugger messing with you. I can feel him all round this place.'

'Can you?'

I cross the bridge, reach her and give her a hug. She smells of peppermints. In fact she proffers a paper bag.

'Have one of these – it'll settle your stomach.'

I've not had an old-fashioned peppermint since I was about ten, so I take one, as much out of curiosity as anything else.

'Thank you.'

'I can definitely feel someone doesn't want us here, can't you?'

I stand as still as possible and I suck my mint. Through the nerves and the strangeness of standing around in Newcastle, late at night without a drink in my hand or belly, I can feel a mocking presence. Mocking and malevolent.

I don't like it.

Not only that, but if this thing – this ghost – was powerful enough to follow Milo home, influence his behaviour and then mess with my sleep, how is a rookie like me supposed to get rid of him? I know Gladys is here, but she's a healer. And Sheila's off-radar, so I can't even ask her. I reach inside my hoodie and stroke my diamond angel with my thumb.

Perhaps this is a stupid idea.

Just then, Gladys links her arm in mine.

'Come on then, let's get underneath this bridge, where people can't see us. I think he's waiting for us to make our move.'

'What are we going to do, Gladys?'

'We're going to do whatever we feel like when the time comes. Didn't your friend Sheila teach you that?'

'She did actually.'

'Good.'

Slowly, so as not to get Gladys's asthma going, we walk back across the bridge and, in the dark, shuffle down the grassy bank to the dark alcove beneath the trip-trap bridge. As we carefully descend, I have this feeling that the air I'm moving through has thickened, like treacle. My feet drag and my chest feels a force against it, a mounting pressure, like I've walked into a wall and I'm pushing against it to move it backwards.

When Gladys speaks next, it's a whisper. We both begin to whisper in fact.

'You know what, love? Some spirits are cheeky buggers, some of them are trying to be scary, and others think women are easy to frighten . . .'

My mind flashes back to the ghost in the cottage that I cleared with Sheila. He seemed to think women were merely property, to be used and abused. In the end, that was his downfall.

'But in this case – and I don't say it lightly – he is a whole other level of nasty. This one was a psychopath in life, and he still is now. There's a coldness at the centre of him. If you believe evil exists, he's pretty much it.'

'Jesus, Gladys!'

'It's good to remember these things, love. Bad 'uns don't always tell the truth, and this one's a bad 'un.'

I think of Dan the murderer. He had a coldness at the centre of him. But weirdly, even after what he did, I'm still not sure he was totally evil. He was mentally ill, but . . . I don't know. His wife loved him so much, and she was a good person. Dan must have had good in him. Funny how I don't think of his second victim much: that awful Carmen. Gutted like a rabbit upstairs and all I really thought was, *She met the end she deserved.* This is probably why I'll go to hell. You can't think that about another human being, can you? *Deserved to be filleted.*

The pressure on my chest is pretty hardcore now. It's like it's me who's got asthma. Gladys is shaking her head.

'Oh, you don't want us here, do you?'

It's very dark down here. We're just around the corner from the place I heard the pub noise and 'felt' all the activity last time. It's hard to see in the gloom, but a bit of light from the sky and street lamps pricks the darkness. We both slow to a stop at exactly the same time. Gladys smiles reassuringly. I suddenly think of something.

'Gladys, we've not done anything to keep ourselves safe.'

'Oh, of course, love. Here we go . . .'

Gladys recites a very short, very effective prayer, offered to our guides and protectors, asking them to guard and look after us and push away negativity. I imagine the brightest silver light around me, keeping out the 'bad'. That's when I hear the serpent's voice.

'Think that'll save you, do you?'

It's like he's whispering right by my ear. He sounds amused. I look to Gladys, but she's staring around us, oblivious.

'I'm not scared of you.'

'*You will be.*'

He sounds plain mean. I wonder why he's so determined to scare me.

'Why are you trying to make me go away? You seem like the scared one.'

There's a small crash. Something fell from a height and hit the ground to our right. I almost jump out of my trainers. Luckily we're sheltered by the bridge above us, so nothing should fall directly onto us. Unless the whole bridge does.

'*I told you. I'm going to smash your head in. Then it'll just be me and you, you interfering bitch.*'

'Gladys, he said something nasty, then that thing fell. Could he have done that?'

'Well, that little boy threw stones, didn't he? Some of them are better at the physical stuff than others. What's he saying to you?'

'Trying to frighten me.'

She looks around again, then speaks out loud.

'I know you're here, you nasty bugger. And I know you did something bad. Very bad. And I tell you what: you're gonna pay for it, whether you like it or not.'

There's another small crash in the gloom, this time to our left. Like he's dropping pebbles from the roof.

'We're going to have a look now, you devil. We're going to stand here and look at what you did.'

'*I'll wring your necks.*'

Gladys jumps at the same time as me. She must have heard that one, too.

'Come here, Tanz, I'm gonna show you somethin'.' She

takes my hands in hers. 'I want you to breathe. Very slowly, breathe. Whatever happens, and whatever you see or hear, breathe . . . and keep a hold of my hands, right? You and me should be able to find out what's going on here if we just close our eyes and relax.'

I hold her fingers, close my eyes and breathe, slow and long, through my nose. I don't really want to close my eyes because I'm scared, but when I do, there's a warmth that surrounds me and I remember that linking in like this provides extra protection. As we stand holding hands, Gladys begins to talk, quietly and gently.

'Tanz, where we're standing there's a lot of activity. I want you to visualize this place as it was. Reach out your energy and touch what it was when little George and this man were living and breathing on this earth.'

I think of the little boy in my dreams, his scared face and his fear. I reach out and send love and try to 'see' anything that might help. Suddenly a picture comes to me.

Gladys tightens her fingers over mine.

'There, can you see it, pet?'

'Yes!'

I can see, and I can smell and I can feel. Old Newcastle has been coming to me – now I'm going to it.

I'm in a room. Barely any furniture, only an open fire and a woman. Not very old. The woman I saw in the window, I 'feel', with the sad, blank face. She's on the bed. It's night and she's lying on her back. When I look closer, her face is covered in blood and she's bruised and battered. I breathe as best I can, trying not to panic, as I see her being dragged by a man whose face I can't see, over to the fire.

He puts her head and shoulders into the open flames and begins to stoke the fire up with a poker. I can't see what else he's putting on there, but the fire builds and her clothes and skin begin to scorch, and I have to look away. When I look back, he's moving burning coals onto the floor around her, starting a fire on the floor of the room. I get a smell in my nostrils, a nasty, cloying, sickly, burning smell as I watch the smoke rise. I've smelled this before, in my nightmares. Only now I know what it is.

Just when I think it can't get any worse, I see a movement from beneath the bed. A little foot, as someone tries to push himself further underneath, away from the horror unfolding before him. Helpless to do anything but watch, I see the man spot the foot and go over to the bed. He begins to reach under it. The child beneath is too traumatized to utter a sound. Soon he's dragged from underneath – not more than six years old and terrified.

George.

The man is laughing. I can feel his enjoyment. I can also feel how drunk he is. He doesn't like this child, and now he can do what he wants with him. The child is struggling and crying hard, having seen his mother on the fire. I can't believe the poor thing has to witness something so awful.

'Gladys?'

I'm whispering and so is she.

'I know, pet. It's hard to watch.'

I hold back the tears as the boy is dangled over his mother's body to get a better look at her burning head and shoulders. Then both of us jump again, as we feel his head connect with a hard surface. The man literally takes him by the feet and cracks him as hard as he can against the brick fireplace. He does it again to make sure, then folds him into a rough sack.

That poor lad.

Before he leaves the room, sack over his shoulder, the man stops and turns, like he knows I'm watching and wants to mess with me. He smiles wide, displaying his yellow teeth and dead eyes. I see his dry, drink-ruined skin, the filthy knotted scarf and the livid scar. I open my eyes in a panic. I try to let go of Gladys's hands, but she's not having it.

'Don't let go. We're stronger as a team.'

I like her very much for that. It makes me feel safer.

'You're not safe, you bitch.'

The snake's voice is back, but surprisingly it's Gladys who replies, so she must have heard it, too.

'We're safe all right, you devil. I know why you're still here. I've worked it out and you're not doing it any more. It's your turn to feel scared.'

There's a movement in the air. I feel his rage, but underneath it I feel something else. Psychopath or not, he has the ability to be worried. And she's rattled him.

'He's mine, you old whore . . .'

Another rock falls, closer this time. I don't know if it's little bits of falling masonry or what. I refuse to get scared, though. If Gladys isn't scared, then I won't be scared. That's always the best policy with bullies. And like the man in the cottage who was causing mayhem, this one is a bully, just on a more epic scale.

Gladys begins to hum. It's not a tune, only a few long notes. Then she whispers to me, urgently.

'Tanz. Picture little George, picture him in your mind. Not the little boy with the scary, burning eyes – that was this devil playing tricks on you. Picture the sad little boy with the beautiful face. George isn't bad at all, are you, son? You're a good boy . . .'

I think of the horrendous end to his pitiful life and try to wrap him in warm light. And then there he is in my mind's eye, his eyes wide with all of the horror he's witnessed. I whisper out loud to him, 'George . . . George, it's me, Tanz. I dreamed about you, remember? We want to help you.'

He looks straight into my eyes. So much pain in such a young face. So much heartache. I wish I could touch him. I imagine stroking a finger down his cheek.

'What happened? Can you tell me? Where are you?'

'I'm a bad boy. I'm stupid. I get in the way. Nobody likes me. I'm bad.'

'You're not bad. Who says you're bad?'

There's a pause.

'Him.'

I feel a rush of energy by my right cheek, like someone is trying to intervene, but Gladys speaks up.

'Step back, you foul bugger. No one wants you here. You're the bad one.'

The energy decreases.

'He . . . he hurt me mam. She wouldn't wake up. I hid when he came back, but he found me. He . . .'

The boy begins to sob. He's so young. Why would anyone hurt such an innocent?

'What did he do with you, George, after he hurt you?'

'He put rocks in the sack. He put me in the river. Nobody knew. They thought I ran away.'

'Where've you been all this time, George?'

'In the room with me mam. But she's dead. So I can't talk to her. I'm all on me own. And it's burning hot in there. But when I look for me body I can't find it, either. It's in the river.'

'So it should be, you whining little cur!'

To my shock, I hear the Bad One's voice and see George's face struck a blow from the left. George screams and crumples.

'Oh my *God*, Gladys, he's still torturing him.'

Gladys's voice takes on an edge I've not heard before.

'I knew it. You're for it now, you bugger. You're off to hell, where you belong.'

Her hands are suddenly hot – almost excruciatingly so. I almost drag mine away, then feel them react in kind. The heat in my palms binds with the heat in hers. And now she's speaking again. This time with all the gentleness in the world.

'George, come here, son. Don't be scared. Get closer. I want to tell you a secret.'

I feel the pressure in my chest and against my throat, as he moves in closer to us.

'Your mam's not dead. He was tricking you. She's looking for you and she really misses you.'

George's voice is filled with mistrust. He must rarely have been shown any love.

'But I saw her. She was full of drink again, then he punched her and punched her until she stopped moving.'

'But she's not dead. She thinks you're such a good boy, and she loves you and misses you every second of every day.'

There's another pause.

'Does she?'

'Oh yes, she does. So much.'

To my surprise, Gladys's voice is thick with emotion. And George is reacting to the emotion and drawing ever closer as he begins to trust.

'She wants a hug, George. She wants a hug so badly, and she wants you to forget all about that horrible man. You don't have to see him any more. You can go with your mammy and never see him again. Look, she's standing over there.'

As she says it, I 'see'. In the darkness of my mind, a door opens and a lady stands there. The one from the window, I presume. But now she doesn't look vacant and drawn and half-dead from lethal, poisonous cheap alcohol. She looks younger and alert, and *alive*. She opens her arms.

'You see, George, she loves you really. She was simply unhappy before. She didn't mean anything by it. She always loved you, and she loves you now.'

'Mam!'

I see the little lad with the flat cap in his hand, running to the open door. I see his mam's arms opening wider and, out of nowhere, I see the dark shape of the Bad One, also

241

running but from the opposite direction. I feel a great tremor inside my head, as his bellow of rage reaches me from whatever bleak place he inhabits.

'NO-O-O.'

But just as it looks like he will intercept George, Gladys lets out a growl.

'You will not have him for another minute! Help me, guides – make him step off!'

And, like magic, as George jumps into his mother's arms – the tattered dress and lank hair not taking away from the joy in her face – a pit, ringed with red like the Bad One's eyes, opens up in front of the man and he falls into it with a scream of fury. As he does so, I feel a huge blow to my head and I fold up onto the ground, and everything goes black.

As I fade to nothing, I see that the door has closed between George, his mam and us and only a wisp of a trail of relieved joy remains.

As I'm disappearing down the quiet corridor of unconsciousness, I feel Frank hold my hand. Without him having to utter a word, he lets me know that soon after I wake up, a door will open for someone else – someone I know. And they will die.

Then the lights go out completely and I don't know anything else.

THE LIGHT

From the darkness, a light comes. It's like a distant star, then it gets closer and looks like the sun coming from behind a cloud; then it's almost blinding, so I close my eyes. A hand tickling my neck makes me open them again.

And here I am, sitting on the usual picnic blanket in Saltwell Park in Gateshead. I often dream of Saltwell Park, my childhood sanctuary, but this is different because I'm fully aware and quite positive this isn't a dream. The blanket is red tartan, the little sandwiches on the yellow plate look like egg-and-tomato, and the sun is warm. Lots of daisies are growing in the grass, just like I remember them when I was five or so.

When I look around me, I see that this is the park of my childhood, with none of the changes that have happened since – none of the new sculptures, and not a trace of the refurb on the fairy castle, which always mesmerized me when I was younger. *A fairy castle in Gateshead: who would have figured it?*

243

Frank is sitting beside me; it's his hand on my neck, and this time I don't cry when I see him. He's looking very handsome in a white linen shirt and washed-out jeans, and what I actually do is punch him on the arm.

'*Ow!*'

'Why don't you talk to me when I ask you to?'

He rubs his sleeve theatrically and shakes his head.

'*How nice. I come for a visit and this is what I get?*'

'And how come you didn't help me with the Bad One? You left me to it, you swine . . .'

'*You're learning, Tanz. You're doing really well. I didn't need to intervene. Plus, you had a helper; plus, I've been busy with other stuff.*'

'What kind of other stuff?'

'*None-of-your-business stuff . . . I thought you said you wanted a cuddle?*'

'That was then.'

'*Charming.*'

I jump on Frank and hug him, knocking a couple of sandwiches flying. After a while I stop and sit back down.

'Why am I at the park again?'

'*It's a good place for a chat.*'

'Fair enough.'

'*How are you?*'

I think. Sitting with Frank in the warm calm of Saltwell Park thirty years ago, it hits me how happy and peaceful I feel. Happier than I have done in ages.

'I'm good. I'm always good when I see you. It's only shit when I have to go back to real life.'

He leans in and kisses me on the cheek.

For a while we eat and reminisce about the time we went to the beach with a bunch of friends in the summer, and Frank chased us with a starfish and threw me into the sea, and I flooded my new watch and slapped him one. We're both belly-laughing by the end of it, and I glory in the feeling of ease that I have in this 'dream'. No troubles at all. And suddenly, as I sit in the park of my childhood and chat with my dead friend, and look at the daisies and let the sun shine on my face, I begin to well up with tears. Frank notices and puts his arm around me.

'What on earth's the matter with you?'

I bite down, attempting to swallow the lump that's forming in my throat. I have no idea where all this emotion is coming from. All at once it's pressing on me that if I were to leave the world behind now, with my parents still alive and relatively young, my career washed up, my friends all meeting people and settling down, no children to traumatize and no partner to break the heart of – well, it would be the perfect moment. Even Inka would have somewhere to live. Maybe if this could become 'my time' to die, then I could simply stay here and hang out with Frank and learn the stuff I'd love to learn from him, minus all the tribulations of real life.

I sniff the aftershave that he always used to wear, even when we were at school. It's such a comfort.

'Frank, I would give anything to stay right here with you. Would that be possible? My usual life is all nightmares, fears and aimlessness. I'm a weirdo, selfish actresstype who can't find a single direction to go in. I love you, and I love the peace of being here. Maybe I could be of use to you? Could I help you with stuff? Maybe I could help the people I love from this side instead? Over there I'm this sad, stupid, pointless idiot. From here, maybe I could help more.'

'You really think that?'

'I know it.'

Frank turns to me, face-on, placing his warm hands on either side of my face. Then he stares into my eyes and his palms pulsate with what I can only describe as pure love. So much so that I want to cry uncontrollably at the sheer overwhelming force of it.

'You don't really want to stay here, Tanz. You need to go back there. You help a lot of people. You just don't recognize your purpose yet.'

Over his shoulder I can see a glint of light, which isn't coming from the mellow sun above us. It's a glint that grows into a straight, vertical line of white light and then develops into a glowing figure. A person made of light, with a rainbow pulsating from her core. No body, nothing solid, merely light and love. I can actually feel the love, like I can feel it through Frank's palms. The joy that I feel as I look at this 'being' is also overwhelming, but in a different way. Such peace.

Frank sits by my side and puts his arm back around me.

'Tanz, meet Mona. She was married to Dan the creepy murderer who kidnapped you.'

My heart leaps in shock.

'Mona?'

The softest of voices, not from her mouth – just from 'her'.

'Hello, Tanz.'

'How come you're . . . Oh my God – you're so beautiful.'

Frank laughs.

'Well, she wasn't going to appear in her old form, was she, and scare the hell out of you? This is the real Mona. This is who she always was, and is.'

'I'm so pleased to meet you, Tanz. I wanted to say thank you, in person.'

'You don't have to thank me for anything, Mona.'

'Yes, I do. I was trapped – trapped by what happened. I couldn't let go of my earthly pain and fear. You and Sheila freed me.'

'That's wonderful. I'm so happy for you.'

Frank squeezes my shoulder.

'Mona is a spiritual helper and healer. It's a great job, but it makes you very, very over-sensitive when you're in human form. So when you get traumatized, like Mona was, you forget your true self and wind up trapped, until someone like you can sort it out.'

'I saw you at Sheila's,' I say to Mona.

'I take care of you both now. You're on my "special" list!'

'Wow, that's amazing. Is that why you helped me at Milo's, too?'

Mona glows brighter. That must be her version of a smile.

'Who were you helping when you were . . . erm, alive, Mona?'

Her laugh is like little bells. She actually *shimmers* when she laughs.

'*I tried to help everyone and everything when I was alive. Especially my horses. I liked everybody, and they liked me back. But especially I was there to help Dan.*'

'DAN?'

'*Yes, he needed as much help as possible.*'

'But he . . . he . . .'

'*Yes, unfortunately there's only so much help and love you can give anybody. Positivity was not enough.*'

Mona doesn't sound upset or sad. Just matter-of-fact. And her energy stays loving and kind.

'*Dan is still recovering from what he did.*'

'Recovering?'

'*Yes. He is in another place. A quiet place away from others, with helpers to guide him. Dan is still in shock at what he did. And he still has a connection with you. He tries to send you love, but first he needs to recuperate more from the life he lived. Dan reaching out to you might feel like he is trying to scare you, but he is not. He wants to make things right.*'

I am fascinated, amazed and a tad creeped-out. I thought Dan would be in hell, or wherever it is you go when you've been very, very bad. Without me saying this out loud, Frank whispers in my ear.

'*People make their own hell, Tanz.*'

And I *know* this is true. I meet people all of the time in their own temple of unhappiness. The ball of light that is Mona suddenly rises slightly in the air, so that I can fully see and feel her. 'Magnificent' is the word that springs to mind.

'*Tanz, every time you comfort someone with a healing or*

a reading, or even a word of kindness, you are completing your mission in life. You are needed there. Everyone who is there is needed, in their own way. You have now found your true path. So many people have already been helped by your insights and intuitions. These intuitions are given to you for a reason. The more you use them, the more they will grow. You will help many and comfort many, often without any thanks. But you must do it anyway. Then you can return. Then you can be like me.'

'Really?'

I look to Frank, who smiles and nods. Mona rises a little higher.

'It will be like the blink of an eye and you will be here again. So don't wish your time away.'

Frank nods again.

'Yeah, Tanz – it's mighty ungrateful.'

Mona's light glows blue for a moment.

'Please don't let fear become your torment. You are very protected. Nothing you're doing is without purpose; you just don't see the healing vibrations of your actions the way we do.'

When she finishes speaking, Frank points to my right. I turn my head. There's a little boy walking towards us. I've never seen him before. He's about four and has enormous amber eyes and a mop of curls. He's wearing a red T-shirt and white shorts with frogs on them. His smile is ridiculously cute, as he has the tiniest, whitest milk-teeth. Without a word he plops into my lap and wraps his arms around my neck. He's all wriggly and warm and I can't help holding him tight.

I look at Frank, who winks. He's gone all winky these days. As he does so, Mona seems to dissipate and grow brighter at the same time, filling more of the air around us with colours and sparkles. I can feel the darkness that has been circling me recently being washed away by her positive light.

Frank ruffles the boy's hair.

'*Tanz, meet Andrew. He seems to like you.*'

'Hello, Andrew.'

The boy looks straight up at me, his arms still wound around my neck.

'*Hello.*'

His voice is teensy and his accent, though not broad, is definitely northern. Which makes him even sweeter. Plus, he has a slight lisp.

'*Will you tell my mamma something?*'

'Erm, yes . . . if you tell me who your mamma is.'

'*Tell her that, when I see her, I'm going to cuddle her all day long, just like this.*'

He holds me tightly enough to seriously dislocate my neck.

'*All right? Just like that. Tell her she's my bestest.*'

'Of course I will.' I kiss the top of his boyish head. 'Who's his mam, Frank?'

Frank leans forward and kisses my cheek.

'*Like I need to tell you.*'

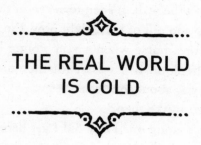

THE REAL WORLD
IS COLD

It's quite a rude awakening, as it goes. One minute I'm in Saltwell Park having a great time with my dead pal, an angel and a gorgeous little lad giving me neck-achingly tight cuddles, and the next someone is screaming blue murder and my eyes are springing open in a sterile white room. I'm on my own, but the room's not posh, like Caroline May's was. And some woman outside is shouting, 'I'm going in to see her. I don't care what you say – she's my sister. I'm allowed, ya bastards!'

Whoever it is sounds more than a little pickled. I hear a man's voice, and then a woman's urging her to leave. From the weird screeches coming out of her, I reckon she's being forcefully ejected. After a minute or two a door opens and her screeches get less loud, as she's presumably dragged away down a corridor.

I take a breath. Bleach smells, covering wee and cabbage. I shouldn't say this, but part of me truly didn't want to wake up. I lift my right hand tentatively, and put it to the throbbing side of my head. There's a lump like an ostrich

251

egg there. Plus, it's light outside. I must have slept here. I have no idea what time it is. I look round and spot a little plastic clock on the wall. It's ten to seven in the morning. I want to get up and out of here, right now. I'm just about to start yelling for a nurse when a very young lass pops her head round the door. If it wasn't for the nurse's uniform, I'd think she was about fourteen.

'Oh, you're awake then?'

'Yes. What's going on? How did I get here?'

'Your mam called an ambulance – you had a knock on the noggin. How are you feeling?'

She comes over and looks at my head, then into my eyes.

'My mam?'

'Sorry, maybe it was your nanna? Lady with the glasses?'

'Oh, Gladys. She's my friend. How come I'm in this room and not on the ward?'

'She said you wouldn't like it. Paid for this. It's an NHS room – like private, but not as fancy. She was in the waiting room eating a couple of Twix last time I looked. I'll go and tell her you're awake. You look better. Bit of a bump, though. The doctors were worried about you, didn't know why you hadn't woken up. Your friend said you simply needed the sleep.'

She bustles out again, and I try to remember exactly what happened last night. We sent poor little George on his way, and we tripped up the Bad One. And then nothing. And then that beautiful dream. Not that it felt like a dream; it felt like a visit that I didn't want to come back from. Even the air in this warm room is cold and harsh, compared to the air I was breathing a few moments ago. Without warning I feel tears rolling down my cheeks, just as they rolled down Caroline's face when she lay there in her bed, wishing she'd died.

But I'm not wishing to be dead. I'm feeling gratitude, because now I know there's a place I'll eventually go where I won't have moods and fears and worries any more. And until that day, I'll actually have a purpose. And that purpose is going to make all the difference. Only it won't have the audience that acting does.

Right then, in walks a very tired-looking Gladys with a fleck of chocolate in the corner of her mouth. She sits in the chair next to my bed, holds my hand and shakes her head.

'That bugger threw a bunch of roof tiles at you. Sideways. We couldn't have predicted that.'

I begin to laugh. She stares at me, then cracks a smile herself.

'What?'

I can't stop giggling for a bit.

'We didn't get rid of him completely, did we?'

'God, no. He doesn't come from the Black Gate and he didn't die there – that's the problem. But still we took little George away from him. He tortured that poor lad in life, and he was still torturing him after death. Now George is at peace.'

'So sad. We'll probably never know the full story.'

'We know a *bit* more, if you want to hear it?'

'Go on.'

'After I got you here, I sat and meditated in the waiting

room and got a few answers. Turns out that bad bugger didn't live at the Black Gate. He was George's mam's pimp. And her boyfriend, after a fashion. She was always drunk and he was always hitting her, and George was always trying to protect her, for all the good that did him. After the Bad One killed the little mite and threw him in the river, people chose to believe that the mam – Reena, she was called – had fallen in the fire herself and that George had run away. They were all so terrified of that bad bugger, you see. And George was so stultified by what he saw happening to his mam, and by how he died himself, that he didn't move on. He kept "guarding" his mam and, after death, she couldn't reach him because he was trapped. Then, when that horrible pimp died the next year in a fight, he fixed onto that poor lad's spirit and kept torturing him.'

'Is the Bad One still around then?'

'Oh yes. He's somewhere, but I'm not sure exactly where.'

'Damn and blast it. He said he'd smash my head in and he nearly managed it. I want him gone completely. He's dangerous.'

'You don't have to think about that now, love. You've just got to get better. Gave you a right knock, and missed me by an inch.'

'Bloody hell.'

I lie there for a moment. My head feels terrible.

'Thank you for getting me this room, by the way. I'll pay you back.'

'No, you will not.'

I'm too knackered to argue. I'll sort it another time. I'm only glad I'm not at work today, as my head is throbbing.

'You were brilliant when you were talking to little George,' I say. 'He only went to his mam because you earned his trust. You're a natural with children.'

Then I see Gladys's eyes mist up, and all at once something becomes clear.

'I had a dream.'

She blows her nose. 'Yes?'

'Just before I woke up. I saw Frank, my friend who died. We had a chat.'

'Oh, that's good, pet. He obviously looks after you.'

'Yes, he does. And I saw Mona, the murdered lady who started that whole thing off with killer Dan.'

'Oh, the one who screamed and screamed . . . ?'

'That's it. Now she's made of light, with a rainbow inside.'

Gladys blinks.

'That must be quite a sight.'

'It is. And there was someone else. There was a beautiful little boy. Cheeky and gorgeous, with amber eyes and curly hair.'

Gladys's eyes suddenly lock on mine, but she doesn't speak.

'He was wearing a red T-shirt and shorts with frogs on them.'

Gladys's chin puckers. Her eyes begin to swim. Behind the thick glass are two paddling pools of emotion.

'He gave me a hug to pass on. He said to tell his mamma that he's waiting for her and, when he sees her again, he's going to wrap his arms tight around her neck and hug her all day long. He said to tell her she's his bestest.'

Water begins to run out of Gladys's nose as well as her eyes. She's gripping my hand so tightly she might break bones. Then all at once she lets out a wail. She tries to stop it, but it escapes anyway, like a Gladys siren. She bites down to stop any more noise coming out, reaches for something in her bag, then buries her face in a grubby-looking tissue.

'My Andrew.'

I swallow. It's hard to see her so distressed.

'He drowned,' Gladys tells me.

'I'm so sorry.'

'I called him "my bestest". He was the love of my life.'

She doesn't say any more, but merely drops her choco-latey face onto the bedspread and wraps her arms around her head while she sobs.

I stroke her as best I can, and whisper to her about how much love I could feel from Andrew towards her. Finally Gladys looks up at me, with snot and tears on her face and her glasses all misted up.

'You have confirmed something I've hoped and wished and prayed for, for such a long time. I'm crying because I'm relieved. And because I still miss him. Thank you.'

She pulls out a tattered little photo from her purse. And there is Andrew, all dimples and dinky milk-teeth. I feel my lip quiver.

'That's him. He's so sweet, Gladys.'

She swallows and attempts to compose herself.

'If I'm going to see his face again, then everything is worth it. Everything.'

What a remarkable woman she is. She's not even mad that I saw him when she didn't. And now I realize what an honour it is to be able to give her this information.

A worthy purpose.

ICE-CREAM CHOPS

They let me out of hospital by 10 a.m. They could see I was perfectly fine. They've given me some painkillers for my head, which are top-notch. Gladys went off to have a well-earned rest. I rang Milo, with the little bit of juice I had left in my phone, and now we're having morning ice-creams even though it's a nippy day. We're sitting on a bench, looking at the river, and I'm trying to process everything. Talking to Milo always helps when I'm doing this. He simply lets me spout.

'So the Bad One, he latched on to you, Milo, and I was trying to figure out why and how. And all I can come up with is that you were drinking a lot and feeling very insecure. Insecurity and fear were his entry points with his women, and they were with you, too. As for little George, that wasn't him throwing stones at us, it was the Bad One pretending to be George, to make things even creepier and stop us investigating. The burning eyes gave him away. George's energy was calling out to me, you see, to free him; and the Bad One didn't want to lose his grip. That's why there was that push and pull. I still don't know why the Bad One wouldn't let George go or why he was so horrible to him, though. George was only a child. Some people are just evil bastards.'

'And the Bad One's still about?' Milo asks.

I lick my pistachio ice-cream and sigh.

'That's the one thing I'm really pissed off about. But I think there's a good reason why we couldn't get rid of him so easily. He's not your usual trapped spook. This one gets off on being nasty, and he's determined not to go anywhere. I can't make him move on if I can't find a weakness; and he's so cruel and violent, it's hard to know where to start. I don't like the fact that he's still hanging about, but I don't have the power to make him leave.'

Milo's ice-cream has caramel chunks in it. I'm starting to get jealous.

'You can't do everything, Tanz. But just think, you saved that poor little lad and sent him to his mam. How lovely is that? Plus, that make-up artist has still got a boy-friend because of you. You're a rinky-dink, class-one, hot-palmed psycho-magic bitch. And I'm proud.'

'Thanks, Milo. It means a lot.'

'You're welcome. Plus, you finish soon, eh? Bonus. We can hang out and go to the cinema and have a few Gin Slings. No more shitty hypothermic costumes.'

'I don't know. I feel a bit bad, not rushing straight back to London to visit Sheila and give Inka a cuddle. Steve's been looking after her for ages now.'

As is the nature of filming, they employed me for a few days more than they needed, in case any of my scenes ran late. But because of Caroline's little hiccup there was a rejig and some rewrites, and my 'character' – if you can call that greasy, monosyllabic twat in shit-sandals a character – is now almost done. Early. Not only is my bank balance happier, but I can go home on Saturday.

'Well, you'd better come back soon then. We need to have some proper fun. It all got a bit heavy there, didn't it?'

'Yes, it bloody did.'

I wipe a fleck of ice-cream off Milo's chin and grin at him.

'I'll tell you what, though. Despite this egg on my head, I feel so much better today.'

'Do you?'

'Yes. Things have shifted. New things are afoot.'

'Look at that – you're even beginning to sound like the wise woman of the village! I love it.'

'Can I have a lick of your ice-cream?'

Milo proffers it.

'Of course. It's started to make me feel sick anyway. What are you doing for the rest of the day?'

I watch the sun sending shafts of light off the river, and the windows and panels of the Sage building opposite, which always reminds me of a gigantic glassy snail.

'Well, I've got my last day of work tomorrow, then dinner with Caroline in Tynemouth, so what I might do is go to bed, have a sleep, then watch Netflix. The knock on the head and the ghost-bust have worn me out – I need to chill.'

'Good plan! I've got work to do, so I'm going to settle

on the sofa with my laptop and a full cafetière of coffee. For at least seven hours.'

'Nice.'

I am so proud of my Milo. He's like nobody else, and he's on form again. It strikes me that I've still not seen any of our other friends since I arrived back up North, but I'll make up for it another time. None of them would have understood what was happening anyway – what with me being haunted and whatnot. And now I just need some rest.

THE CALM

O f course the thing about lying in bed watching an American horror series all day is that by ten o'clock at night you're a bit more awake than you should be. My head is heavy. I don't want to move, but I'm not sure I'll sleep. I get up and open my window. It's chilly, but not unpleasant. At precisely twelve minutes past ten my phone rings. I have no idea who could be calling me this late. The phone doesn't identify the caller, but I pick it up anyway, in case it's an emergency. Always the optimist.

'Tania – sorry, *Tanz*. How are you?'

The cut-glass voice, sounding mighty perky, is unmistakable.

'Caroline! Hello.'

'Hello, how are you?'

She's hidden her number so that it says 'Caller withheld'. Getting back to her old paranoid self then.

'Erm, quite weird actually. A ghost threw a bit of roof at my head last night and I've got a bump bigger than Kilimanjaro. I look like John Merrick.'

She giggles. Caroline's giggling!

'You really are a character, aren't you?'

'This time last week you wouldn't have phrased that quite so nicely, Caroline.'

'This time last week I wasn't the same person.'

That's quite a statement.

'You sound happy, Caroline. Which is strange, considering what you've just been through.'

'Do you like your angel charm?'

'Oh, I love it. I already feel like she's my protector.'

'That's exactly what I hoped. Wear it and it'll keep you safe.'

'Thank you. By the way, there's no use withholding your number. I can simply get it off the call sheet.'

She laughs.

'No, you can't – it's not on there, nor will it be again.'

'Sorry?'

'I've opted out.'

'What?'

'I'm fine with it. I'm fine with everything. These past few days have opened my eyes completely. You and your chips, and that ridiculous plant. Dave giving me another chance, after I treated him like a badly paid skivvy. I found some things in me that I forgot existed. People are kind, and I like at least two of them. So now I'm ready to spread my wings.'

'Oh my goodness, Caroline. That is so-o-o cool.'

'Yes, it is. It's "cool". What you did – coming to see me in that hospice – it started a trail of events and . . . well, you know. I'm very grateful. You've changed everything.'

'Pack it in, will you, or you'll have me bawling in a minute.'

'I know. Sentiment isn't usually my thing; it brings me out in hives.'

'So, are we still doing Tynemouth tomorrow night?'

'Oh yes, Dave will contact you about that.'

'Okay.'

'I just wanted to say good night and to wish you a happy day at work.'

'Bloody hell, Caroline. You've gone a bit crackers, haven't you?'

'I certainly have. I think it's called freedom. I'm heady with it! Thank you again, Tanz. And much love to you.'

She puts the phone down. *Much love?* She's turned into a honey-haired hippy. Good on her. Better than a suicidal sociopath.

As I stand there, a breeze creeps through the window, which is open a crack, and I feel peace descending on me. It's like Mona, the light-being, is here, making me feel sleepy and content.

I hardly get my head down on the pillow before I'm spark out.

FLOWERS BLOOM
AND BIRDS FLY

When I wake up I'm in a panic. My car to work is due in twenty minutes and I've slept for nine hours straight. I don't think I woke up once. I actually feel groggy from too much sleep. I run to the shower and lather myself with tea-tree-and-mint gel. That gets the blood pumping through my veins. Also, to my shame, after putting on some comfy clothes, I grab an ice-cold Diet Coke from the minibar. It should be water I'm grabbing, but I already had a glass when I woke up and I can't resist the brown fizz.

As I exit the hotel and jump into my cab, I feel a chill. It's proper nastily cold today. My good cheer and my surfeit of sleep can't disguise an ill feeling that I have. I keep glancing at my phone. Something suddenly niggles me. It was what Gladys said at the hospital. That if she was going to see Andrew's face again, then everything was worth it. It occurs to me that maybe she'd choose to see him sooner rather than later. What if something has happened to her when I've just got to know her? What if staying up all night at the hospital when I got my head injury has made Gladys ill? I finger the digits on my phone, wondering if it's too early to give her a bell. Eventually I text her:

How are you after the other night's shenanigans? Nice and rested?

Then I put the phone back in my pocket and finish my can of pop. One more day and I'm free. Exactly like the newly hippified Caroline. Maybe I should take a leaf out of her book, sooner rather than later, and stop acting now. Let other younger, prettier and, let's face it, much more enthusiastic women show off for a living. Maybe I'm not into all of that any more. My phone buzzes. I take it out of my pocket, expecting a text back from Gladys, but finding one from Sheila:

I'm so sorry not to speak to you this week. Chest was bad. Been in hospital.

Oh my God. My tummy flips and quivers. Sheila's even worse than I am about hospitals. She once told me she'd rather swim in a cesspool than spend an overnighter on a ward. Still, at least she's in the hands of professionals now. I'd better drive back to London first thing tomorrow and see her, which means I'd better not partake of too much of Caroline's fizz tonight. I hope it's not pneumonia. Maybe my hot palms can help? I text her back:

I hope you're okay. Hopefully see you tomorrow,
if you're up to it?

My thoughts are racing, partly due to the fizzy caffeine
for breakfast. I need to calm down. I suddenly feel fucking
odd and really cold. I'll ask Kelly if I can have one of the
big Costume coats between takes again because, of course,
I'll be in my shit costume one last time. It dawns on me that
they're going to have to do something about the bump on
my head. The greasy hair hangs down over it, so it might
be fine, but I reckon Vicky's going to have a fit when she
sees the size of it. Thank goodness it's a standalone scene,
my last one, or she'd have continuity to deal with as well.
Oh dear, the bump is probably why I'm feeling so sick all
of a sudden.

As I step out of the car, a whole flock of geese pass overhead. They are so noisy and chatty. How many times have
I wished I could fly? When I was a girl I was always dreaming I could take off into the sky. I'm still, to this day, jealous
of birds. A moment later, as I approach the Make-up van, I
notice one very perfect pink rose on a bush. I bend and put
my nose close to it. Its scent is heady and strong. I love that
it's there, waiting to delight anyone who takes a sniff.

After deciding that picking the rose would be an act of
vandalism, I step up the wibbly-wobbly stairs one last time
to enter the Make-up truck. But there's no one there. In fact
Vole was nowhere to be seen when my car arrived, either.
Which is unusual. I peek back out and eventually spy a few
members of the crew leaving the tiny production room.
Vicky is among them. None of them is talking. She reaches

the foot of the stairs and looks at me. Her face seems to be crumpling into her mouth.

'Caroline died last night.'

I don't think I heard that right.

'Sorry?'

Fell asleep and didn't wake up. Her heart, they think.

'*What?*'

'Dave wants to talk to you.'

Right then Dave appears at the production-room door and looks straight at me. He's ashen. Without another word, I pelt over there, slipping through the wet sod on shaky legs. He takes my elbow and leads me to a quiet bench at the side of the field. I sit heavily.

'Dave? I don't understand.'

He has a tissue and is making a monumental effort to hold it together.

'She just fell asleep, Tanz. I can't . . . I can't believe it.'

There's a ringing in my ears. He nods to himself.

'She was on the bed on a load of cushions, reading her book, like Lady Muck in her silk pyjamas. I left her and went out for a smoke. I said I'd bring her a green tea after, then I was going to my room to ring my wife. She's been giving me grief for not calling home enough, you see. So I go outside and have a smoke, and send a couple of texts to my daughters. Then I go back and make the green tea and take it to Caroline's room. And her reading glasses have fallen down her nose and she's fast asleep.'

His ears have gone red. And his nose.

'So I take them off her face. Then I see her chest isn't moving . . .'

His own chest begins to heave as he speaks. So does mine. We both just sit.

'And . . . and . . . well, later the doctor says her heart simply gave out. Years of starvin' herself and drinkin', and she used to smoke a lot, and then the pills she took the other night – apparently it's natural causes, but . . . she was so happy and fine. She was talking about you, Tanz, said she'd ring you in the morning.'

'She said you were going to ring me today.'

'Oh no, she said she wanted to ring you herself. Wanted to ask if you liked the angel. Like a kid she was, about that. She really took to you, you know. Never seen her like that before. It was lovely to watch. A privilege to spend time with her the past few days . . .'

'But she did ring me. She rang last night. We had a chat. She must have done it when you were outside. We had quite a laugh.'

Dave stares at me.

'Really? Well, I'm glad she got to speak to you. She was so excited about tonight. Was going on and on that I had to let her have some champagne to celebrate the new life we'd given her. Kept saying that. She was the happiest I've ever seen her.'

I'm so shocked. The lump in my chest is solidifying. How could this be? Caroline sounded so alive and so well when she called.

Dave shakes his head again, like he's trying to clear something that's buzzing about in his ears.

'How can you be chatting and happy at eight o'clock, and dead by nine? What the hell is it all about, eh?'

That halts me in my tracks.

'Nine o'clock?'

'Yeah. Doctor pronounced her dead at nine o'clock. Just when she was ready to start living. It's a bloody travesty.'

Dave sobs to himself. I breathe. Breathe again. Calm my racing brain. I looked at the clock, I know I did. Twelve minutes past ten. I'm positive of it. She called me an hour and twelve minutes after she was pronounced dead. I don't know what the hell is going on here, but there's not a person on the set that I'm divulging this information to. Not one of them would be able to process it. Including me. My bottom jaw is wobbling. Then I have a very strong feeling.

'Dave?'

'Yeah?'

I can't breathe properly. Am I actually going to faint, like they do in films?

'This might sound wrong, but . . . can we go to Tyne-mouth anyway? Tonight? Toast her with a glass of champagne? If she was so excited, I don't want to call it off.'

I remember now the way she dodged the question about tonight, said Dave would be in touch today. Little did I know it would only be two of us going. Dave looks at me and swallows.

'I think that's a really lovely idea.'

It's not until I'm in my little room, hair greasy, clothes horrendous, eyes ringed with shock and purple make-up, that I fully take in what has happened. My grief is inexplicably raw. I feel like someone ripped my heart out. I allow myself to cry, but only a bit. If I properly let go I won't be able to stop, and I have work to do.

As I swat my tears away, I begin to pace. I can't sit still. I check my phone, look at my 'recent' calls. There's an 'unknown' at 22.12 last night. This proves nothing. It could have been one of those computer-generated calls I get sometimes, trying to get me to claim some money or other that I'm supposedly owed. I could already have been asleep when it happened, phone on silent. There are no other calls from last night. But crucially it's not a 'missed' call. They're highlighted in red. This one's black. According to my phone, I answered the call.

I know exactly who phoned me. I *know*. Caroline called to tell me she was free and she wasn't sad to go, and that she'd not had to kill herself – she'd waited until her time was up, like I told her to.

And then I can't help it. I stop pacing and lean against the decrepit mini-sofa. The tears become a waterfall and my racking sobs are probably audible from the Make-up bus. But I don't care. The world is *not* always fair and I am *not* always calm, and I am going to miss Caroline bloody May. Vole taps at the door at some point, looking horribly out of his depth, and says I'll be going to set in half an hour. Asks me to go back to Make-up in ten minutes. I nod and he makes a swift exit. I try to meditate, to calm myself down. I attempt to speak to Caroline in case she's around. I know people aren't usually ready to talk for quite a while after they die, but she managed it last night so it's worth a try.

'Caroline? Why did you bugger off? Get back here, immediately.'

Nothing. But I suddenly see that flock of geese in my mind's eye, flying overhead, and I wave them off as they disappear into the distance.

THE CHANGING TIDES

It's half-past seven and we're nearly there. I stood outside the hotel at seven o'clock feeling like someone had kicked me in the face. I am still completely in shock. When the limo arrived, I realized that Dave was in the back, in a suit, and there was a different driver. Dave's mate runs an executive car service apparently, and seeing as Dave won't drink a drop when he's driving, he's got us this car, which will wait and bring us back tonight.

Dave's not spoken a whole lot, but at least he's not crying and neither am I.

When we arrive at the fish restaurant that Caroline was so excited about and park, something doesn't feel right.

'Dave, why don't we buy a really good magnum of champagne from that posh wine shop over there, get some chips and go and watch the sea for a bit?'

He nods gravely.

'A girl after my own heart. Do you mind if I get a few beers in, though? Champagne gives me awful heartburn.'

He chokes on the word 'heartburn' as he struggles not to weep.

'Of course not. More fizz for me.'

So we make our way to the same bench that I led Caroline to just a few days ago, and pop the champagne and put it in the little plastic flutes that they had in the off-licence, and we hold our drinks aloft to the starry sky and toast Caroline, then eat chips. This time with curry sauce. I can't believe I'm having chips twice in the same week, but these are extraordinary circumstances.

We are slow as we eat because tears are falling, but we do our best and I manage to only sob really loudly twice.

When I've dumped our rubbish (and most of the chips) in the litter bin, I sit back next to Dave, cross my legs on the bench and lie against his arm, because I just know he's feeling wretched. The drink has insulated us from the cold and I'm glad to be close to the sea, again.

'Did you love her, Dave?'

He glances at me, then looks back out to the horizon. He takes a while to answer.

'She was a one-off. She could be so bloody rude. But I could see past that most of the time. The crazy woman who attacked the director of the show was the bad side: the frightened, angry little girl. The woman she was this week is the woman I always knew she was. And what would that magnificent woman want with a geezer like me? A driver in a hat.'

'She loved you, too. She was lost without you.'

He sighs and pats my leg.

'Thank you. You're a lovely girl.'

We sit in silence. Then he sips from his can, having abandoned the champagne after the initial toast.

'What I can't work out, right, is how she managed to phone you last night, then pass away so quickly. I mean, I was only out of the room ten minutes at most. How long was she on the phone? How did she sound?'

I hesitate. But the drink has made me bold.

'She sounded happy as Larry, Dave. And she phoned me at twelve minutes past ten.'

He looks at me and narrows his eyes.

'Nah, she couldn't have – I told you, she died—'

'Before nine o'clock, I know. But I am telling you, on my mother's life, the phone call came at twelve minutes past ten. I checked the clock. And there's a call logged in my phone at that time. I can show you . . .'

So I do. And he looks at it. Then at me again. Blows out a long breath.

'She sounded happy?'

'She said we'd freed her. You and me. We'd reminded her of things she'd forgotten. She was happy and free.'

He takes another slurp of lager.

'That's good to know.'

I can tell he's crying again. He's just doing it silently.

'You believe me?'

He shrugs a tiny shrug. Goes quiet for a bit.

'My old auntie was a medium. All kinds of people used to visit her house. I used to sit under the stairs and watch 'em. I saw things that would make your hair curl. For all I know, you were dreaming last night. But either way,

Caroline came and told you she was okay. I only wish she'd come to me . . .'

I put my head on his shoulder and listen to the sea, and the cars passing and the voices of people as they walk their dogs and go out to dinner and plan their lives, and probably don't even give a passing thought to how fleeting it all is.

'Dave. I know it's no comfort, but at least she died happy and contented, wearing her silk pyjamas. Not a miserable ninety-year-old, living out of a car and going to a soup kitchen.'

'Yeah. Like that Holy Jesus Hospital next to where we're staying. Caroline was telling me about it being a soup kitchen. She thought it was an amazing building.'

I freeze.

'The what?'

'The old almshouses next to the turn-off for the quayside . . . Used to be the Holy Jesus Hospital.'

I remember the dream. The flowing water and the little boy. Kids crying and women gossiping and men fighting. I could feel the cold and I could smell something . . . soup – I smelled soup. 'Holy Jesus, Holy Jesus . . .' The sobbing boy, he'd kept repeating it.

When we pile back into the limo, I've had all of the champagne to myself, except for one tiny flute, and I'm all over the place. I lean forward towards the driver.

'Could we make one more stop before we go to the hotel, please?'

'Of course. Where'd you want to go?'

'The almshouses near the quayside. Do you know them?'

'Oh aye.'

'You can park round the corner. I'll be as quick as I can.'

'What's going on, Tanz?'

Dave is quite woozy with drink now, too, you can hear it in his voice. But he knows I'm suddenly on a mission, from the way I've dragged him back to the car.

'Something you just said – I think it's a final message from Caroline. And I've got some unfinished business with an evil bastard.'

'Who?'

'He's a ghost.'

'Bleedin' hell, girl. What kind of ghost?'

'The Bad One. He's a twat and I'm going to sort him out.'

'Are you sure you're in the right frame of mind to be sorting him out?'

'He's dead, he's a bastard, and I've never been in a better frame of mind to sort him out than I am now.'

Dave narrows his eyes and half-smiles.

'I wouldn't wanna cross you, dead or alive.'

Then we both laugh. Not because we're happy but because it's better than crying again.

ROTTEN BASTARD

Sometimes when I drink, I 'connect' better. In this case I may be too drunk. But I couldn't care less.

Turning down Dave's offer of 'help', I storm over to the front of the almshouses. It's a Friday night, I'm next to an underpass and there are very few people around, which comes as a surprise. The building itself has always seemed very sad to me, but beautiful. It's a long block with windows at the top, then lots of brick arches leading to front doors and more windows. I knew that it had been used to feed and look after the poor, as the almshouses and as a soup kitchen, for many years. I just didn't know it was called the Holy Jesus Hospital. I can imagine a lot of people died around here in despair and poverty; it's like there's always been a cloud hanging over it. Right now I can smell booze and decay and beaten hopes, all around me. And I think the Bad One died in a brawl outside here. I can feel it.

I reckon the Bad One made life even harder for those who were already desperate. He was a cruel man and a murderer. He frightened people, and I hate bullies; and for once I have someone to vent at. I am so angry he's still around, causing trouble. Lovely people die and that's them gone, but he died and carried on hurting others. I am *incandescent*.

I place my palms against the cold bricks and close my eyes. My head is spinning the tiniest bit, but that doesn't make any difference. And I don't bother speaking inside my head, either. Everything I say tonight will be out loud.

'Where are you – you drunken psycho?'

I know, I haven't got a leg to stand on with the drunken thing, but I don't particularly care right now.

'WHERE ARE YOU?'

I slow my breathing and stand stock-still, forehead against the bricks, side-of-the-head bump still aching, feeling pissed and ready for a barney. I can't bear that his appalling energy is still out there, when life is already unpredictable and cruel enough. He tortured that little boy, killed him, then tortured him some more. How can he be allowed to get away with it? I have to stop him. I'm not sure how, but I'm going to wing it.

And then I see a sparkle. A trace in the air of the glow that I saw in my dream – Mona's beautiful light. And a gentle voice in my ear begins to talk.

'*His name is Keenan. Nobody knows his first name. He was beaten from the day he was old enough to walk, and he didn't have a mother. She abandoned him and his brothers when he was a baby. I will now show you something. It's the key. His one weakness.*'

And as I stand with my head against the bricks, listening

to the off-tune song of a wizened old tramp who has arrived at the mouth of the underpass and is watching me curiously, she shows me. It's a grainy film in my head, with sights and sounds and smells, and I remember another dream and realize what it was that I saw. Now I understand things a little better and, despite my disgust and horror at what the Bad One did and is still doing, I feel the tiniest spark of empathy for Keenan the boy. Just not for the man.

Now I think I know what to do.

I walk a little further up the building, closer to where the limo is (it's around the corner) and I place both hands on the walls of this sad place and call his name.

'Keenan. KEENAN!'

The rough old voice of the tramp with the wispy beard echoes me from twenty feet away, 'Keenan! She's lookin' fo' ya, man! Keeeenan!'

I *feel* him first, rather than see him. A blast of bad air against my neck, and the pressure of cold rock against my heart.

'Hello, Keenan.'

The tramp, seeing that I'm talking quite loudly to thin air, stops calling and stares. He probably doesn't meet people madder than himself that regularly.

'How are you?'

'Go away, bitch, before I brain you again. This time I'll do it properly.'

I don't believe him. He's already lost George. And throwing stones isn't the same as caving in someone's head against a wall. He might be strong, but he's not that strong.

'Oh reaallly? Going to brain me, are you, you massive

bastard? Well, you didn't make much of a go of it last time, did you? Because here I am, right as rain. And now little George has gone off with his mammy, you've got no one to bully. Poor little diddums!'

The tramp sniggers and sits down on the freezing concrete, watching everything.

'*I have killed many people in my life. More than you know. When I kill you, you won't be such a hoity-toity whore!*'

'But I'm not a whore, am I? And you're not alive any more, so what now, Mr Big Stuff?'

Just as I finish my sentence I swear I feel a blast of angry, fetid wind against my face. Then, oh joy, it starts to rain. If the thunder comes, it will match my mood perfectly. I feel a stone land at my feet. A small pebble. The Bad One has lost power, I'm sure of it. But I'd better watch out in case he does attempt to brain me. It could be potentially embarrassing if he managed it.

'I know why you did it, you know. I know why you were so horrible to that little boy. Because your dad and your brothers were horrible to you. Classic psychology . . .'

'*Stop speaking in riddles. I know what you want – that's why you called my name, you filthy slut.*'

Suddenly my whole body flinches as he pushes me against the wall. More strength than I expected, but weirdly it only scares me for a second. Then something else kicks in. Blind bloody-minded determination to end this once and for all.

In my head I call on Mona, I call on Frank, I call on

everything I've ever learned from Sheila, I call on Elvis
Presley, two of the Bee Gees and my grandma Lily, who I
never met. I smack my fists off the wall, turn exactly
towards the place I'm *positive* he's standing and open my
third eye like a cavern, then stare straight into the place
where his hot-coal eyes would be, with my own eyes
closed.

Then I fill my mind with a picture.

A picture of a scruffy little tyke with no shoes, ragged
shorts and a threadbare shirt, playing in filth and muck in
a hovel near the banks of the Tyne. The little tyke that
Mona just showed me. And I strip away the drink and the
fighting, and the bad reputation building, and the beatings
of women, and the lack of any empathy or kindness, and
the bar brawls, and I force him to be that little boy again – a
little boy covered in bruises and hardly any clothes. A little
boy with one friend. A tiny black-and-white cat with one
eye. And I hear him as I bring this ridiculous little cat into
the picture, I hear him in the right side of my brain.

'*Don't try to trick me, bitch . . .*'

But I keep on picturing the scene and I build up the
energy in my body and begin to talk.

'Coal Dust. That's what you called him: Coal Dust. And
he was warm and sweet, and at night when you were lying
on the hard floor, he would curl up against your belly and
purr; and by day you'd watch him chasing mice and rats,
and you'd wish you could be his size and run away with
him and catch food, and escape the blows and the cold and
the loneliness . . .'

'*Shut up. Shut up, you whore.*'

But the Bad One's voice has changed. It's more desperate than it was before.

'You cared for Coal Dust more than anyone or anything you ever met in your life. And that's why your dad wrung his neck. Just to spite you, while he was drunk. Just to laugh in your face. Poor little helpless Coal Dust was murdered because you loved him. And the last and only light in your life was snuffed out.'

Now he's stopped speaking. I can hear him groaning. I don't know if it's anger or sadness, but I don't want to stop to think about it. The rain is really whipping up and it's stinging my face. Keeping my energy high, I visualize the world of darkness and shadows that Keenan lives in. And I paint a door there. An old arched wooden door. Then I open it. It creaks slowly on its hinges. Behind it is a glowing light, and standing there at its foot is a scruffy little cat with one eye, waiting for his master. And then Coal Dust begins to purr; and the purring gets louder and louder until it sounds more and more like a heartbeat. The heartbeat of a baby in the womb. And I wait. And I keep my eyes closed, and my third eye fixed on the shadow that is a man. And I wait some more. And then, at last, the shadow shifts, and the brooding presence that is Keenan moves tentatively to the door and bends and holds out a dirty hand. Coal Dust approaches and puts his head in Keenan's palm and closes his one eye with pleasure. For a horrible moment I think Keenan will crush his skull.

But he doesn't. Instead he speaks quietly.

'Hello, little fella. It's been a long time . . .'

The purring softens and Coal Dust looks up adoringly

and, with one final sigh, Keenan shrinks to the size of a filthy little ragamuffin and steps through the door to pick up his kitten and cuddle it to his chest. Quickly I close it behind him. Then I seal up the edges, until all I see is the darkness and all I feel is the rain whipping my face.

Then, with my eyes still shut, I see the glowing light of Mona floating before me, a look of such intense understanding in her eyes.

'Where did I send him?'

'Somewhere he'll get help for his soul.'

'Is that good?'

'It's right. It's the right place. You did well, Tanz. So well.'

Her voice is growing faint. Then suddenly the light has gone and I open my eyes and see the rain falling fast through the orange rays of the nearest street lamp. There's a whoop from the tramp, who jumps up and gives me a round of applause. God knows what he thinks he just witnessed.

'Good lass! He was a right horrible bastard, him.'

I double up in the pissing rain, all of the emotion of the past few days spewing forth in sobs, and vomit from too much fizz. The tramp stays where he is. Transfixed by my display.

Suddenly Dave is by me, helping me to stand. He wraps his arms around me as we get more and more soaked. Then he pulls back and looks at me.

'Are you done here?'

'Yes.'

'Good, cos it's bloody freezing.'

When we get back to the car, the driver makes us sit our wet bums on bin bags, and I feel like I did something good. I truly hope Caroline would approve, because it was kind of in her name.

Well, not the vomiting bit.

OPEN CHANNELS

It's taken about an hour to stop shivering. I ran the hottest, most fragrant bath when I got into my room and I've sat in it for forty-five minutes, letting some out and topping it up with toasty water every time it's cooled.

Not that I think the shivering is necessarily only from the cold. The past couple of weeks have been outrageous. I exorcised Milo, shagged an idiot, got clouted by a murderous ghost who I eventually managed to get rid of, I met a light-being, I saw my Frank, I met Gladys's son, I finished my job, which was driving me nuts, and my friend died.

My friend died.

Baths are good to cry in because they're already wet, so it doesn't matter. Plus, sometimes when I'm drunk I sob my heart out, just for the sake of it. But I find that the vomiting and crying at the almshouses have cleared me out. Now I merely have a rushing in my ears and a huge amount of gratitude that I received that call from Caroline last night. It makes it all a bit more bearable, knowing she's happy.

When I'm out and dry, and wrapped in the biggest,

thickest, most fantastic hotel bathrobe, my phone rings. It's after midnight. I'm not sure I can bear to look, in case it's more bad news. Or a ghost. I check the screen. It's Gladys. Phew!

'Hiya, Gladys, you all right?'

'I'm fine. Lots of sleep, lots of tea, lots of Battenberg and I'm right as rain. What about you? What the hell have you been up to?'

'What do you mean?'

'Don't play the innocent with me. I was sitting there watching a documentary on otters, on Sky, and I started feeling strange. I couldn't work out what it was. Then I realized . . . *him*. He's gone. You bloody did it, didn't you? On your own.'

'Erm, yes. I think I did.'

'Do you realize how dangerous that was?'

'It wasn't. I knew he couldn't do anything. It was his time to move on.'

'You are a naughty girl. But I'm very proud – well done.'

'Thank you.'

'You sound a bit weird, love, are you all right?'

'No. Caroline died last night.'

'Who?'

'Caroline May, the actress off the show. Died in her sleep. Called me on this phone about an hour later.'

'Are you joking? No wonder you've been so connected to the spirits this week; when someone you know is about to die, it opens all the channels up.'

'Does it?'

'Oh yes. Get round here first thing tomorrow – you need some healing. And I want to hear all about it.'

'Okay. I'm supposed to be driving straight back to London, to visit Sheila, but I suppose I could delay it for a few hours.'

'Yes, better drive back feeling all aligned.'

'Right. I'll come over when I wake up.'

'Good. And, Tanz . . .'

'Yes?'

'I saw Andrew in my dreams last night. Got my first hug off him in years. He called me his bestest.'

'That's lovely.'

There's a little pause as Gladys gathers herself. Looks like I'm not the only one who's been crying today.

'See you tomorrow, pet.'

I'm about to put the phone away when I see a message sign. Someone must have called when I had it on silent earlier. I listen to the voicemail. To my surprise, it's my little mam. It's short and to the point.

'I just nodded off on the settee. Saw you chasing some horrible man with a scar and bad teeth, in my dream. Woke up in a right lather. You better not be messing with them ghosts again, young lady. I'll speak to you tomorrow.'

Despite everything, I can't help but laugh as I climb into bed. God, I'm bone-weary.

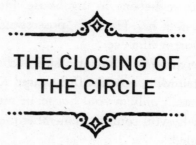

THE CLOSING OF
THE CIRCLE

On the M1 back to London I have a giant mix-up of kid's sweets, an even more giant super-hot cappuccino, and some cheesy seventies rock to sing along to. I'm not in the hurry I thought I was, because Sheila messaged me to say that she's feeling better, but tired from the medication, and will be open to visitors tomorrow instead of today. That means she's on the mend and that I can spend this evening with my cat. Double bonus.

Just before I left I asked Milo to come along with me for the ride, but he's right on the edge of finishing his new play, then he'll have rewrites and the like to do. I told him he could do it at my flat and could arrange some face-to-face meetings in London instead of always using Skype, but it's pretty hard to get him to leave the North-East when he's on a roll, and I can hardly blame him. Anyway I reckon I'll get him to move southwards eventually. He can't quite grasp the concept of not living next to his mam yet, but he'll get there.

I mull over our last chat, as I chew on a jelly cherry.

'Tanz, I was wanting to ask you something?'

'Okay.'

'That bloke – the one in my house. He wasn't only haunting me, was he? He was "possessing" me, like in every awful horror film ever.'

I didn't know what to say at first, but then I figured it was okay to tell Milo, now that I'd cleared Keenan.

'Yes. He wasn't only in your house, he was also in your head. That's why you couldn't remember much.'

Milo whistled.

'So it was that bastard who made me wear jogging bottoms?'

'Yup.'

'He was pure evil, eh?'

'Yup.'

'Are you okay, Tanz?'

The healing at Gladys's had been incredible. I lay on her little bed as she put me into a deep state of relaxation by placing her palms on different parts of me, then basically injected so much peace and warmth into my body that it shifted the shock of the past fortnight and seemed to make it all less traumatic. Afterwards I cried again, but it was like a 'shedding', and now I feel more my old self than I have in weeks. I'll never get used to people dying, but I don't feel as crippled as I did yesterday.

'Yeah, I'm coping, Milo. Gladys sorted me right out.'

Gladys is a find and no mistake. I roll my angel pendant between my thumb and forefinger as I drive and think about all the new things I've learned in a short time. I've promised Gladys that I will still my mind at least once a day, and that I will get 'gentle exercise'. Gladys doesn't hold with gyms and says the only exercise she needs is her walks in the country. In my case, she says my obsession with not getting fat will be helped if I do some yoga. She says I should never worry about eating chocolate again, as people who don't eat sugar are unnatural and overly judgemental of others. Everyone should have a Gladys in their life.

As I got into the car, I'd asked Milo one last thing.

'Milo, should I quit acting for good?'

His reply was an eye-opener.

'I think you should get on with solving ghost cold-cases. That's the second time you've solved a murder in less than a year.'

'I never thought of it like that.'

'It's dead exciting. You can be Miss Marple for the undead.'

And I did, didn't I? I solved a murder. Granted, it happened more than a hundred years ago and no one knew it had happened, but I still solved it – and that has to count for something, doesn't it? Like a clean-up job for karma. After all my years of reading magazines about murderers, I've now been involved in solving two cases. I suck on a pear drop and smile. I'm a crime-fighter.

A little later, as I'm approaching Sheffield and I'm eating foam bananas and singing along to the Electric Light Orchestra, my phone rings. I have my earbuds and wire plugged in and I see that it's an unknown number. Fleetingly I think, *If this is Caroline May giving me an update from the Other Side, I am going to crash the car*. Then I come to my senses, turn the music down and press 'answer'.

'Tanz?' It's a man's voice. I recognize it, but I can't place it.

'Hello?'

'It's Neil here. Remember me?'

Neil, Neil, Neil? My mind is drawing a big fat blank.

'St Albans bobby? You thought I looked twelve.'

Oh my goodness: *Neil.* Last time I spoke to him he was imparting confidential police information about Dan's murder/suicide scenes and asking me out.

'Neil? Hello, how are you?'

'I'm great, thanks. How've you been since your little adventure?'

I blush at this, because I sort of said I'd give him a ring and go for a drink, after the whole Dan thing. But I'd got in a right flap afterwards and then didn't call anybody.

'Sorry I didn't get in touch. I think I went into shock for quite a while. It suddenly hit me.'

'Happens a lot.'

'Then I got a job on a TV show in Newcastle. Just finished it actually.'

His voice perks up, like a terrier wagging its tail.

'Really? What was it?'

'*Pendle Investigates . . .*'

'Actually I don't know why I asked you that, because I don't watch TV shows. I watch films.'

A man after my own heart.

'Me too, usually.'

He laughs.

'Well, you've had plenty on your plate then?'

For some reason I blurt out the truth.

'You don't know the half of it. I also met a clairvoyant healer called Gladys, got haunted by Newcastle circa 1890 and cleared a century-old murderer from the earthly plane while I was there. Then my friend died.'

His laughter turns into a shocked whistle.

'Bloody hell! That's rough.'

Sodding tears are threatening again.

'She died with a smile on her face. It could have been worse.'

'Right . . .'

There's a lull. I don't want to be rude, but I have no idea why Neil's calling. If it's for a chat, I'm not really sure what to talk about.

'Anyway you're probably wondering why I'm calling.'

Thank Christ for that.

'I thought you just wanted to hear my dulcet Geordie tones,' I reply.

'Yes, well, apart from that. I . . . erm, it's funny you should mention murder. I mean after that nightmare up the road, the fact that you've been involved with another homicide-thing – well, maybe it's something you could help us with again. On the quiet, you understand? If you fancied it? I've got a mate, right: Charlie. He's on the Met. We trained together. He's working on something. It's a case they never solved. He's looking for some help, and by the nature of the case, I think it could be right up your alley.'

The hairs on my neck prickle up. Milo tells me I should

work on ghost cold-cases, and then this call comes in. I'm starting to wonder if Milo's more psychic than I am.

'Wow! Tell me about it. I'm driving to London right now, so I've got plenty of time.'

'Why don't you come to St Albans for lunch in the week and I'll tell you face-to-face?'

And as I'm stopping the call and squinting at the sun, I hear Frank's voice in my head, loud and clear, and cheeky as always.

'This is all going to be very interesting.'

'Oh, is it now? And I'll bet you're not going to tell me how, Mr bloody Cryptic.'

'Of course not.'

'Well, thanks for nothing.'

'You're welcome.'

A hazy rainbow forms in a cloud. I've never seen anything quite like it before – just a wash of colours over the woolly off-white. I think of Mona, translucent with her core of healing light; and of Caroline, who wanted to stop living and got her wish. I think of the bigness of that sky up there and the smallness of me. And I turn up my CD as loud as it will go and sing at the top of my voice.

Because if there's any time to do it, it's right now.

ACKNOWLEDGEMENTS

I want to extend gratitude to everyone who has encouraged me on this bonkers, knackering, inspiring, LONG journey. Thank you Don for taking up the slack and bringing me medicinal wine while I bashed at the laptop for eight hours a day, writing my first two books. Thank you to my wimmins, so many of you, who believed in this tempestuous witch a lot more than I believed in myself. Thank you to my family for being an endless goldmine of funny one-liners. Thank you to the glorious Pan Macmillan team for being complete champs. And thank you to my closest pals for just being wonderful. Finally, many thanks to every single one of you who has bought this book. Turns out that in a dark world there are many pinpricks of light. You just have to look up.

THE ACCIDENTAL MEDIUM

Tanz is a wine-loving, straight-talking, once-successful TV actress from Gateshead, whose career has shrivelled like an antique walnut. She is still grieving for her friend Frank, who died in a car crash three years ago, and she has to find a normal job in London to fund her cocktail habit.

When she starts work in a 'new age' shop, Tanz suddenly discovers that the voices she's hearing in her head are not just her imagination working overtime, but are in fact messages from beyond the grave. Alarmed, she confronts her little mam and discovers she is from a long line of psychic mediums.

Despite an exciting new avenue of life opening up to Tanz, darkness isn't far away – all too soon there's murder in the air.